PRAISE FOR *ANNAKA*

WITHDRAWN

"Reading *ANNAKA* allowed my beliefs about what it means to be a young woman of African descent living in Nova Scotia to relax. Although parts of Annaka's speech were unfamiliar, her imagination of and love for Clay was a comforting escape. The themes of confronting one's self, working through inter-generational conflicts and secrets, and learning to trust and lean on friendships were very relatable. Annaka offers hope to the misfits of the world. Annaka's relationship with Tia confirms that two women can rely on each other in difficult times, without malice. The pain that Annaka's grandfather held onto speaks volumes of what it means to be the rock of the family, despite what one may have experienced. He did all of this with love and goodwill, which is a true reflection of many real-life grandparents. I was happy to see these nurturing dynamics. A huge thank you to Andre for this work of art that offers a pleasant escape with real-life takeaways."

–Jade H. Brooks, author of *The Teen Sex Trade: My Story*

"*ANNAKA* has a fantastic hook (what if your imaginary friend from childhood came back just when you needed them the most?) but quickly evolves into a multi-layered exploration of what it means to seek belonging when you straddle many boundaries. Andre Fenton has crafted a wonderful and heartfelt love letter to childhood, memory, and the people and places that mean home."

–Tom Ryan, author of *Keep This to Yourself*

"*ANNAKA* tackles two of life's biggest challenges: death and adolescence. Fenton weaves together joy, grief, and discovery through the eyes of Annaka Brooks, a sixteen-year-old African Nova Scotian woman. The story brings to the forefront the achingly familiar feel of loss through a world tinged with magic. With characters and perspectives often left out of YA fiction, Fenton not only centres his characters' community and history, he does it with both humour and heart."

–Rebecca Thomas, former Halifax Poet Laureate (2016–18) and author of *I'm Finding My Talk*

ANNAKA

ANDRE FENTON

NIMBUS
PUBLISHING
——— NIMBUS.CA ———

Nimbus Publishing Limited
3660 Strawberry Hill St, Halifax, NS, B3K 5A9
(902) 455-4286 nimbus.ca

Printed and bound in Canada
NB1430
Cover design: Jenn Embree
Interior design: Heather Bryan
Editor: Emily MacKinnon

This story is a work of fiction. Names characters, incidents, and places, including organizations and institutions, either are the product of the author's imagination or are used fictitiously.

Library and Archives Canada Cataloguing in Publication

Title: Annaka / Andre Fenton.
Names: Fenton, Andre, 1995- author.
Identifiers: Canadiana (print) 20200160206 | Canadiana (ebook) 20200160257 | ISBN 9781771088923 (softcover) | ISBN 9781771088930 (HTML)
Classification: LCC PS8611.E57 A76 2020 | DDC C813/.6—dc23

 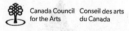 

Nimbus Publishing acknowledges the financial support for its publishing activities from the Government of Canada, the Canada Council for the Arts, and from the Province of Nova Scotia. We are pleased to work in partnership with the Province of Nova Scotia to develop and promote our creative industries for the benefit of all Nova Scotians.

For those who feel grief
For those accompanied by loss
For those trying to heal

This is for you.

———————

CHAPTER 1

THEY SAY THE FIRST STAGE OF GRIEF IS DENIAL, AND I speak from experience when I say that's true. When I heard the news, I felt numb. Like someone unexpectedly hit the pause button on my feelings. I guess we always carry the expectation that the people we look up to will never die, but when they do you begin to realize how mortal the rest of us really are. When I heard about my grandfather, I was in the main office of my school. There had been a call waiting for me. It was Mom, and her voice was cracking but it was strong. It's blurry, but I remember not being able to answer when she told me. I just sat there. Frozen.

"Anna? Anna, can you hear me?" I heard Mom's voice. She was in her minivan, on the way to pick me up.

"I hear you," I said quietly. "But I don't want to believe it."

"Me neither, babe. I'm coming to get you. We have to head home."

Home. That's a tough one.

––––––––

A COUPLE OF DAYS LATER, Mom and I packed her minivan. We were heading to our hometown: Yarmouth. When we turned on to the highway I sunk into the passenger seat with earphones in both ears, trying to erase the fact that my grandfather's funeral was the next day. You would think losing someone I shared some of my earliest memories with would cut deep, would make me want to cry or slam my fists on the van's dashboard, but I still felt more numb than anything else. I felt anywhere but present, and being on that highway felt like existing in between fiction and reality, between Halifax and Yarmouth. I knew when we made it to Yarmouth, everything would hit. I had to face the fact that grief had made it home before I ever did. It had been ten years, and we were finally going home. I wanted to soak in that highway of ignorance for just a little longer. This was new territory for Mom and me; we let silence fill the air, not really knowing what to say or how to translate our feelings. I had never lost anyone before, but I guess that's because I never really had too many people to lose.

When I was a kid, my mom and I lived with my grandparents until I was seven, my Mom moved to Halifax and brought me along with her. Even though I've lived there for half my life, Halifax never really felt like home to me. Home was where the magic was, and Yarmouth was a place of magic for me. A place where my grandfather built me a tree house and I could stay up there all night looking at a sky illuminated by the stars. A sky that looked like it was full of freshly lit matches. In Halifax, they were always dying out.

I had always wanted to return, but under the circumstances I was more fearful than anything else—fearful that the person who made Yarmouth magic was gone. There'd be no more giant hugs that kept me better grounded than gravity ever has. No more riding downtown in the passenger seat of Grampy's antique truck, feeling the cool air of the summer breeze blowing in from the waterfront with him. Those moments always meant a lot to me, and now I had to come to terms with those moments only being memories.

I began to drift off. Sitting in the passenger seat did that to me, but also Mom and I had spent the majority of the previous night prepping for our trip. She had told me that she didn't know how long we would be gone for, but to "be prepared." I didn't know what that meant, so I brought a lot with me. We were in a minivan; we had the space.

My earliest memories were all tinged with magic. Not that it amazed me, or anything. When you grow up around it you just sort of assume that's the way life is. It's not until you leave it behind that you realize it isn't exactly normal. When I was a kid, my best friend was magic.

Don't freak out quite yet.

He could cover the lake outside of my grandparents' house with ice, even on a July day. How did he do it? I never knew, and didn't question. I just remember my hand wrapped around his as the rest of the world just disappeared; the lake stayed, though, and we would skate beneath the stars. When I first met him, his hands were soft and grey, so I called him Clay. He came into my world as I drew him in my journal: two arms, two legs, and a lot of heart—but always too innocent. I knew I had to hide my imaginary friend away from the world. He was both my best friend and best kept secret.

Clay could recreate anything I wrote in my journal. It was almost like dreaming, but I was always wide awake. This wasn't just any journal, either; it was the journal my grandfather gave me on my first day of grade primary. He told me that it used to be his, and now that I was starting school, he was passing it along to me. He was a teacher, and a big believer in writing journal entries. He drilled that into me as a kid, said it was important to keep track of ourselves. I got tired of it pretty quickly, and often let my imagination run wild in that thing. There were more drawings than entries, and that's how Clay came about.

I remember spending a lot of time with Clay in the tree house. Some nights we were accompanied by a summer breeze, other times we were surrounded by the fall's red leaves. We shared some timeless moments up in that tree house, and there I was wishing those nostalgic moments would last forever. But one thing I have learned is that magic always finds an end. I want to say I grew out of it, but the truth is my mom and I left it behind.

I wasn't ready, and neither was Clay. I didn't want to leave Grampy and Nan. My grandfather and I had a unique relationship—he was my first superhero, and the only father figure I ever had. I never met my father, but Grampy was always enough for me. Every Sunday we had our routine: I'd climb in his big red truck on the passenger side. He'd put it in drive, turn to me, and ask: "Are you ready, co-pilot?"

I was sad to leave them behind. Mom told me I couldn't stay, and I knew I couldn't bring Clay along with us. What good would it do to bring him to a small city apartment where he couldn't be seen? He was better off in Yarmouth—a safer place. So I left Clay behind with a promise. I promised him I would return that summer. Mom had said we would, and I looked forward to spending warm summer nights in the tree house with Clay, looking at the galaxy above our heads....

But it turned out that wasn't a promise I could keep, because we didn't return. Mom, an artist, kept getting gig after gig after gig. After a while, I assumed Clay had taken the hint and moved on to somewhere else in the world.

I still remember the last day I spoke to him. I told him I was moving away, but he could stay with grandparents as long as they didn't see him. We had just finished playing hide-and-seek, our favourite game. He cried all afternoon. For ten years, the look on his face has stayed with me. Then Mom and I went off to a place that never quite felt like home.

Yarmouth wasn't exactly light years away from Halifax, so I don't know why we never returned—or even visited. Mom didn't speak about home too often. But there had to be a reason. Most summers Mom claimed to be stacked up with work, and didn't trust that I was old enough to go alone.

But back to Clay: I guess I always assumed that, with age, he just… went away like other kids' imaginary friends. I was always told that my imagination would get the better of me, but I thought of Clay as the best part of me. The hardest part of all of this was knowing I didn't keep my promise.

"Anna," Mom said, causing me to stir.

I took out my earphones and shook my head. "Yeah, Mom?"

"I know this is weird for both of us. But we need to talk about your grandmother."

This was a conversation I wanted to avoid. I sighed. "I know. You're going to say that she might not remember me, right?" I was blunt. Better to get straight to the point.

Mom didn't reply right away. She kept her eyes on the road. She had kept strong since finding out that her father had passed. I think it didn't feel real to her either. Or maybe she was just better at hiding it.

"Yeah. That's what I'm trying to get at," she said quietly. "I just—I just don't want you to get there and have your hopes up."

I had just found out that my grandfather had a heart attack in his driveway and died as soon as he got to the hospital. My hopes weren't exactly high, but I replied, "I know. I'll try not to."

I sunk back down into the passenger seat and shut my eyes again. I dreamt about a good day. A day when we sat on my grandparents' porch as Nan braided my hair and Grampy was trying to blow away the smoke from his charcoal barbecue.

"Why don't you throw away that stupid thing and get a propane one already?" Nan asked him.

Grampy tried to hide the smile on his face. He could certainly afford to upgrade, he just liked being stubborn.

"If it works, it works," he replied, taking a cloth to wipe his face.

"Stubborn," she said back. "Girl, I hope you aren't half as stubborn as he is," she said to me.

"I hope she is! It'll save her a lot of money for college."

Nan laughed at that.

Then Mom came out the front door saying, "The smoke is getting all in the house! The next thing you know you'll have the alarm going off."

"That's what I'm trying to tell your daddy," Nan said. "Soon enough we'll be bunking up in the tree house with you, Annaka."

"Hey! There's no room up there for all of us," I pointed out.

Nan and Grampy both let themselves go in a gentle laugh.

Even if they were dysfunctional at times, they made me feel at home. I still remember one morning waking up to Grampy and Nan arguing outside. Grampy was keen on painting our house yellow, a bright alternative to our basic grey. Though Nan and Mom both wanted a baby blue, they talked about it for weeks, and eventually Grampy came around. He even said he had picked up the blue paint and was going to get started early in the morning. As the sun rose, I moved to my window to see Mom and Nan both looking speechless in front of a fresh coat of yellow paint on our home. I still laugh at the memory from time to time. As stubborn as he was, he was also a gentle man. He used to sing me lullabies, and would tell me the story about how he met Nan. He told me that he won her over on a dance floor with his moves. I would love to see it for myself. He was a gentle giant who showed his soft side. He wore his heart on his sleeves, but also rolled them up as he checked the closets for monsters. But after Clay came around, I told Grampy to leave the closet alone.

"What if they aren't mean monsters?" I would say. "What if they're friendly?"

My grandfather paused with a hand on the doorknob and I could hear a grin in his voice. "Your imagination gets the better of you."

"No, it is the *best* of me."

He let laughter fill his lungs and left my closet alone.

Thinking back, maybe my imagination did get the better of me. When Grampy noticed all of the drawings in my journal, he showed me how to "properly" journal, according to him. He began having me write about my day each night before I went to bed. I wrote a lot about the time he and I spent together, and the adventures we got into. As an English teacher, this was his way of trying to get me to read and write at an early age. One time he had taken me on an adventure to Cape Forchu so I could write about it. Later on he peeked over my shoulder to see my doodles of his truck driving up the hill of Cape Forchu with the lighthouse sitting up top. I could tell it wasn't what he expected, but he gave me a smile and a pat on the shoulder anyway. Maybe that's how I was stubborn. I always wanted to do things my way—I must have learned that from him.

I woke up as rain began pelting against the windows.

"I thought you were my co-pilot," Mom said as I stretched and yawned. "You hungry?"

"Yeah, a little bit."

Mom nodded and turned off at the next exit and made her way to a burger joint drive-through.

"What do you want?" she asked.

"A cheeseburger with—"

"I'll get a cheeseburger, fries, and a large coffee," she ordered on my behalf. Then she said to me: "I need you to stay awake with me, okay?"

"Fine." I shook myself awake. I guess the least I could do was keep Mom company on a three-hour drive.

Mom gave the drive-through employee a ten and told him to keep the change. I devoured the burger and fries immediately and sipped away at the coffee as Mom made her way back to the highway. Her body language was tense. Her hands tightly gripped the steering wheel, and I watched as her shoulders began to tighten up. I knew she was about to say something I wasn't going to like.

"I know our family has always been a tight unit. For a long time it's only been you and me, and I thought we'd be returning to Yarmouth much sooner than this. I'm sorry that we didn't. I really am." She said all this without taking her eyes off the pavement.

"Mom," I cut in, "what are you getting at?"

"I'm trying to say that I know you're a sentimental person. I know who you are, Anna. I'm just worried about you right now. You loved Yarmouth, and I know you have wanted to return for a long time. But it might not be the place you remember, and we're probably going to be there for a long time."

"How long is a long time?"

"I don't know yet." Mom kept her eyes on the road.

I let out a breath of air, and let worry fill my lungs. I wasn't ready to go back home to bury Grampy, and I wasn't ready for the possibility of Nan not remembering who I was.

"Does she remember you?" I asked Mom.

Mom's eyes were still on the road and she didn't answer right away.

"When I called a few days ago, she asked me to bring my report card."

I took in a deep breath. *Shit*.

"This is going to be hard, Anna. But we're in it together, okay?"

"Okay."

After a few more kilometres, Mom pulled over.

"What are you doing?"

"I want you to drive the rest of the way. Driving helps soothe the soul—trust me," she said as she got out of the car.

"You can't be serious. I don't know how to get to Yarmouth."

She was opening my door. "Easy. It's a straight shot. Just stay on the highway until it ends. We're more than halfway there."

I got out and walked around the van to the driver's side. "What are you going to do?" I asked while I buckled my seat belt.

"I'll be your co-pilot. I got your back." She smiled.

"Whatever you say." I put the van in drive, making my way back to the road.

CHAPTER 2

I DIDN'T NEED THE GPS TO TELL ME WE WERE ABOUT fifteen minutes away. I could tell from the bumpy road and painted rocks that lined the highway. Mom was sound asleep in the passenger seat beside me. I rolled my eyes at her plan of getting me caffeinated so she could take a nap. I knew she hadn't slept much in the past two days, so I cut her some slack and tried to avoid potholes. The sun began to creep through the clouds as we closed in on our destination. Maybe it was the town's way of saying, "Hey, Anna and Jayla, thanks for not forgetting about us. Completely." I wondered what had changed about the town, if anything had changed at all.

I wondered if Mom ever regretted leaving Yarmouth a decade ago. Mom took me with her when she moved to Halifax to study illustration and fine art at NSCAD University. She would take freelance gigs and commission work to pay the bills. Some months were easier than others, but she always made it work. A few years after she graduated, the university wanted her to return as an instructor. She jumped at the idea of a stable income while also working in the arts. At first glance you'd probably assume our minivan made us some soccer family, but Mom had bought this to transport large canvases and art supplies between our apartment, her studio, and the school. As much of an imagination as I had, my doodles often felt like nothing compared to the worlds she could create on paper or canvas.

It takes a lot of strength to get up and leave your hometown as a young single parent. My mother could have very well left me with her parents, but she didn't. I have never met my father; all I knew is that he was from Yarmouth too. And coming back ten years later, I realized that Yarmouth isn't a big enough town to be surrounded by strangers. I did think about how life would have been different by having a dad. I wondered if he ever thought about me, if he told his friends that he has a daughter—heck, I even wonder if he had another family and I have half-siblings I've never met. As much as I tried to convince myself otherwise, I wish I had a relationship with him, but Mom told me at a young age that lingering on those thoughts was dangerous. So I tried not to.

"What did I miss?" Mom yawned.

"Oh, you know. Ran a red, police chased us for three miles until I shrugged them off on the last exit."

"Not funny."

"A little funny. We're actually just about there." I signalled and took the next exit.

Mom sighed and leaned back. She still looked anxious. Maybe she was nervous about returning? After all, she had more history in Yarmouth than I did, and returning after ten years because of losing a parent is tragic on its own. Mom always knew what to do for us, but this was something we had never experienced.

I could see fishing docks and warehouses—I even noticed there was a new bar just by the coast called The North Crow. I had read somewhere that crows have long-lasting memories, so I hoped that meant there'd be a few folks here who remembered us.

"There it is." Mom pointed.

A sign read, *Welcome to the Municipality of Yarmouth.*

We were welcomed to town on a rocky dirt road surrounded by homes you wouldn't find in the big city. I was happy to see Yarmouth not being gentrified. In Halifax it felt like a constant struggle: condos and businesses popping up out of the blue that didn't serve the community and always made finding a home a fight. Mom and I were lucky, but a lot of folks weren't as fortunate. So I was glad to see Yarmouth didn't have hipster cafés or craft breweries on every corner.

"Keep following the GPS, you can go sightseeing later," Mom reminded me.

I suddenly felt nervous in the driver's seat. Add the fact that we were finally here, and emotionally I felt like a house made of cards. I continued on the road towards my grandparents' house. We drove past the old playground with the green slide that always gave me an electric shock, and Mr. Phillip's house that still badly needed a new coat of paint, and Ms. Layton's corner store that always had good deals on Freezies. It made me want to jump out of the van and soak in my surroundings. Once we passed the waterfront, that's when it really kicked in. I remember Grampy taking me down there every Sunday afternoon after church. He would buy fish and chips, and we would throw rocks in the water. He told me to wish on them, but never tell him what I wished for.

"You feeling that too?" Mom asked, looking out towards the water.

"Yeah. I'm feeling it pretty hard," I replied, confirming the nostalgia that filled the air around us.

I made a left turn at the next intersection and could see houses lined up against the ocean. We didn't get that in Halifax. Halifax was more concrete than evergreen, there was no fantasy, only loud cars and city noise, and I didn't miss it. Soon we'd be to Nan and Grampy's—well, just Nan's now—place. She lived on the edge of a lake not much farther from where we were.

"It's this street right up here," Mom said, pointing.

I turned right and we made our way up a dirt road with houses on each side. I could see Ms. Layton's house. Then there was Mr. and Mrs. Evans's house—they were sweethearts. Nan and Grampy had them over a lot when I was young, and I had been close with the Evans's granddaughter, Tia. Mrs. Evans was a doctor and used to bring me stickers when she and her husband came over for dinner. I wondered if Tia was still around town. Maybe paying her a visit wouldn't be a bad idea once I got settled in. Gosh, I missed her. I regretted not keeping in touch as much as I should have. For the first few months after Mom and I left, we would chat on the phone every Saturday afternoon. Eventually every Saturday turned into every second Saturday, to once a month, to once every six months, until Tia Evans and I faded away from one another.

I took a deep breath as I tried to drive straight down the path. So many memories flooded my head all at once, and in front of me was the biggest one.

"Here we are," Mom said softly.

I could see Grampy's crappy charcoal barbecue on the front porch. The top of my tree house could be seen just around the corner of the house, and Grampy's red antique truck was parked in front of the garage. I got out of the van and walked straight to the old thing. I rested my hand on the aging hood. I noticed it was beginning to rust by the wheels. I loved that thing so much, and so did he. It was more than a truck; it was our airplane, rocket ship, dream-mobile.

"Hello!" I heard Mom calling out. "Anyone home?"

"Who's that I hear?" someone replied, opening the front door. It was an older white man wearing a golf cap and a blue button-up shirt.

"Mr. Evans!" Mom smiled.

Mr. Evans looked a lot older since the last time I saw him; he now leaned on a cane and his once-brown hair was distinctly salt and pepper.

Mom gave him a warm embrace and he said, "Jayla, you've known me long enough to call me Ben." He smiled. "Lillian is inside with your mother."

"Thank you so much for taking care of her," Mom said. "And thank you for handling the arrangements for Dad."

"We're always here, dear. I'm so sorry for your loss. Rudy was family to us, and so are you."

"Thank you, Ben."

"And is that Annaka I see?" Ben asked.

"Hey, Ben." I waved. "I just go by Anna now."

"Well, hello, Anna. I have to say, I prefer Annaka."

"It doesn't matter what you prefer," I let him know. "My name is Anna."

Mom gave me a look, but I was over letting people calling me what they think I should be called. I could let a lot of things pass, but I don't let people decide my name for me.

"Okay, Anna," Ben said, looking a bit stunned. "Hey listen, Tia is still around. She works at Ms. Layton's convenience store just down the way. Would be nice if you popped in to say hello."

I wondered if she even remembered me.

"It would be nice to see her," I replied. "I'll try to stop by in a bit."

"I should probably go inside," Mom said. "You coming, Anna?"

I shook my head. "Not yet. I think I'm gonna take a minute. It was a long drive."

"All right, I'll be inside, hon."

After Ben and Mom went inside, I went around to the backyard and looked at the lake. I remember Nan teaching me how to swim in that lake. That's a memory I held close. I didn't want to go inside because I feared it was a memory she no longer had. I wasn't ready for that. I knew she was in there, and I didn't want to be a stranger to her. Not yet. I wanted to take some time and spend the last bit of ignorance I had to enjoy a sunset. I didn't want to think about the future, or Grampy's funeral, or Nan not remembering who her granddaughter was. I wanted to remember the woman who taught me how to swim, and the stubborn man who didn't know when to throw away his crappy barbecue. I wanted to be in a place where I didn't have to worry about the rest of the world. I was scared that Yarmouth probably wasn't the place I remembered.

I couldn't hide my smile when I turned to the tree house. I climbed the ladder and could see the sun sinking beneath the lake. Everything outside was just the way it always was, but I knew inside everything would be different. I didn't want to cry yet. The world was slowly taking everything away from me but I wouldn't let it take away that view. I remember Grampy and I would use his old binoculars to look across the lake from our perch in the tree house. And on warm nights I would sneak out here with Clay and we'd use them, trying to follow the stars while the Milky Way was visible above us. The binoculars weren't there now, but I looked across the lake and in the fading light I could just make out small boats and folks relaxing on a dock in beach chairs. I wish I felt as relaxed as they looked.

I sat there for a while. Eventually the moon made its way to the sky, and I saw constellations I hadn't seen in years; I was happy to know they hadn't gone anywhere. Unlike the stars, Clay must have moved on a long time ago. I sighed. It was time go inside and face my fears. I climbed down the ladder and walked back towards the porch. I heard Mom's voice from inside as I passed an open window.

"It's worse than I thought," she was saying.

I paused and heard another voice, which I assumed was Lillian's.

"I know, darling. This is a difficult time and you haven't had an easy go. There are options, though." She paused. "Have you thought about moving her into a home?"

I made sure I was out of eyesight and sat down so I could continue listening.

"She's my Mom, Lillian. I can't leave her to die in an old folks' home. I just lost Dad." Her voice started to give out. I had never heard Mom cry before.

"Oh, come here, sweetie," I heard Lillian say.

I could hear Mom sobbing. I felt those tears flood my heart; it was beginning to sink. I just sat there feeling helpless. There are few things more uncomfortable than hearing your mother cry. Moms are supposed to know how to deal with everything...and if this broke *her*, what impact was it going to have on me? I was scared to see her—both of them—but I knew I had to stand up and make my way inside.

"This way, Tanya." I heard Ben's voice before I turned the corner.

"Nan's name." I whispered to myself. I could hear them sitting down on creaking chairs on the front porch. It was now or never. I made my way toward the creaking and said, "Hey" in a shy voice.

"Anna," Ben greeted me awkwardly. I knew he didn't want to be there for this. "I thought you were in the backyard."

"I was, but it's getting late and we've been on the road all day." I made my way up the steps, and that's when I saw her. She looked a lot older and a lot smaller. Her hair was white. She didn't even acknowledge me.

And that's when I choked up.

"Anna, maybe go inside?" Ben suggested.

Nan looked over at me. Her face didn't light up when she saw me this time. She observed me for a minute and then she turned to Ben and asked, "She's the other one? She's moving in too?"

The other one? My name is Anna, I wanted to scream, *not The Other One.* I looked into Nan's eyes but they were blank. She looked at me as if I was a visitor.

My arms and my legs felt completely numb after that. That was the only confirmation I needed. The memories of Nan teaching me how to swim, of her braiding my hair, of her teaching me how to play cards, of watching TV with her on the couch, and the memories of all the times we spent together…were gone.

I closed my eyes and let out a heavy breath.

"Anna," Ben said. "Anna, I think you should go inside to your mother."

I fought the tears as best as I could, and turned back down the path. The tears started rolling down my cheeks. I was a stranger to her. I didn't want to see my mom or be in that house. I just wanted to get away from it all. For so long, I had wanted to return to Yarmouth. But I wasn't ready for any of it. I wasn't ready to return to a memory that didn't remember me.

CHAPTER 3

I WALKED TO THE MAIN ROAD AND COUNTED THE STREET lights for a while. I couldn't believe I was nothing more than a stranger to my grandmother. I knew deep down it would happen, but I really didn't know how much it would actually hurt. Mom had been trying to prepare me for the last couple of days, but I don't think anything could have eased that blow. I felt aimless walking down the road but I eventually found myself in a familiar surrounding. I decided to keep going, I needed a clear mind.

I eventually made it to the downtown area and noticed most shops were closed. I remembered Main Street pretty well from my childhood. Every street corner I could look down and see the ocean. The weather was warm, but it wasn't summer by any stretch, so I wasn't sure if the vendors on the waterfront were open yet. Fish and chips didn't sound like a bad idea, but then I saw the lights were still on at Ms. Layton's corner store across the street. I hadn't eaten anything since the burger I'd scarfed down on the road, and I could feel my stomach rumbling for a snack. It was half past eight, so I assumed I had at least a half hour before they closed. Small town hours. I didn't see anyone near the cash so I went straight for the candy section.

"Uh…hello?" I spoke to the universe. "Anyone here?"

"Oh shit, fuck. I thought the door was locked," I heard a whisper from the other end of the store. The whisper turned into a woman's voice at the end of one of the aisles. "The store is closed." This was followed by footsteps coming in my direction.

"We close at eight," she said as she turned the corner. Her look of annoyance froze as she recognized my face.

It was Tia Evans, my fearless, rebellious childhood best friend.

"Woah! Annaka Brooks?" She was a lot taller than I remembered, and her hair was a lot shorter.

"Tia? Is that you?" I could not hide the grin sliding across my face.

"You get that from my name tag?" She pointed at it while laughing.

"No, I got it from your potty mouth." I pulled her into a tight hug.

"Dude, what the hell? It's been so long!" She hugged me back with a big squeeze.

It had been a while since I had one of those, and I didn't realize how much I needed it. Tia was my "real life best friend," if that made sense. No stage lights or special effects—what you see is what you get with Tia. I remember when we were kids she would stress out her father, Jonathan, so much when he watched us. If you took your eyes off her for a second, she was already a block away. Sure, she could sometimes be a handful, but she was always fun.

"It took you ten years to grow taller than me," I teased her.

"Pffft! It actually only took one. I had a growth spurt after you left. Sorry, I didn't mean to kick you out of the store," she continued. "When did you get in?"

"Just today actually. I needed a walk after being on the road all day. Guess I've been soaking in the surroundings."

"Not much has changed, as you can see." Tia shrugged.

"That's not always a bad thing," I replied. "I should probably get out of here so you can close." I made my way to the door.

"Wait, what are you doing? Like, right now? My car is just in the parking lot. Let me close up and I'll buy you some fish and chips and we can catch up on the waterfront."

"I like that idea a lot." I smiled.

A LITTLE WHILE LATER, WE sat on a bench at the waterfront eating fish and chips from takeout plates. I looked around and it felt like stepping back in time. I looked down the same docks Tia and I played on when we were young. I still remember her dad chasing us when we'd run off. It was a fun memory for us, but I'm sure it raised his blood pressure. The weirdest part of it all was that nothing changed. The waterfront, the docks, the building surrounding it all, looked exactly the same. But there I was with Tia, both of us knowing we had a decade's worth of catching up to do. I guess we changed even if our town didn't.

"God, I really didn't expect to see you tonight, dude," Tia cut into my thoughts. "Did you run into my grandparents?"

"Yeah, I saw your grandfather earlier. He was with my grandmother on the front porch."

"How's she doing?" Tia asked, taking a bite of fish.

"Not how I remember her." I paused. "I was a total stranger to her."

Tia put her fish down. "Damn, Annaka. I'm really sorry. We don't have to talk about that if you don't want to."

"It's just Anna, now. And thanks. Today has been one of the longest days of my life." I looked up at the sky. "Are you coming to the funeral?"

"Of course," Tia replied, not even giving me a second glance because of my name change. I appreciated that more than she knew. "Your grandfather meant a lot to this community and to this town. Hell, half the high school will be there—all his students. Everybody knew him, everybody loved him, and everybody will want to show their respects."

"Thank you."

I looked up to see the stars bright and alive, not shying away from light pollution. In Halifax that was a sight we could never see.

"It's been a while since I've seen that." I soaked it in.

Tia rested a hand on my shoulder. "Welcome home, Anna." She was quiet for a minute and then turned to me with a devilish grin. "I know you're going through a lot right now. And a real friend raids their parents' liquor cabinet for a pal who needs a drink. You game?"

I let out a laugh. Tia was always ridiculous. I was glad to see time hadn't changed that.

"Let's go," I said.

When we made it to Tia's place, she parked the car outside of the garage and took a breath. I remember how by the book her parents were—always followed the rules very closely. Tia was one who would always bend them. It's safe to say she didn't really take after her parents too much.

"Feeling like a people person today?" she asked.

"Can't say I am," I replied honestly.

"Well, I'll need you to distract my parents while I raid the liquor cabinet. Just be cool. Tell them about Halifax." Tia smiled. "Since you're a city girl now."

I shook my head and sighed. Tia had always been braver than me. I let my imagination do most of the scheming while she was more about the groundwork. As soon as we got out of the car, Tia grabbed my hand and made her way towards the front door.

"Hey! Look who I found!" She busted through the front door, pushing me to the forefront.

Tia's mother, Clare, turned around on the couch and squinted. "Annaka, is that you?"

"Hi, Clare," I said with a smile. Clare stood up and pulled me into a hug as Tia made her way out of sight.

"Oh, dear," Clare said as she let go. "I'm so happy to see you, but I'm sorry about the circumstances."

"Thank you, Clare. I didn't expect to see you—or Tia—tonight. How are you?"

"I've been good." She smiled. "I just can't believe how fast you and Tia grew up. Time is escaping us."

She was right about that. "And how's Jonathan?"

"I'll let you see for yourself. Jonathan, come see who turned up at the door!" Clare called.

"I'm coming, I'm coming," I heard as a tall black man in plaid made his way past the living room. A smile cracked his face when he saw me. Both of Tia's parents presented as black, though Jonathan was mixed. Jonathan's mother, Lillian, was black. And his father, Ben, was a white man. Both Tia and my families held a close generational bond through the years. We were basically one big family.

"Annaka." Jonathan gave me a hug. "Come sit down, do you want a coffee?"

"No thanks—bit late for that," I declined. "And actually, it's just Anna now. But I could use a seat after today."

In the kitchen Jonathan made a coffee for himself. Then he turned to me and said, "I'm going to miss your grandfather. I love him and I always will. He left behind a beautiful family of strong people."

In a way it felt awkward, because I wasn't quite sure what to say. I hadn't lost anyone before, so this was all new to me. "Thank you," I said quietly.

"How's Jayla?" Clare asked. "We're all rooting for her down here. I heard she took a leaf out of Rudy's book and teaches now."

"Yeah," I replied. "Everyone knows Mom in Halifax. She's always being featured in articles or stories, and has her worked showcased all the time."

Being the daughter of a sought-after artist wasn't exactly an easy task. I wasn't Anna Brooks; I was The Daughter of Jayla Brooks. I didn't hold resentment because of that. I was just tired and wanted to be my own person, form my own identity. But when your mom is a nationally recognized art superstar, it isn't exactly easy to find your own voice.

"That's great to hear." Clare sounded proud. "She left here with so little, and made so much of herself. She was always so driven and strong, and I can see it in you."

Everyone always expected me to follow in my Mom's footsteps, and that weighed on me. I had great grades in school, but I didn't know what I wanted to do with my future. I wanted to use this summer to find a job and save up money for university; I was hoping I'd find my path through there. But I learned that plans can change in a blink of an eye.

"I'm still trying to find what direction I want to go in," I replied.

"Go wherever your heart tells you," Jonathan said.

Such generic advice didn't really help. But then again, Jonathan was a real sitcom kind of Dad.

I heard a door slam, followed by Tia entering the room wearing a baggy hoodie and coming straight towards me.

"Yo! Glad y'all had a chance to catch up with Anna, but I'm going to be stealing her now. Thanks for coming to the party."

"Aha. Don't stay up too late, you two. Good to see you," Jonathan said, smiling at me.

I smiled back.

Tia took me downstairs to the basement. When we got down the steps, I was immediately hopped on by something big and furry. It was a big brown, black, and white dog.

"Woah! Calm down, big guy," I said as I gently let him down.

"And that's Taz. You probably remember him as a pup." Tia petted him. "Who's a good boy? You're a good boy." The dog barked like a good boy.

I remember Tia took Taz in right before Mom and I left. Tia had found him as a puppy; he had been wandering alone in the parking lot of a grocery store, abandoned. Tia had always had a soft spot for puppies. It didn't take long for her parents to come around, and just like that, Taz had a new home. He probably didn't remember me, but I'm sure he was just excited to see someone new. I stood up to see that the basement had been transformed to look more like a small apartment. There was a carpet underneath a sofa and reclining chair with bright red and green Christmas lights stapled to the walls. It was spring, but I guess Tia had free rein to let her imagination go.

"Make yourself at home. My parents let me live down here now instead of that small bedroom on the top floor," Tia explained.

"This place is pretty lit," I admired. "So, what'd you get?"

Tia pulled a bottle of rum from her baggy hoodie. "Score! There's some cola and glasses down here, sit tight."

I sat on the chair, Taz flopped down below me, and I admired Tia's set-up. I couldn't believe she still had a CD player; I looked at her collection and it was full of bands I'd never heard of before. Before long she came back with two drinks and handed me one.

"Hey, who are these bands?" I asked.

"Oh, those ones? Just local bands. I buy their merch when I can. Maybe someday they'll make it big and I can sell their crappy first EP and get rich. You never know when you're sitting on gold." She shrugged.

I sipped my drink and sat back in the chair. I wasn't a big drinker.

"So…how is Halifax anyways? A big city girl returning to her small hometown must have stories."

I laughed. "Halifax isn't a big city, but if you're into hipster cafés, craft beer, and gentrified neighbourhoods, you can check it out." I paused. "Not much has changed here. I'm happy to come back somewhere that's easier."

Tia cocked an eyebrow. "Easier? In what way?"

"In Halifax everyone cares too much about what everyone else is doing, thinking, who everyone was friends with. I was lucky to keep my head low."

"Must've been hard when your Mom is Jayla Brooks."

"Yeah, it was. Everyone would always have this large expectation of me. When you have a parent who's well known, I guess it makes it harder to find your own way."

"Why do you say that?" Tia asked.

I have to say, I appreciated the bluntness Tia offered. Most of the time I find myself cautious about opening up, and it was nice having someone who just wanted to skip right to the point. Even after ten years, she was super easy to talk to.

"Everyone thought I wanted to follow in her footsteps. But I want to be the main character of my own story. I want to have my own great journey." I paused and shook my head. "Maybe that's egoistic, I don't know."

"I don't think there's anything wrong with that. What are you looking forward to while being back?" she asked. "Stupid question," she cut back in. "You're here out of grief, not on a vacation."

"To be honest, with how my nan is doing, I don't know. I think I'd rather head back to Halifax. I got a life to pursue, and I was hoping this summer could be the stepping stone for it all."

"What kind of stepping stone?"

"Y'know, saving money. Next year is grade twelve, so I guess I wanted to be a step ahead for college. But then this happened and it shook everything up."

"Well, if you're here for a while then you're always welcome here," Tia smiled.

I took a swig of the drink and smiled back. "So what have you been up to, Tia Evans? What's life been like in Yarmouth?"

"That's a good one." Tia shrugged. "I guess everyone is kinda like you: they wanna save up money, go to college, and leave town."

"How about you?"

"Not quite my plan, I guess. As small as this town is, I love it here. I don't want to be thought less of for wanting to stay, y'know?"

"I get that." I immediately felt bad for telling her my plan. I loved Yarmouth too, but the idea of staying here seemed impossible, even as I was stuck there.

"Well, what do you wanna do?" I followed up.

"I wanna create a music festival!" She sat up with bright eyes. "I want to create a reason for more people to come down here, and stay hopefully. The music scene here comes and goes, but I want to build some type of longevity, y'know?"

I smiled at that. "What are steps are you taking?"

"I started reading lots on music business and grant writing. I'm hoping to get something going by next summer, even if it's small. Gotta start small before we get big, right?"

"That's the spirit." I smiled.

I looked across at the CD player; beneath there was a frame and inside there was a picture of Tia and Jonathan. Jonathan looking proper, smiling at the camera while Tia had her tongue sticking out with two peace signs up in the air.

"I'm wondering if my dad is still in town," I said. "I never met him. But I do know that Yarmouth is too small a town to be surrounded by strangers."

Then I paused. I don't know why I had to say that out loud. God, I hadn't even been here for twenty-four hours and I had already let that cat out of the bag.

Tia looked at me with non-judgmental eyes and asked, "Do you think about your dad a lot?"

"I mean, sure. As much as anyone else who hasn't grown up with a father. Christmas, birthdays, Thanksgiving, Father's Day. Every time I get into an argument with Mom." I usually wouldn't say things like that out loud, but Tia made me feel like I could. But that didn't mean an awkward silence didn't fill the air.

"Sorry if that's kind of a lot," I said, embarrassed. Sure, Tia made me feel like I could be open but I forgot I hadn't seen her in ages; dropping heavy shit on her like that probably wasn't always welcome.

"No, not at all. Don't worry about it, Anna," Tia reassured me. "Those feelings are real and honest. I think it's natural to think of that when coming back. It's the town where you're from, but also where he's from too. I'm sorry if there isn't much I can offer, but if things ever get heavy at home, you can crash here. This place is a lot bigger than my old bedroom. And besides, company is nice."

"Just like when we were kids," I mentioned. "You still hang with our crew? Laura, Taylor, Lucy?" To be fair, they were never "our crew" as much as they were Tia's. They kind of thought I was weird. I guess maybe I was. I mean, I was the only one who never outgrew my imaginary friend.

"Yeah, we're still all pretty close," Tia said as she got up and stretched. "I'm sure they'll be happy to see you if you stick around."

I lay back in my seat—I didn't realize how tired I was, but it had been a long day. The Christmas lights Tia had up were a nice touch.

I closed my eyes, but heard Tia messing around with her CD player, and music began to fill the air. A low melody broke the silence. There is always something intimate about finding out what music your friends listen to. Sharing music was sharing the rhythms and beats that got you through difficult times. I took another drink. I pretended the lights above my head were stars in the sky. I thought about the idea of heaven and wondered if Grampy was there. I didn't believe any of that stuff, but the thought was nice; if heaven were real, I would want Grampy to be comfortable there. I guess I was worried in a weird way. I didn't like the idea of Grampy just not existing anymore.

"Do you believe in heaven?" I asked out of the blue.

Tia sat up; the question caught her off guard.

"Okay, that one is kinda heavy," she said. She turned down the music with a remote. "Uh…I don't know. Maybe."

"Meaning?"

"I don't think so, no. But it's not something I would ever say to my grandmother. Being black and being an atheist aren't really two things that mix well, if you get what I mean."

I nodded. "I feel that."

She had a point. Sometimes being black and being a non-believer didn't sit well with the elders. Often, it's a conversation that never happens because we never know what will happen if we decide to bring it up. Grampy didn't believe in God. He didn't talk about that much, but that didn't stop Nan from dragging him to church often.

"What do you think?" Tia asked. "You think there's something after all of this?"

"If we're lucky then maybe it's a bottomless ball pit in a burger joint," I joked to break the tension.

Tia giggled. "You always had weird thoughts."

"What do you mean, weird thoughts?"

"I mean, dude, you were the only kid who had an imaginary friend when we were young. What was his name? Clay?"

I hadn't heard anyone say his name out loud in years. I was surprised Tia remembered.

"Yeah, Clay. How do you remember that?"

"This is super dorky," she said with a chuckle. "Be right back." She left the room.

I waited, unsure what she was doing. I took another sip and Tia returned with a dusty shoebox. She blew the dust into the air around us.

"This," she whispered, "contains secrets from the past."

Tia placed the shoebox on the table and opened it up. She began taking things out of the box:

A rubber band ball.

"Wow, I always wanted one of these," I said, reaching for it.

"Too bad, it's mine," she said, moving it away.

A piece of paper with a heart on it.

"Ooohhh, what's that?" I asked swiping it out of her hand.

"Hey! Give that back!"

I opened it up before she could grab it.

All it read was: *Bee Mine*. It was a Valentine with a heart-shaped beehive in the background. It was signed by Bobby Noah.

"Ooohhh, Bobby from elementary!" I teased. "You had such a crush on him."

Tia swiped the Valentine from my hands and threw it back in the shoebox.

"Yeah, before I realized that all men are trash."

"What's he up to nowadays?"

"Just being a douchebag on the football team. We, well…actually, we went to a dance together recently."

I glanced at her. "Juicy."

She snorted. "It really wasn't. He only went with me to make his ex feel jealous. It was bad enough he asked me how many guys 'I've been with.'" She rolled her eyes. "Which is none of his business. I just felt super used. *And* I caught him making out with his ex outside later that night."

"Oh, dude. I'm so sorry." I lowered my shoulders. Why are teenage guys such disappointments?

"Don't be," she cut in. "I made sure he got his."

There was the Tia I knew and loved. "Oh yeah? What did you do?"

"Well, I walked away in a mood. He followed me like, 'Wait, wait, Tia, it meant nothing!' He grabbed my arm then I turned around. Kicked him in the nuts in front of everyone and yelled, 'I hope you get kidney stones, douchebag!'"

I couldn't contain my laughter. God, I had missed Tia. She started laughing too.

"You're the most amazing person I've ever met," I told her.

"I'm all right," she replied with a shrug and a grin. She took a sip of her drink. "But that story is besides the point." She reached into the shoebox and took out a piece of loose-leaf and showed me.

"You drew this the week you left. I held on to it."

She handed me the piece of paper. I unfolded it to see it was drawing of Tia, Clay, and I standing in front of my tree house.

I had drawn myself with long braids and brown skin with goggles; Tia had long black hair, brown skin, and a cape. Clay was bald and grey. I had totally forgotten I drew that for her.

"Wow," I said, looking at her. "I can't believe you held on to this."

"Yeah, I'm one of those sentimental people. I like to hold on to the past as much as I can."

I smiled. "I'm really glad I ran into you today."

Tia smiled back, turned up the music, and poured me another drink.

The drinks led to laughter and memories. It was exactly what I needed. I needed a friend that day—someone who remembered me. I'm glad it was Tia. I just wanted to feel connected somehow, after all the years that had passed. I guess someone did remember me.

"You can crash here tonight if you like," Tia offered. "The sofa is all yours—my bedroom is down the hall."

"Thanks, but with the funeral tomorrow I think I should be home tonight. I'm def down to hang out again soon, though."

"That makes sense. I'll be there tomorrow. You okay getting home?"

"Yeah, it's only a short walk. I got this." I stood up and stretched, and Taz did the same. I bent down and scratched behind his ears. "See you tomorrow, Tia. And thank you for tonight. I appreciate this a lot."

"Any time." She walked me to the basement door. "Oh! Also, don't forget your phone." She handed it to me.

"Why'd you have my phone?"

"So I could put my number in it, of course," she said with a smile. "Text me when you're safe."

We hugged, and then I started down her driveway.

I took a breath of the night air and heard a car driving slowly down the dirt road. I followed the moon to my grandparents' place and counted street lights glowing through the trees. Some Yarmouth side streets didn't have crosswalks, so I walked as close to the side as I could; local traffic was smart enough to drive closer to the middle of the road. I could feel the alcohol make its way through my veins and I had a smile on my face from spending time with Tia. I still couldn't believe she'd held on to that drawing. It was nice to connect with her, and it was even better to just…get away from everything else. As I got closer, I was sad knowing how broken my childhood home felt.

But broken or not, this was our home for the next little bit.

I found the road towards Nan's place, and when I got close, I finally checked my phone. Two missed calls, and three texts from Mom.

Mom: *Where are you?*

Mom: *Anna, you just ran off. I need you to come back.*

Mom: *Call me.*

I'm usually fast at texting back, but my phone had been on silent. I hope Mom would understand.

All the lights inside were off, so I assumed she must have already gone to bed. When I got inside, they suddenly flicked on.

"Shit," I muttered to myself. I saw Mom waiting for me.

"You know, it only takes five seconds to reply to a text," she said. "I've been stressing about you."

"Sorry. I was at Tia's."

"And you couldn't have told me that?" She crossed her arms. "It's really not that hard to communicate, Anna." Then she came closer and smelled my breath.

"And you were drinking?"

"I...."

"Don't lie."

"Yes. We had one drink."

Mom gave me a serious look for a moment, then it was followed by a sigh.

"I'll let it go. This one time. I know the last couple days have been difficult, but don't make this a habit, Annaka."

I hated my full name. Mom only used it when she was upset, and this was my warning.

"Yeah, yeah, yeah. It won't happen again, all right?" I said as I tried to make my way upstairs.

"Anna, wait," Mom called out. "We need to talk for a minute."

My shoulders dropped. I didn't know what else there was to talk about.

"What is it?" I asked, coming back down the stairs.

"Listen, I was talking to Lillian today.... Your grandmother —she's, well, she's doing a lot worse than I thought."

"What do you mean?"

"And I heard something happened outside earlier tonight."

I sighed. "Yeah." I wanted to forget that happened, but I knew I couldn't lie to myself. "She…didn't know who I was. Treated me like a complete stranger."

It hurt. A lot. My eyes began to tear even thinking about it. Nan's eyes didn't light up the way they used to when she looked into mine. She didn't ask me how my day was, or even wonder if we shared a past. I was a stranger to her, and it dug deep. More than I thought it would.

"I'm so, so sorry, Anna." Mom looked at me. "I know what we spoke about on the drive, but a part of me was holding hope." She shook her head. "I wanted you to have more time with her before this happened. I'm sorry."

I didn't know what to say. We had so many opportunities to return here and visit, but Mom never wanted to. Mom had Halifax as her home base when it never felt like home to me. Home was in Yarmouth, where the houses were by the shore, where a community actually felt like family, where we could rest in a field to see the stars in the sky. Yarmouth was a place of magic and nostalgia, but now it was filled with so much grief and loss. This wasn't home anymore. I wanted to go back to Halifax, finish school, and leave the past behind, as much as it hurt.

I shook myself back to the present. "What else did you want to talk about?"

Mom paused, and then she sighed and said, "Listen, we're going to have to get comfortable here."

I narrowed my eyes. "What does that mean?"

"It means we have to stay here for a while."

"What do you mean 'a while'? I have to finish grade eleven. I was planning to get a job and save up money this summer. For university."

"I know, I know," she replied, putting her hands up like she was surrendering. "But we can't always catch the curveballs. Life isn't always as straightforward as that."

"You mean not for me," I retorted. "You always did what *you* wanted to do. I never had a say. I never had a say about moving to Halifax. I never had a say about leaving Grampy and Nan. I never had a say about any of it." Maybe it was the alcohol, maybe it was the long drive, but the idea of staying made me feel anxious. I loved the Yarmouth of my childhood, but with Grampy gone, and with Nan not even remembering who I am…I felt like I could barely process any of it.

"Listen, Anna, I know this is a lot—"

"It's always a lot with you," I growled. "It's never anything easy."

I stormed up the steps and made my way to the room at the end of the hallway. I opened the door to see fading yellow walls, blue blankets on the bed, and the familiar curve of the ceiling. It was the first bedroom that I ever called mine. Most nights Grampy would read to me until I fell asleep. It dawned upon me that tonight wouldn't be one of those nights. It would be a sleepless one. I noticed a black dress lying across my bed beside my suitcase. I wish Mom didn't feel like she had to micromanage me.

I moved my suitcase towards the closet. When I pulled open the door, I could see my name on the wall in Grampy's handwriting. Beside my name were measurements with their corresponding years: 2007, 2008, 2009, and 2010. My frown faded when I saw it; they never erased it, never painted over it. They kept it all there. I remember Grampy was always so excited every few months to see how much I'd grown. I always wanted to be as tall as him, but I seemed to stop growing a few inches shorter than Mom. Seeing that took me away from my anger, and put a smile on my face.

I moved my suitcase into the closet and as I got further inside, I saw even more measurements.

"Wait a sec, these aren't mine," I said out loud.

It was my childish printing instead of Grampy's neat script. Above the measurements I read his name in my messy writing: Clay.

Could he still be here? I wondered. As soon as I did, I tried to bury that thought. There was already so much going on, and I couldn't carry that question on top of everything else.

I tried lying in bed but sleep was the last thing I could focus on. I couldn't come to terms with the fact that Grampy was gone. I couldn't admit that this house was missing a loud voice. Moonlight splashed on my bedsheets through the window and I could hear crickets chirping. It was almost the same feeling I had ten years ago. I want to say that it felt like home, but everything was different. It took coming back to know what emptiness felt like. As angry as I was, I was starting to catch my breath as cool spring air made its way into my room. I sat up and looked at the lake outside my window. How bittersweet that view was. I shouldn't have taken everything out on Mom the way I had. I knew she was trying her hardest, and that was probably the last thing she needed to hear from me.

As the anger left, I could feel regret taking its place. As messy as this entire situation was, it was a surprise to all of us. I had never seen Mom cry until that night; there was a world of vulnerability inside of her that I never got the chance to see.

It didn't take long for the cool air to become chilly, but I liked the cold. I tried closing my eyes again. Then I heard a creak above my head. It sounded like it came from the attic.

I was pretty sure Mom was asleep, and I doubted Nan would be up there this time of night. So I ignored it. But it didn't take long for it to happen again, and this time a bit of dust fell down on my forehead.

"Ugh." I sat up and could hear more creaking. "Mom, is that you?" I called.

There was no response.

A piece of me was curious; it had been forever since I was up there. Birds would sometimes get stuck up there when I was younger, and

Nan would have to go up and open the window so they could fly out. I didn't want a little bird to stay trapped.

I made my way up the steps and at the top, the first thing I noticed was the smell: lemons and cigarette smoke. Grampy was a smoker but tried to hide it most of the time; the attic wasn't the smartest idea. He would use lemon-scented air fresheners to hide the odour. We all knew what he was doing anyway. He thought he was being sneaky, but men always think they're one step ahead when they're full of shit.

It was cold up there but everything still looked more or less the same. Just with more dust and a few extra spiderwebs. But there was no bird up there that I could see. The cigarette smell was still strong—Grampy must have been smoking up here just a few days before. A part of me held hope this was just a bad magic trick, but it wasn't.

When I walked on the floor it creaked beneath my feet, and I knew there was no way a bird was heavy enough to make that sound. My curiosity piqued when I saw an old trunk at the other end of the attic. Something told me to go for it, so I did. I popped it open and found old blankets, folded-up curtains, and I could feel a few things at the bottom. I pulled up an old photo album. My heart almost leaped out of my chest as I sat down and opened it.

The first photo was of Grampy and Nan kissing outside of the house with a "Sold" sign in front of them. They both looked so young and happy. It must have been when Grampy started teaching. I flipped a few pages and found a baby photo of Mom that made me smile. I had never seen her baby photos before. I moved farther along to see her first day of school. She was wearing overalls and her hair was in braids just like me. It made my heart melt. Mom usually wore her hair in a natural Afro these days, but it was cute to see her rocking my iconic look. I continued until I saw me. I looked real young, about four or five. Mom, Grampy, Nana, and I all stood in front of the house—and I could see it was the family that made this place a home. I really needed that. I kept flipping, close to the other end. I found what looked like a photo from ages ago; it showed a young woman, a teenager. I had never seen her before. She was a little bigger, and had long dark hair and skin. She was sitting, smiling, in a rocking chair.

"Who are you?" I asked aloud. After a moment, I put the album away and kept digging.

I eventually felt another book. I pulled it up to see it full of dust, but recognized it as the dark grey journal Grampy had given me on my first day of school years ago.

"Woah, there you are," I said with a smile.

It wasn't in the best shape—the pages were wrinkled and looked water damaged. They felt real stiff but I flipped through it anyway. I opened up to the first few pages and found a drawing of what I thought looked like me. Not to brag, but most kids' drawings were pretty bad. In my case, it didn't take too long for me to learn a thing or two from Mom. I flipped through a few more pages to see the small grey boy I had drawn when I was a child. Clay.

"Miss ya, buddy." I smiled and put a hand on the page. I moved past the drawings and found the entries I made each night. Beside one entry was a drawing of Grampy giving me a piggyback by the lighthouse that said "Cape Forchu" above it. It was a bittersweet feeling. I think the hardest thing about seeing it, was realizing I'd never get a piggyback up that hill again. I didn't want to think about it, so I closed the journal.

I had never said it out loud until tonight, but deep down I'd always resented how Mom took me away from Yarmouth. I hated how she never wanted to come visit. I hated how I was always an afterthought in her story. I never got to see Grampy or Nan before everything changed. I had so much deep-rooted anger towards her because of it. The only family I ever had was either gone or was slipping away.

I thought about the what ifs, and what life could have been like if I had stayed—I could have spent more time with Grampy, I could have made more memories with Nan. I remember asking Mom when we might return, and it was the same old script:

"This summer isn't likely," she would say after I asked eagerly.

"You say that every summer," I'd reply, annoyed.

"I promise, we will visit soon."

But we never did. And that was the hardest part about being back now—everything that ever meant anything to me was gone. I dropped the journal on the ground, tears landing beside it.

My life could have been totally different. I could have had a family—more than just me and Mom. I could have even met my dad. As it was, the only father figure I ever had known was going to be buried in the morning.

I reached for the journal, but before I could touch it, I heard rustling from the other side of the room. It startled me so bad that I stumbled back, landing on the floor.

"Who's there?" I called out.

There was no reply.

It was probably a raccoon, and those things were terrifying—my absolute least favourite animal. When I reached for the journal again, I noticed its spine was damaged. Once I touched it I felt resistance, like someone was pulling it.

"What the hell?" I was beginning to scare myself. I got to my feet and pulled, but was met with an equal amount of resistance. Then suddenly, I was pulled so hard I fell forward onto the ground.

The journal hit the floor too. I scrambled to grab it, only to see it had fallen open to a page with a drawing of Clay and me sitting on the front porch of the house. The last journal entry I wrote before we left. God, that had been such a bittersweet day; bitter to be leaving, but with sweet thoughts of coming back.

I looked up to see who was there, but everything was gone. I found myself surrounded by a pitch-black darkness. The walls, the floor below me, the ceiling, they were all gone. Only the journal was lying in front of me.

"What the hell is going on?!" I looked around in a panic.

The darkness formed into new shapes around me. My surroundings shifted, transformed, and faded into existence. Suddenly, I felt the rocky path outside of my grandparents' house beneath my knees, and the smell of warm summer air touch my face; crickets chirped in the distance, and I watched as wet grass started to sprout around me.

How was this happening?

Then I heard a voice that made me freeze. Someone from my past. An innocent, shy, playful voice.

"How long are you going to be gone?"

It was…Clay.

My heart sank to my stomach. I looked down the path that formed beneath me and could see the two of us sitting on the porch of my grandparents' house. Clay was wearing one of my old T-shirts—we used to share clothes—and I wore a dress that Nan had given me for my birthday one year. I was only a kid.

"Not forever, silly," I heard my younger voice answer. "We'll be back soon. But I want you to stay here; it's safer. The city can be a scary place." I heard my own voice echo in my ears.

"I don't wanna stay. I wanna go with you. I don't wanna be alone." His plead echoed too. This was the morning I told Clay Mom and I were leaving.

"I know, Clay," I soothed. "But Mom said we'll be back before you know it. She said the apartment we're moving into could be small. I don't know if you'd be comfortable there."

I was the only one he ever wanted to reveal himself to. He was afraid bad things would happen if he showed himself to Grampy or

Nan. And maybe he was right. But I knew if I brought him along, there would be a greater chance of him being seen.

"You promise you'll be back soon?" he asked with teary brown eyes.

"I do." I raised a pinky finger, and he wrapped his grey one around mine, followed by a hug. That was the last memory I had with Clay before we left.…

I sat there with those bottled feelings as everything around me disappeared again. I closed my eyes, placing my head in my hands.

When I opened my eyes again, I was back in the attic like nothing had happened. I touched the wooden floor to make sure it was real.

"Okay, okay," I said aloud. "What the hell was that? What just happened here?!"

"I really didn't expect to see you today."

I heard that voice again, and it caused a shiver to go down my spine. His voice wasn't as playful, shy, or innocent. It was deeper, more mature, and…sad. I looked up to see a familiar face. It was still soft and grey, but older.

"What the hell." I moved back and couldn't say anything. My heart began pumping. Why was he still there?

"Cl-Clay?"

"You remember me," he said with a surprised, but not happy, face.

He was so much bigger than the last time I had seen him. He was wearing a light brown V-neck that was a bit baggy on him, and black dress pants where the legs touched the ground before his feet. Were those my grandfather's clothes?

"You have something that's mine," he said as he picked up the journal. And then, just like that, he vanished, along with it.

"What the hell?!" I ran down the steps as fast as I could and crashed into Mom.

"Anna, what happened?" Mom asked me groggily. "What's going on up there? It's two in the morning. I don't want you to wake up your grandmother."

"It's nothing." I caught my breath and thought fast. "I just wanted to see some old photo albums and got spooked. There was a bat; it flew out the window."

"A bat?!" She was alarmed. "Oh no." She started shaking her head. "Was there just one? If there's more, we may have an issue…." Mom had that stressed look on her face.

"There was just one, and it's gone now. I promise," I lied. I made my way to my room. I shut the door to my bedroom and covered myself with the blankets.

I couldn't believe what had just transpired.

Clay was here all this time.

I had so many questions I couldn't process, while my heart was beating out of my chest. It felt like I had motion sickness but I kept myself under the blankets with one eye peeking out. There was no sign of him.

That…couldn't have just happened, I said to myself. *He's still here?!* I was breathing real heavy and checked my phone: 2:23 A.M. I had to be up in less than six hours. I looked across my bedroom again and saw the inside my closet. There read *Clay* above some measurements, right beside mine.

CHAPTER 4

T HE NEXT MORNING IT FELT LIKE MY VERY BONES were shaking. Clouds covered the sky, and I was filled to the brim with grief and confusion. Today was Grampy's funeral, but what I had seen the night before...I couldn't get that image out of my head. I knew what I saw—someone who looked like Clay. He spoke like Clay. Except he was older. What could he want with my journal? Grampy had given me that journal, and it was the only thing of his I had left. I knew I had to find it.

These thoughts were filling my head while I sat near the entrance of the church. I wasn't in the mood to talk to anyone. I felt so out of it. I looked across the funeral home at the giant photo of my grandfather, and it made me think back to the last time I actually spoke to him. It had been my sixteenth birthday. He called me, as he usually did. And he told me the story he always told, about the first time he heard my voice. I loved the way he told it. That night I had lain on the roof of our apartment building in Halifax speaking to him. At one point he asked if I could see the same stars he was looking at. I replied, "You can't really see the stars too well in Halifax."

"That's a shame," Grampy said. "But I'm sure there's more opportunity over there for you."

"Maybe," I replied. "But it isn't nearly as fun. Not much space for campfires."

"Oh, so you're looking for a story, are you?"

"We do this every year." I laughed at his slick transition. "You're going to tell it to me either way, so let's get it over with."

"All right, all right, well here it is. The first time I heard your voice, I drove you, your mother, and Nan to the hospital. We were waiting and your stubborn butt wouldn't come out." (He would always say that line.)

"I inherited that from you," I shot back. I had been waiting a good six months to use that one.

He laughed and continued. "A little later, your grandmother told me to head home and clean up the house. She said she knew you'd be coming any minute. And I replied, 'We've been here for eight hours, what makes you say that now?' She said that she had a feeling. So I drove home, cleaned up the entire house. Top to bottom. The floors were sparkling."

"Sparkling?" I cut in. "That's some serious elbow grease."

"Oh, believe me when I say sparkling. I put in so much work that I fell asleep on the couch and couldn't hear the phone rigging."

"That sounds just like you," I said with a roll of my eyes.

"I wasn't asleep forever, only about an hour. But when I woke up, I saw a message was on the answering machine. It was from your grandmother and she was shouting, 'Rudy, Rudy! Pick up the phone. Come meet your granddaughter! And dress nicely.'"

That was something Nan would say. I smiled.

"And in the background," he continued, "all I heard was you crying up a storm. I thought to myself that you had good lungs. I knew you had something to say and always would. When they told me your name, a tear came to my eye. They told me, 'Her name is Annaka.'"

Grampy had always really liked my name. A lot more than I did. I never knew why, and I never thought to ask...and now I'd never be able to. I guess the saddest part of that memory was knowing that was the last time I would ever hear his voice.

Fast-forward almost a year, and here we were. I could see Mom on the other end of the church with Nan. There were lots of black folks around. There is a big misconception about Yarmouth having no black people, but that's where Nan's people stem from. Nova Scotia isn't as white as people think it is, even if it is pretty white sometimes. Though I didn't remember any of them, they all remembered me.

"Look at how much you've grown, Annaka," an older black woman said to me. "I'm so sorry about your loss, dear."

"Thank you." I nodded, not knowing what else to say. I didn't correct her about my name; I wasn't in the mood for the response it would bring.

"I'm your distant cousin, Carla," the woman continued. "Not sure if you remember me."

I wish I did.

"I remember," I lied with a smile. I didn't want to be rude, and it was probably a lot easier to just lie. To be honest, I didn't feel like hearing stories about everything that happened in the last ten years, or having to explain why I didn't come visit, or what I should have done to make more of an effort. I wasn't in the mood for any of that, so I wasn't opening any door that led to that conversation.

The service was starting and I made my way to a seat in the front pew by Mom. An older black man named Pastor Dennis gave the eulogy. He has known our family for years. I sat and watched the pastor speak about my Grandfather's life while I was trying to mourn the loss of him.

I think deep down I would have liked to say something. Lots of other people did: Carla told a story about the first time she met

Grampy when Nan brought Carla to a Christmas dinner at the house. She spoke about how shy he used to be, and how different he became. I only ever knew him as the loudest person in the room. I could never imagine Grampy being shy; it almost made me laugh. Tia's parents, Jonathan and Clare, spoke too. They talked about how he used to be their high school English teacher, and how he had also been teaching Tia before he passed away. I wondered what it'd be like having Grampy as a teacher. He must have been awesome because there were a lot of students present; all dressed in black, most repping Yarmouth High buttons. Shortly after the Evanses finished, Mom went up in front of everyone. I could tell she was nervous. She knows how to speak publicly—heck, she did it often—but that experience wasn't useful for a funeral.

"My father spent most of his life with a smile across his face," she began. "Even when the world tried to take it away. Coming to Canada from England with little family, he knew he had to be brave to find his way here. And judging by how many people are here, a lot of you cherished him." She paused and looked out at the sea of faces. She took a deep breath and went on.

"Dad's presence could chase away a cloudy day, and bring warmth to those who needed it most. I remember how supportive he was. Contrary to popular belief, my teenage years were always somewhat of a roller coaster. I wasn't always setting the best example, and I sometimes got into a little bit of trouble." Mom shrugged at the last part while the crowd let out some giggles. "But I always knew I could call Dad, regardless of the situation. No matter what happened. He would get in his big old truck, pick me up, and he'd buy me a cheeseburger, some French fries, and a coffee. And we would just talk it out." Here she smiled, and a tear leaked out her eye and rolled down her cheek. "I think it was those small moments that left the biggest impact on my life. As stubborn as he was, he was wise.

Rich in knowledge, and always could say the right things. He never shied away from his family in the difficult moments...the vulnerable ones. My father always rose to the occasion when it mattered most. I'm lucky to have been raised in such a loving home; he always treated my mother with love, respect, and cherished her even in the moments when she wanted to rip his head off." The crowd laughed at that.

"I know that without his patience, love, and understanding, I wouldn't have become the woman I am. He always had a special place in his heart for my daughter, Annaka." Mom smiled while looking at me. I didn't even mind that she had used my full name. It suited the moment. "I still remember how his face lit up the first time he met his granddaughter, and how joyful he was being able to watch her grow. He stepped in to be a positive male role model in my daughter's life. He was so excited to have her around, and grow in the same household that he raised me in.

"My father was an anchor not only for his family, but also his community. He taught most of the people here, I'm assuming?" Almost everyone in the room nodded or raised their hand. My mother smiled and nodded. "My father cherished working with young people because he knew how vital those teenage years are, how important it is to make a lasting impact on a young person's life, and how far that can take them into the future. All he ever wanted was the best for everyone. He did that by instilling hope in those who will be the future. I need every young person here to listen closely to the words I'm about to say. You hear?" She looked out at the audience again, scanning for the students. I could see the young people in the back saying yes as a way of acknowledgment.

"Embody the hopefulness he planted in your school hallways, in the classrooms where he spilled his knowledge, and use that as a foundation to build upon when you lead the future. Be kinder to one another, never shy away from fear, and be brave in this world, especially when the world is trying make you anything but. He believed in all of you, and right now, he needs you to be the future. He needs you to be the now. So jump into the world, and ignite a fire behind you, lighting a path for others to follow. I know you won't let him down." She paused to let that sink in, before finishing: "Thank you all for being here on this day. I want to give others the opportunity to share their memories of my father. God bless." Mom nodded her head, wiping the tears from her eyes, while the attendees applauded.

That last part did warm my heart. Mom had the voice of a giant, and the strength of one, too. Grampy was an immigrant who came to Canada as a child. He never spoke about his family, nor did anyone else. When I was a kid, the only extended family who ever came over were great-aunts, uncles, and cousins on Nan's side. The funeral was full of them. Add to that the large presence of students from Yarmouth High, and it just went to show that he didn't need blood family to have a large funeral.

AFTERWARDS I FOUND MOM AND Nan on a bench by the entrance. Tia's grandparents, Ben and Lillian, and her parents, Clare and Jonathan, stood close for support.

"How you doing, hon?" Mom asked me.

"As good as I can be, I guess." I shrugged. "You did great up there."

She smiled. "Thanks, babes. Have you talked to any of the family?"

"Barely. Everyone here knows me but I barely remember any of them."

"I know. You haven't seen most of these people in years. I saw you with Carla, though. She's going to be coming over later. Did you eat this morning?"

"No. I wasn't hungry."

"You should grab a bite to eat," Lillian said. "There's tons of food over there."

I could see Tia standing by the food table and she waved me over. She gave me a big hug and I squeezed her right back.

"How you feeling?" she asked.

"Like I saw a ghost last night."

She looked at me. "Odd choice of words."

"I know. I'll explain later."

Had Clay actually been waiting for me all those years? I was still spooked from my experience the night before. And what exactly could I say to Tia? *Hey, I saw my imaginary friend last night. You know, the one you have a drawing of?* It didn't exactly roll off the tongue.

"You remember Taylor, right?" Tia cut into my thoughts, bringing me back to reality. It was Taylor Bell, one of Tia's friends growing up. I was glad to see she came.

"Hey, Annaka," she said. "Good to see you. I'm sorry for your loss—Mr. Brooks helped me out a lot last year with English, I felt honoured to be one of his students."

She extended both of her hands, and I grabbed hold of them and genuinely thanked her for coming. It was nice to see someone else who I remembered from elementary. I was sure there'd be more, but suddenly, I was more interested in food. I grabbed a plate and surveyed the spread. They had everything from ham to sandwiches, to meatballs.

The rest of the reception was full of warmth. Many folks offered me their condolences. I kept my distance from Nan. I couldn't bring myself to speak to her and have her think I was a stranger. I felt so awful about it. I also felt bad because I hadn't called home since last year. Maybe if I had, I could have had a proper goodbye with Nan. But that never happened, and I had to live with that.

I wandered, and finally made my way to Grampy's urn. I knew I had to; I wouldn't be able to forgive myself if I didn't. I lost my breath when I actually saw it, but I knew I had to be brave, just like he would be. Although I was chasing each breath, I knew I had to keep moving. I tried going to a happy place, thinking back to Grampy taking me to the lighthouse while giving me a piggyback, and the way we used to run to the edge of the rocks and see nothing but blue: ocean under sky. We did that every Sunday. Those were memories I wanted to carry in my heart for the rest of my life. When my eyes closed, I was on Grampy's back, on top of the hill that I pretended was a mountain, and we watched the sky meeting the ocean in a distance that stretched further than I could see. When I opened my eyes, my hand was on the urn that his ashes would be buried in. I know Mom wanted me and everyone there to leave feeling hopeful, but right now, hope felt like a daydream at best.

When things began to wind down, someone collected the urn and everyone made their way towards their vehicles. We were on our way to the burial. I decided to ride with Tia. It was a quiet ride, and I began to feel a hard weight making itself comfortable in my chest. The feelings were beginning to settle in. I just wanted to hug my grandfather again. I just wanted a piggyback. I wanted to hear his voice and I wanted to tell him that I loved him. But I'd never get that chance again.

"You okay, Anna?" Tia asked, her eyes on the road.

"No." I closed my eyes, wanting to be anywhere else. "No, I'm not." I could feel my chest tighten as I became short of breath—I was doing my best trying not to cry. The funeral was more than I thought it'd be, and I wanted to just let it out. All of it.

Tia extended a hand and I grabbed hold of it, tight.

"What are you feeling?" Always to the point, Tia.

I shrugged and looked out the window so she wouldn't see my eyes welling up. "Scared."

"What are you scared of?" she probed gently.

"Forgetting what his voice sounds like." Tears rolled down my cheeks.

Tia kept her eyes on the road but I knew she could feel the pain—it was radiating off me. Grieving felt so awkward. Even at the best of times, I couldn't open up to people. Mom and I only ever talked about school, work...the day-to-day stuff. Never emotions. I didn't know how to allow myself to be fragile. I guess I kept everything bottled in, like Mom. After all, Tia and I barely even knew each other anymore. We spent a lot of time together as kids, but the years had created so much distance. I wondered if all of that felt uncomfortable to her as well. If it did, she didn't show it. She just held on to my hand tightly. I was thankful she was giving me space.

I kept looking out the window and tried to focus on what was out there. The cars were driving in formation to the graveyard. It was a little ways outside of Yarmouth, and the clouds weren't breaking away. Raindrops began to pelt against the window. I didn't want to say goodbye to Grampy. Not in the rain. Not today.

We arrived. Walking the path to the gravesite was the hardest part. I read my grandfather's name on the tombstone. *Rudy Brooks. Beloved Husband, Father, Teacher, Leader, Grandfather.* Everything about him reduced to a handful of words. But he was more than anything that could be written on a tombstone—he was the sky that held everything, and everyone, together.

Tia's grandfather, Ben, carried the urn and placed it in front of the grave. He wiped the tears from his eyes. These two had been best friends. They talked daily, and I couldn't even imagine how Mr. Evans felt having to carry his friend's ashes.

"I'll miss you, buddy." He knelt down and placed his hand on the urn for a moment.

Everybody else did that too, as a way to say goodbye. I was hesitant at first. Something inside of me didn't want to—I knew if I did then all of this would be real. I wanted to wake up from this bad dream and call him. But when I placed my hand on the urn again, it hit harder than before. This time it was all…real.

I took in a deep breath and started crying again.

"I miss you, I love you, and I'll never forget you," I whispered.

And then the floodgates opened. I couldn't stop crying. He was the man who taught me how to read and write. The man who told me ghost stories when Mom warned him not to. The man who taught me to tie my shoes. The piggybacks, the long drives, they were all gone. My tears splashed on the urn as Mom came up and wrapped her arms around me. She was crying too.

"He's gone, and I want him back," I wept.

"Shh…it's okay, hon."

I cried and I cried hard. The worst part of it all was knowing my birthday was coming up, and I wasn't going to receive that phone call.

CHAPTER 5

MOM KNEW I WASN'T IN ANY SHAPE TO HEAD BACK to Nan's house for the reception. There would be lots of company who would ask me the same questions, tell me the same stories, and would want to know why I only wanted to be called Anna now. I was in no mood for exhausting questions while dealing with grief. So instead, Mom asked Tia if I could chill with her for a bit. So there we were, back in the basement. Eventually night took over the sky, but it was still cloudy. I was lying on the couch covered in a blanket with Taz lying on top of me. We hadn't said anything since we got there, and I could tell Tia was feeling a bit awkward about it.

"Hey, Anna? If you need some space, that's all good. Do you want me to leave for a bit? I could go for a drive or—"

"I don't think I want to be alone right now."

"I see. I see. Just not in a talking mood?"

"Not really."

"Oh."

Tia took a breath, got up, walked over to her ancient CD player, and put on something soothing. I could tell her life was somewhat of a playlist. She always had music for different moods and it was what I needed right then. I closed my eyes and I thought about Grampy.

"I just want to give him a hug," I let out.

"Hey, hey." Tia sat next to me. "I know."

She got close and I rested my head in her lap and held on to Taz.

"It's just weird that he's gone. The last time I spoke to him was on my birthday. Almost a year ago. I've been meaning to call, but, but—"

"Life gets busy, Anna, it's okay," Tia cut in. "It's easy to take in all the guilt of the world, but is that what he would want?"

"No," I replied. She was right. He'd want to have a big cookout, a celebration of his life. "He'd want a parade in his honour." I laughed through my tears.

Tia smiled and nodded. "Yup, that sounds like the Mr. Brooks I knew."

We laid there for a while as music filled the air and Christmas lights lit up the room. I wanted to be in that moment forever. It was a comfort zone for me. Tia hummed with one arm around me as she checked emails on her phone.

"D'you think it's weird that I kinda wanna meet my dad?" The thought had been swirling in my head since Mom told me we were coming back to Yarmouth, and it just kind of slipped out. I could never ask that kind of question around Mom, but I felt safe with Tia. A part of me wondered if he'd show up to Grampy's funeral, but I wasn't sure if Grampy even knew him. I sure didn't—Mom never wanted to speak about him, so a lot of it was left up to my imagination.

"No," Tia told me instantly. "I don't think that's weird at all."

I knew that my father probably wasn't a perfect man by any stretch of the imagination, but the what-ifs filled me. I always wondered what it'd be like to have a dad. Growing up and seeing Tia doing father–daughter stuff with Jonathan made me wish I had that, especially once we were in Halifax. With Mom being out most of the time, it would have been nice to have someone to be silly with, have someone to give me guidance, or someone to tell me that the world could be anything I wanted to make it. But the only man to tell me those things had been a world away in Yarmouth, and I only spoke to him once a year.

"I think that's a normal feeling. And whatever you do I got your back. But—" Tia paused.

"But what?"

"I guess what I'm trying to say is, maybe don't keep your expectations too high, y'know? I mean, has he ever tried to contact you while you were in Halifax?"

"No."

He never did. Every Father's Day in school I spent time making cards for Grampy. When we made the switch to Halifax I would mail them to him. So I know Tia was right. I shouldn't hold someone who never put in the effort to introduce himself to a high standard.

My mind drifted back to the attic. I knew I couldn't tell anyone what I had seen; they'd think I was out of my mind. I moved off the couch and saw the shoebox from the other night was still sitting on Tia's table. I opened it up and pulled out my drawing. I saw all three of us again, and looked at Clay. Maybe I had just been seeing things that weren't really there. In the drawing, Clay was holding onto the journal.

Something clicked in my brain.

"I think I'm going to get some sleep," I told Tia.

"Wanna crash here?"

I shook my head. "I think I should stay close to home tonight."

"That makes sense. Need a lift?"

"Nah. Thanks, though," I said as I made my way to the door.

She followed me and gave me a big hug. "I'm always here for you, Anna."

I was overwhelmed with guilt. I hadn't always been there for her like she was here for me now. I wished I had kept in better touch with

Tia after we left, but I couldn't change the past. All I could do was attempt to be better in the present. She understood that when not many people did. Tia was a real one. I had to keep her close.

———

WHEN I APPROACHED HOME, I saw the last few cars leaving. I kept my head down because I didn't want to talk to Mom or Nan. I managed to skip past them by going in the back door and heading straight upstairs to the attic.

Everything was the same as the night before, full of dust and memories. I didn't exactly know how to summon an imaginary friend—it's not like there were any professionals on the subject. So I just spoke.

"Hey. I know what I seen last night. If you're around, I'd like that journal back, please."

There was no reply.

"You're not going to make this easy for me, are you?" I took a few steps. "Listen, dude. Can we cut the bullshit? I'm sorry I left. Can we talk? It's been a while."

Still nothing.

"This is so stupid." I put my face into my palms.

Maybe it had just been wishful thinking after all. Everything else was still in the same place, the photo albums, the blankets, and the trunk.

But the journal was still gone.

I went outside to get some fresh air. The cool ocean air felt nice, and it was so quiet out here. Then I noticed that the side door to the garage was open. I made my way inside.

Inside was Grampy's big old red truck. I guessed Mom had parked it there so guests had more room to for their cars. God, I loved that truck, even if it was rusty and even if it was old. I climbed up the passenger side and blew a thin layer of dust away from the dashboard. I lay back in the seat to look around the garage. It was beat down, not well kept, and it made me sad. Clay and I would play hide-and-seek in the garage when we were young. I remember getting in trouble one time when Nan found me in here alone, because she thought I was making a mess. Maybe we were, but she never found Clay. He was always the better hider—me, I was always the seeker.

I got out the truck and looked around a bit more. I could see Grampy's toolbox on the floor. Behind it was a box of books. I searched it and found a bunch of old muscle car magazines, which made me giggle. Grampy was never much of a car guy, and I always made fun of him for having these magazines. There were also some textbooks in there that he used to teach his English class at Yarmouth High. I kept moving the books until I came across it again: the journal.

"There you are." I smiled.

I felt the cover—so soft. I opened it for the second time in ten years and saw the drawings of me, Grampy, Nan, Mom. I continued flipping through the journal until I came across Clay again. I found a drawing of him and I standing outside of our tree house holding hands. I looked at the journal's damaged spine again, and this time I noticed pages were missing from the back. It was definitely already worn out by the time Grampy had given it to me, but I'm sure time hadn't helped the thing either.

I hopped up in the bed of Grampy's truck and scanned more pages. There was a drawing of the lake iced over in the winter, and I was skating across it, holding hands with Clay. It made me smile. I guess some of Mom's talent did rub off on me. I didn't end up the worst illustrator in the world, that's for sure.

"Where did he go?" I wondered out loud.

I found a drawing of Nan braiding my hair on the front steps while Mom painted on a canvas. I chuckled. I loved having my hair in braids. There was a drawing of Grampy and I sitting in his truck. We had gone on so many adventures, all of them better than the last. Maybe that drawing represented the last one we went on. I closed the journal and tried not think about it.

But I couldn't stop thinking about the funeral. When I had touched Grampy's urn, that's when everything became real. That's when I knew I couldn't escape the moment, and it was full of pain.

Above my head a light bulb flickered. I ignored it at first, but then it flickered again.

"Who's there?" I called out. "Clay, is that you?" There was nothing.

Before anything could happen to the journal I stood up on the bed of the trunk and grabbed it, but again I could feel resistance. I pulled and pulled and eventually I got it but fell on the floor of the truck.

"Ouch!" I closed my eyes.

Before I got the chance to stand up, I heard rattling from the other end of the garage. I got to my feet and held the journal, ready to use it as a weapon. I kept twisting and turning, looking behind me and in front of me. I held the journal with a tight grip, until it felt like someone else had a grip on it.

"Hey! Let go!" I tried to keep it in my hands, but the pull was stronger than I was. The journal was yanked from my hands and I fell forward, yelling.

Then everything froze. It felt like someone was holding me in mid-air. I looked around wildly.

Nothing.

"What the hell is going on?!" I yelled.

I heard a voice, and all it said was, "The journal is staying with me."

I looked up to see a face alongside a body making itself visible, standing on the bed of the truck with me. It looked like—

"Clay?"

The grey boy I had imagined as a child wasn't a boy anymore. He was bigger, taller, and he looked around my age.

Clay stood me up softly. Even though I had been looking for him, I still couldn't verbalize what I was feeling in that moment. It's not every day you come face to face with a grown-up version of your childhood imaginary friend. I looked at his dark eyes, grey skin, and his curly black hair in braids that could use some tightening. I didn't know what to say or how to respond. His face said black man, but his skin told a ghost story.

"Holy, crap. Clay." I tried reaching out to him but he moved back, still holding the journal.

"Wait, don't go." I took a step forward.

He jumped off the truck, and continued to walk towards the door. I couldn't let him leave, not again.

"Hey, Clay! Come back." I stepped off the truck.

He didn't say a word, but he looked back at me, his eyes full of anger.

"What's wrong? Clay, it's me. It's me, Anna." I paused. "Sorry, it's me, Annaka."

He stopped. He let out a loud sigh, looked back, and said, "I know it's you. You never came back."

That hit my heart. I had promised him that Mom and I wouldn't be in Halifax for long. But then ten years passed; somewhere in that time, I thought he would have left.

"I'm sorry." I didn't know what else to say.

He only shook his head and went for the door; he let in a spring breeze and looked towards the lake.

"Where are you going?" I ran after him.

He didn't reply. He was focused on being anywhere but there, I could tell. A decade may have gone by, but I still knew him.

"Hold up." I grabbed his hand. He turned to look at me with a frown.

"Clay, I—"

"You came back for the funeral, right?" he cut in. "You're heading back to Halifax shortly, right?" He crossed his arms and waited.

I thought for a minute. It was true that I had ultimately wanted to leave. But that was before I knew Clay was still here.

"No," I said firmly. "No, we're staying." I looked into his eyes. "Clay, I didn't know you waited." I tried to touch his shoulder but he moved back.

"You said you'd be back sooner than later…it's way later."

"I'm sorry, Clay. I tried."

He gave me a long look. I could see the sadness in the way he carried himself; his shoulders dropped, his face held a long, sad frown. I noticed he was still wearing my grandfather's clothes, and they were a bit big for him. I guess he must have grown out of my clothes a long time ago. He turned to the lake.

"Wait!" I yelled. "Clay, this isn't ideal for either of us. I'm sorry, okay? I know what I said. I know I told you that I would be back, and I wanted to come back. I really, really did."

"Save it."

"Wait!" I yelled again. "You have something of mine. That's my grandfather's journal."

"You can't have it," he replied in a grim tone.

"No, you don't get to take it." I walked towards him. "It's mine." I tried to grab it but he was faster than I remembered. Next thing I knew, he was behind me. I moved again but he was swift.

"Clay, seriously. I'm not kidding." I turned around to face him.

"Neither am I."

"All right, all right. Whatever," I said in mock surrender, hoping he would let his guard down. "It's yours, if you want it. Take it. Whatever."

He did let his guard down—he was still gullible, even after all those years—and that's when I jumped at him, causing him to drop the journal. I grabbed it and tried to run. I didn't make it too far though, he tripped me, and I stumbled forward out of the garage, tossing the journal in the air.

"Shit," he muttered.

It was the first time I heard him curse, and it caught me off guard. I caught my balance and saw the journal hit some rocks by the tree house. I looked back at Clay; he held onto his arm as if he was hurt.

"What was that about?" I called out.

He didn't reply, he only glanced at the journal and I knew he was going to dart for it. So I ran first; I could feel him behind me, but I jumped for it and got a hold of it. I rolled so I could jump to my feet, and I dashed towards the tree house. I climbed the ladder, Clay close behind me.

"Hold up!" I whirled around when I got to the top. "You have some explaining to do."

"I don't owe you an explanation!"

"Maybe that's true, but the journal is mine." I held it tight. "Why are you holding your arm like that, are you hurt?"

"Because whatever happens to that journal happens to me, all right?" He showed me a mark on his arm. "That's why I took it last night." He showed me his other arm where a dark bruise bloomed on his grey skin.

Oh, man, I thought to myself. When I dropped the journal it must have hurt him. "Did it hurt when I dropped it last night?"

"It didn't tickle." He crossed his arms.

"I'm sorry."

"Just give it back." He put his hand out.

"I can't. Grampy gave it to me. I want to hold on to it."

"You're not going to make this easy, are you?"

"I never do." I backed away from him.

He gave me a hard stare; I knew he was still angry. But I was hoping I could make him budge. He was breathing heavy, I remember that was a thing he did when he was frustrated. I sat down on the floor of the tree house while he stared at the journal. I knew if he caught his breath then he would be able to talk.

"Just breathe, Clay," I spoke while extending a hand.

"I *am* breathing!" He said, his breaths getting heavier and heavier.

"No, like me." I took a deep breath, and he watched. "Like this, c'mon."

He didn't look impressed, but he did as I said, and I could tell he was beginning to calm down as his shoulders relaxed.

"You good to talk? Like adults?"

"Whatever," he said. "Fine."

"Okay. Let's go back into the garage where no one can see you." I gestured at the ladder. "C'mon."

Back in the garage, Clay paced with his arms crossed and a frown on his face.

"Okay, what d'you wanna talk about?" he asked.

"You were here? The whole time?" I sat back down on the back of the truck.

"I was waiting…for you." He stopped pacing and pointed at me.

I looked down at my feet, a twisting feeling of regret in my stomach. So Clay spent ten years in this place alone while I was away living a new life in the city. God, that's horrible.

"Clay." I put my hands on my head. "I didn't know. I just assumed—"

"You assumed wrong." He took a breath.

"Why did you stay?"

"For a while it was hope, but I lost that a long time ago," he said as he shot me a look. "A lot of it was safety. I couldn't last out there, in the real world. This is the only place I've ever known. And if that journal ever gets wrecked, I'm toast." He sighed.

I never knew that when I was younger. I had always thought Clay was just…Clay. I didn't know that if the journal got damaged, he'd be hurt too. But it made sense now. Partly.

"Did…did my grandparents ever see you?" I was honestly curious. Some folks can live for a long time not knowing they have mice, but how did my grandparents not know a large grey figure the size of a young man was staying in their home?

"They've never seen me," he assured me. "I wasn't exactly always here. It's kind of difficult to explain."

"I'm all ears."

"It'll be easier to show you," he said. "Open the journal, pick an entry."

I opened it up, and thumbed through until I found the entry where I had a drawing of Grampy driving me to Cape Forchu. That was the one I had been thinking about when I walked to Grampy's urn at the funeral.

Clay walked towards the truck and got in the driver's side.

"What are you doing? That's not yours."

"Get in."

I hesitated. But then I moved one foot forward, and the other followed. I opened the passenger's side door and climbed in.

"Okay, so what's going on?" I asked.

"Open up that page in the journal again."

I flipped through the pages. There were drawings and journal entries above each one.

"Find the one where you were riding to Cape Forchu," he said.

"It's here," I said, opening up the page.

"All right." He looked straight at me.

Clay extended an open hand. His eyes began to glow blue. "It's just like when we were kids, remember?"

It was not exactly how I remembered it. I didn't know what would happen, but I took his hand and closed my eyes.

Suddenly, we weren't sitting in the garage anymore. I could hear birds chirping and feel a warm sun pressing against my skin. I opened my eyes and I was standing on damp grass with morning air. I looked around. We were in the park just off the Yarmouth waterfront.

"Holy shit," I said out loud. *What is happening?*

"Annaka! Who taught you to speak like that?" I knew that voice.

My eyes widened. That voice—the one I was so afraid I was going to forget. It felt real, but it couldn't be. This had to be a trick. I closed my eyes and opened them again, trying to wake up from this dream, but then I felt a hand on my shoulder and I turned around.

And there he was: large in appearance, dark skin, grey beard, and a smile that took all my fears away.

"Gramp...Grampy?" I managed to say while taking steps back. I tripped over my feet and fell back into the grass.

"Always tripping on your feet," he said with a chuckle. He leaned over and pulled me up; his skin touched mine and it felt as real as anything.

"No more language like that. But I'll keep it a secret if you promise not to repeat it. Deal?" He smiled.

"Deal," was all I had the courage to say.

I didn't understand any of it. One second ago I was in the garage with Clay, and now I was...in the park...with my grandfather. But I wasn't the same. I was younger—a *lot* younger. I looked at Grampy and gave him a big squeeze.

"Hey! Thanks for the love, hon." He hugged me back. It was exactly how I remembered it. He was a soft, giant, gentle man.

"Want a push on the swings, Annaka?"

Logically, I knew I was still a sixteen-year-old young adult, but I also knew that if I was going to spend one more day with my grandfather, I was going to take that swing push.

Grampy pushed me on the swings and I got to see the world from a kid's perspective again. Was I in the past? I didn't really understand how this was happening. There was no sign of Clay; it was just my grandfather and me. This was what I had wanted for a long time.

We played for what felt like hours. I stopped questioning it, and just enjoyed the moment for what it was. Eventually I lay down on the grass, tired from being in the sun. I could see Grampy standing over me with a grin.

"You look all tired out. Do you want to head back home or go for a ride up to the lighthouse?"

It was exactly how I had written it in the journal: Grampy had taken me to Cape Forchu, and he had given me a piggyback up the path towards the lighthouse.

"To the lighthouse, always." It almost felt automatic.

"Then let's go!" He pulled me up and piggybacked me to the truck. I held on tight. I never wanted to let him go again.

Once we were buckled in, Grampy looked over at me before he put the truck in reverse. "Ready, co-pilot?" he asked. "I need you to be my eyes and ears on the right side."

God, I couldn't believe what I was seeing: the way he gripped the steering wheel with one hand, the other one resting out the window; his slight grin; and the scent of his truck—it always smelled like peaches.

"I'm ready," I replied.

He pulled out onto the road and I rolled down my window, putting my hands in the air. It felt like a dream, but the dashboard, the seat belt, and the late-afternoon air felt very real.

"Maybe some day you'll be the captain of this ship," Grampy said as we drove down by the waterfront. We took the road down to the 304 and made our way to Cape Forchu. It felt so different from Halifax, being near so much green, more ocean than harbour, and being the co-pilot again. Before I knew it, we were there. Grampy parked his truck and I got out to see the big red lighthouse at the top of a hill.

"Ready for another piggyback on this old man?"

I climbed on and he carried me up the hill. I wanted that moment to last forever.

"Grampy?" I said as he walked up the hill.

"Yeah, hon?"

"Is this real?"

He paused, and I could see a look of confusion from the side of his face. "Yeah, hon. I know you're in your imagination a lot of the time. But yes, this is real."

I shook my head. "That's not what I mean."

"Then what do you mean, Annaka?" he asked gently.

"I don't know. But can you make me a promise?"

"What would that be?"

"Never leave me." I held on tight.

"You don't have to ever worry about that." He chuckled as he made it to the top. The sky was pink and the water stretched as far as our eyes could see. Black rocks piled beneath the cliff's edge and above us, the lighthouse flashed.

This was the homecoming I wanted.

My arms wrapped around Grampy, and a clear view was illuminated from above. I held on tight and never wanted to let go. This was the home I remembered. The home I loved. I felt so tired holding on to him that I closed my eyes, and his humming put me to sleep....

When I opened my eyes again, it was back in the truck in Grampy's garage. Rain was hitting all sides of the garage and Clay's hand was still attached to mine.

"Holy shit!" I said as I let go.

I was back in the present.

"Are you okay?" he asked.

I couldn't catch my breath, nor could I believe what had just happened. It had felt so real. It *was* real. I had been holding on to Grampy.

"I saw him. I saw him! I was riding in his truck. He took me to Cape Forchu."

I looked at my hands and could tell I was sixteen again.

"He told me I wouldn't ever have to worry about him leaving," I whispered.

I looked over at Clay and tried to rationalize what just happened. But I don't think I could. He knew I was feeling down, and he knew I was looking at that memory from the journal. In that moment I didn't want to think about the how, I just wanted to accept that it happened.

"Thank you for that," I said as a tear rolled down my cheek.

"You haven't had a good day today, have you?"

"No. It was Grampy's funeral today."

"I'm sorry."

There was a long silence and we just sat there listening to the rain. Memories came back to me. I couldn't believe Clay had always been there. I told him I would return years ago, and he grew up just like me. I could see that he carried a lot of hurt, and I tried to avoid eye contact until he finally said, "I missed you, Annaka."

"I missed you too, Clay." We looked at each other for a long moment, and I said, "I just go by Anna now."

"Okay, Anna."

I began to weep. Clay slid over and gave me a hug. I held on to him just as tight as I'd held on to Grampy. I was home, and finally felt close with someone I didn't have to hide anything from.

CHAPTER 6

I WOKE UP THE NEXT MORNING IN THE PASSENGER SEAT with a stomachache. Clay was gone, but the journal sat on the driver's side seat. I had no idea where he went, but I had a feeling he would be back. I put the journal in the glove compartment for safekeeping. When I got inside the house I saw Nan and Mom sitting at the kitchen table with bacon, eggs, and sausages. I was still shaken up by everything that happened the night before.

"Hey, where were you last night? Did you spend the night at Tia's?" Mom greeted as I came in.

"Yeah...I spent the night at Tia's place," I lied. It would be weird to say I slept in the truck.

"I thought as much. Are you hungry?"

"No. I think I'm gonna go lay down." I didn't know what made my stomach ache, but it wasn't a good feeling.

Mom walked over to me, put a hand on my shoulder, and said, "Listen, I know everything is hard right now. But I would like you to eat something. Making sure you're fed is part of self-care, and right now we all need to take care of ourselves and each other."

I sighed. "Fine."

Mom put a plate of food in front of me, but I felt sick to my stomach. Nan was a slow eater, and Mom asked me to sit with her while she went to go make Nan's bed. I kept silent because I didn't think we had much to talk about. On the table was a photo of Grampy; he was smiling, wearing a nice button-up. It was his school board photo. Eventually Nan picked up and observed it.

"It's a shame what happened to Rudy," she said.

I didn't reply, only listened.

"What a handsome man." She spoke about him like a stranger, putting the photo down. That made my heart ache as much as my stomach. I remember Grampy had told me where he met Nan. When I was younger, he told me he met her while on summer vacation away from university. He visited Yarmouth on the off chance of taking a ship to Maine. It turned out he missed his boat and ended up at a local bar. Nan was there, Grampy asked her to dance, and the rest was history, I guess. Key word: history. I was sad it was a memory Nan probably didn't carry anymore.

I couldn't sit around all day in the house. I thought about getting some sleep, but being there put me in a bummed-out mood, so I shot Tia a text instead. With everything that happened the night before, I needed to vent.

Me: *Hey dude. Something happened.*

Tia: *Everything okay?*

Me: *There's no way I can explain over text. Wanna meet up?*

Tia: *Sure. My parents actually suggested I take the day off school to see if you needed anything. Come over.*

Me: *Well I definitely need a friend. Be right over.*

I went to my room to get changed quickly then darted for the front door. I made it down the front steps of the porch before I heard Mom's voice coming out the front door.

"Anna. Are you leaving?" She stepped out.

"Yeah, I was gonna go to Tia's place," I replied.

"Didn't you just spend the night there?"

"Uhhh…." *Shit*. "I think I forgot my phone there." I managed to save myself, knowing my phone was in my pocket.

"All right." Mom gave me a suspicious nod. "Anyway, you weren't here yesterday, but we read your grandfather's will."

I didn't say anything.

"I wanted to let you know that he left a little something in there for you."

"What was it?" I genuinely didn't know. I just hoped it wasn't his crappy old charcoal barbecue.

Mom threw something in the air that tinkled—I caught it. It was a set of keys. Not just any keys, they were…the keys to his truck.

"What?!" was my only response. "You can't be—"

"He knew how much you adored that truck growing up, hon," Mom said with a smile. "You were his co-pilot, remember? But I know how you drive, so just don't perform any crash landings, all right?"

I wanted to cry thinking about that. When Mom and I left, she would call me her co-pilot too. I think she did it so I would feel more comfortable about leaving. We all had a duty, and Grampy left me his truck to take care of. It was a huge responsibility but he must have had faith in me.

I didn't know what else to say besides, "Seriously?"

"Yes, seriously, babes. And besides, driving can soothe the soul. It might be good to ride around town for a bit. Maybe you can pick up Tia and head on a small road trip or something? Just don't go too far."

I knew right away where I wanted to go: Cape Forchu. After what happened the night before, I couldn't stop thinking about going up the hill holding on to Grampy. It would be nice to grab Tia and Taz and spend the day out there. I couldn't bear to sit in that house and listen to Nan rambling.

"Thanks, Mom."

"I'm not the one to thank," she replied. "Be safe, all right?"

"All right."

When I got to the garage, I stared at Grampy's truck for a moment. *My* truck. I opened the door on the driver's side and slid in. I held the steering wheel. It was way wider than Mom's minivan. I knew Grampy kept CDs under his front seat so I reached under. I chose one that said "Jazz 2006" and stuck it in the CD player. As it played, though, I realized I wasn't a fan, so I turned it off and blasted music from my phone that I "forgot at Tia's house" instead. I put the keys in the ignition and revved the engine, giving me goose bumps that fuelled my smile. It felt like I was sitting in a rocket ship getting ready to blast off. It was almost the same thing, right? I took a deep breath, put the truck in drive, and hit the gas. I never thought I'd actually be driving this thing.

"I promise you I'll take care of it," I whispered out loud as I drove towards the path and onto the main road. I couldn't wait for Tia to see. My big old truck would be better than her stupid car.

Tia was already sitting out front with Taz.

"Look at you, Anna!" she said as I pulled up. "This yours?"

"It is now." I got out to pet Taz. "We always used to joke, y'know? He called me the co-pilot, and said one day I'd be the captain of this ship." I put a hand on the hood of the truck. "God, we had some great memories riding around in this thing."

"Keep them close." Tia smiled. "So, what did you wanna talk about?"

Right. There was no way to tell Tia about what had happened the night before without her thinking I was out of my mind. After all, the real reason I drove to Tia's was to get everything off of my mind.

"It was nothing."

Tia narrowed her eyes. "Nothing, huh?"

I shrugged. "I don't know. I just didn't want to be alone. Maybe I needed some puppy time." I hugged Taz and he licked my face.

"Well, we could all go for a ride. You could drive this time instead of me being your chauffeur."

"You know I think more of you than that."

"Says the daughter of the one and only Jayla Brooks," Tia said with a laugh.

"Oh, stop that," I said as I climbed in the driver's seat. "You guys coming or what?"

Tia, Taz, and I all fit in the front of the truck and we took off. There was some traffic, but nothing like back in Halifax. Here everyone seemed comfortable and relaxed; back in Halifax everyone was always in such a rush and traffic downtown gave me anxiety attacks. It felt nice being on an open road under a clear sky. It was soothing, and that's exactly what I needed to smooth down my rocky thoughts. I never felt present back in Halifax, but coming back to Yarmouth was forcing me to live in the moment instead of waiting for one.

"Hey, remember back when we used to play here?" Tia asked as we drove by the waterfront. "Dad would always freak out when we got too close to the edge."

"Yes." I laughed. "I remember how he always looked prepared to jump in. Did you wanna head to the lighthouse?"

"Heck yeah. I haven't been there in a while."

"You? I haven't been there in years."

Tia grinned. "More reason to go."

I switched onto the main road and we made our way out of town. We drove for a while and admired some of the homes along the way—a bit more upper class and pretentious than the ones in town.

"I go to school with someone who lives out here," Tia brought up. "She had a party out here once. A bunch of the folks who went got too drunk and had to walk back to town that night. It was a disaster."

"I can imagine," I replied. "Beautiful scenery, but it looks like this road stretches forever."

Taz was curled up on Tia's lap and I focused on the road. I didn't even need directions; it was all muscle memory for me.

I couldn't contain my smile when we rolled up to the lighthouse. Just like the night before, it felt good to be back. Taz stood up in the front seat and began barking.

"Woah, calm down, big guy." Tia petted him and opened the door. Taz darted out and made his way straight to the water.

"Figures," she said. "Lets go to the top!"

Tia grabbed my hand and pulled me towards the path. I didn't know what had happened the night before. Was it time travel? I didn't understand how it worked, but I knew I had to be there.

"You look ridiculous right now." Tia pointed out the smile plastered on my face.

I didn't care. The lighthouse was beautiful. The sky was grey, unlike the pink from my memory, but it still felt great. No buildings, no loud cars, no shitty neighbours—just me, a friend, and a lot of open space. We could see Taz at the bottom of the hill sniffing other dogs' butts and chasing birds, barking happily.

"My dog is the biggest dork," Tia said with a laugh.

"He has personality, and that's all that matters."

"What did you really wanna talk about?" Tia cut into my thoughts.

I hesitated. I couldn't just say, *Hey, Tia. Last night I ran into my imaginary friend and he brought me back to the place where we're sitting now, only it was ten years ago.* To be fair, I had tried telling her about Clay when we were kids, but she didn't believe he was actually real.

"C'mon," she pressed. "It's gotta be something. I'll pry it out of you."

I knew she could. But that didn't mean I would let her.

"I don't know. It's just weird being back here after being away for so long…everything I knew here is gone. I actually had a dream I was here at Cape Forchu last night."

"Oh, yeah? Is that why you wanted to come here?"

"Yeah, I guess. But it wasn't like other dreams. It felt so real."

"Was it, like, a lucid dream?"

I didn't know how to explain something I didn't understand, and I knew if I told Tia the truth it would sound ridiculous. So I just shrugged.

"I don't know. Everything is just weird. It's home, but everything is different, y'know?"

Tia nodded and looked out at the ocean again. "That is a rough place to come back to, and you have a lot going on. I guess it makes sense to dream about it. What else would you really be thinking about?"

She had a point, but it wasn't the point I was trying to make.

"You said your dad was still here," she continued. "Have you been thinking about him more?"

That question threw me off guard. I suppose it was an easier segue then speaking about an imaginary friend.

"Yeah…I have been thinking about him," I said in a low voice.

"This town is small."

"It is. I know. Mom never speaks about him."

"I'm sure she has her reasons."

"And I have mine for wanting to know."

"Fair point." Tia shrugged.

I didn't even know what he looked like. I wondered if I had his laugh, or his smile, or his eyes. All I really knew was that he was white, and that's why my skin was lighter then everyone else's in my family. I didn't look white by any stretch; my brown skin and long braids made it clear who I was. But I was always curious about my other half. Being half black to us always just meant you were black. But I knew I must have a bunch of white cousins somewhere. I wondered if they would like me—not that I needed their validation, but they were still blood, whoever, and wherever, they were.

"I always wanted a father–daughter relationship," I admitted. "When Mom spent a lot of time away, I spent too much time daydreaming of fatherly figures from sitcoms."

Tia gave me a sympathetic nod. "Is that what you're hoping to find with him?"

"I don't think it'll end up like that," I explained. "At the end of the day, he'll still be a stranger." I thought for a minute. "I guess what I really want is clarity. I want to know why he wasn't around, why he chose not to be in my life. He must have had the opportunity. I don't know…sorry to just unload."

"Don't be sorry," Tia said. "Those thoughts are normal, and real. Are you hoping to search for him soon?"

"It might be a lost cause, it probably is. But we'll see I guess."

We sat and watched the water for a while. I wanted to tell her what was actually on my mind, but I knew deep down I couldn't.

LATER THAT AFTERNOON I WENT back home to explore Grampy's study. He loved calling it that even though it was just a spare room on the ground floor. I just wanted to be near a space he'd spent time in. His desk was full of papers I wasn't supposed to go through, but I did anyway. They were marked grades he never got around to logging in his computer. It was actually really sad. Curious, I went through some of them. I came across an essay by Tia. I skimmed most of it but I saw she received an 89 percent. Not bad.

I opened up one of his drawers to find a picture frame. The photo inside showed the same woman who was in the photo album in the attic. The photo itself was different, though: the woman looked a lot skinnier and she didn't have any hair. But she still had a large smile. I tried not to overthink it since I already had enough on my mind.

I put the papers and frame away and made my way towards my bedroom, but I could hear R&B drifting up from the living room. I followed the noise and saw Mom in her own space, completely zoned out. She didn't even notice me come in. She had a canvas standing in the middle of the living room and she was creating a new world. Mom created worlds like I did, only in a different way—I required a journal, she had her canvas.

"Anna." Mom noticed me. "I didn't hear you come in. How was hanging with Tia?"

"It was fine. We went to the lighthouse." I looked around. "Where's Nan?"

"Lillian took her for a walk. Said she wanted me to relax a bit...so I did this." She moved out of the way and showed me what she was working on. I saw the backyard recreated. It had everything—the tree house on the right, lake in the background, firepit in the foreground, and a lawn of bright green grass.

"They say one of the best ways to help with the grieving process is to create," she said, considering the canvas. Then she sighed and turned to me. "I haven't seen you much since we made it back. How are you keeping up, Anna?"

"As well as I can, I guess. A week ago I just...wouldn't have expected any of this."

Mom nodded. "I know. It's hard to adjust to changes like this. I wanted you to get out today and get used to the town a bit again, because there are more changes to come."

I looked her in the eye. "What do you mean, more changes?"

Mom sighed. "Remember when I said we were going to be here a while?"

"Yes. How long is a while?"

"Well, long enough for you to register for school."

Everything just slowed down when she said that.

I was supposed to finish grade eleven in Halifax, and this summer I would start saving up and applying for colleges.

"What?"

She rushed to explain: "Most schools wouldn't take in a student this late in the year, but Grampy was well loved here. You're lucky."

"I'm *lucky*? Mom, I don't want to stay here."

"I know, sweetheart. But we don't have a choice right now. Your grandmother is in a bad spot. Your grandfather was her main caretaker and Ben and Lillian are getting up there with age."

Everything inside me dropped. I was frustrated, mad, and wanted to be anywhere but there. I wanted to cry, but I kept my composure.

"Mom, I can't just leave my life in Halifax behind!"

"You're not. You're starting anew." She paused. "Look, I know you wanted to save up money this summer but maybe you can get a job here? I'm sure there are some shops you can apply to. We just need to be close. For Nan."

"I don't want to be close. Nan doesn't even remember me. That's messed up, for real. I can't handle it. Being near her makes me want to burst into tears and—" my throat began to tighten up and I knew tears were coming. I tried my hardest to fight it.

"Anna, I know." Mom put a hand on my shoulder. "It hurts me too—she's my mom. But she's going through a difficult time."

"There's no one here for me!" I managed to get out. I knew that wasn't true, but I also wanted to make a point. "Everyone I cared about is either dead, or doesn't remember me."

Now all of a sudden Mom wanted to be close? If she wanted to be close, she shouldn't have made us leave in the first place. If she wanted to be close she should have brought us back here before Grampy died.

"I have to go," I told Mom in a frustrated voice.

"Where?"

"To be alone."

I stomped up to my room and slammed the door.

I ended up just lying in my bed for a while. The mental gymnastics of navigating this last week made my body ache, but my mind was wide awake. I didn't know if I could handle school in Yarmouth. I didn't really know anyone here besides Tia. I was sure people would recognize me from elementary, but no one would really *know* me. I would just be the sympathy case—Mr. Brooks's granddaughter. I was a loner in Halifax, but I could get away with it there. In a small town? Not remotely.

I felt lost and didn't know how to find a way out.

Eventually I drifted off and awoke to moonlight crashing through my window and lighting up the room. The closet door was open and I could still see *Clay* written on the wall inside. I wanted to find him again, but wasn't sure when he'd come back. I knew where the journal was, and that he was attracted to it. I had parked the truck back in the garage and the journal was in the glove compartment. I knew I had to be gentle, so when I went out to the garage, I took the journal out and just spoke to it while sitting in the back of the truck. Somehow, I knew that would get his attention.

"Hey, dude. Wanna talk about last night?" I asked. "I'm going to be in Yarmouth a while, I guess, so it looks like I have lots of time."

There was no ta-da moment where Clay appeared. It's not like he was a genie in a bottle—he was his own thing. I lay in the bed of the truck thinking of a way to make him come out.

"You know, we had a lot of adventures when we were young," I spoke aloud. "Clay, I'm so sorry I left. I honestly didn't think you would wait all this time."

I didn't realize how awful that last part sounded until I said it out loud.

"Listen, I know. I'm an asshole. You have every right to give me the silent treatment." I stopped to gather my thoughts. I just wanted him to understand. "I do appreciate what you did for me last night, though. It felt like a gift. And honestly, Clay, so much has changed in ten years. I wanted to come back but we just never did. Some things are out of my control. I never wanted to hurt you, and I'm sorry that I did."

Still nothing.

I waited a few more moments and said, "What is it that you want?"

I felt him swipe the journal out of my hand from above. I looked up, and there he was.

"Holy crap!" I screamed. I dropped into the bed of the truck "You scared me." I said. "What's your deal, man?"

"So, everyone you loved is either dead or forgot about you?" He was upset. "Last time I checked, Anna, I'm alive. And I never *ever* forgot about you!"

"Wait, what are you talking about?"

Then it clicked. I had said those exact words to Mom earlier. "Clay, I didn't mean that, I was just angry. And anyway: how did you hear that?"

"You think I'm not always close by?" he demanded. "Did you forget that about me?"

Right, I thought, *Clay can make himself invisible*. Given what I said, I felt a hundred times worse knowing he was there and had to hear it.

He still had that look of hurt on his face. God, I had really messed up with him. There was a lot I had to own up to, and be accountable for. In some weird way, I had brought Clay into this world, and I had abandoned him in it.

"I'm sorry," I whispered, even thought I knew full well the words weren't enough. "Is there anything I can do? We can go for a drive? Buy some food?"

"It isn't that easy." Clay let out a breath. "You couldn't have just sent a letter I would find? You couldn't have asked your grandparents to send you the journal?" He looked like he was fighting back tears.

"There's so many things that I could have done differently, Clay, and believe me, if I could have, I would have. Please, please believe that."

"You're only saying that because you thought I would be gone." He wiped the tears from his eyes. "Well, here I am. A little bigger than when you left."

"But I'm back now," I said. "I'm here to spend time with you."

He scoffed at that. "You're here because your grandfather died, Anna, not to see me. I'm the afterthought of your story, so you'll forgive me for not jumping for joy and riding off into the sunset with you. You never cared. You don't even wanna be here!"

Ouch.

"Clay, please. I know what you're going thro—"

"No you don't," he cut me off. "How do you know what it feels like, waiting for someone who doesn't even think about you?"

The truth was I *did* know what that felt like, but I didn't think it was my place to say so. Not then.

"What do you even want from me?" Clay asked me.

He had waited for me all those years and he grew just like me. He looked to be around the same age as me, had similar hair, and was dressed in my grandfather's old sweater. I knew I had been a bad friend. Not just to him, but to everyone. I was flaky, and I recognized that I sometimes only put in work towards friendships if it benefitted me. I thought about Tia's thoughtful questions and patient presence, and wondered how I could be more like her. I knew had to work on it.

But there were also a few things I needed to know.

"How did you do that thing last night? Did we time travel?"

"No," he said. "It's not time travel." He looked between the journal in his hands to my face. "When you were young, you filled most of these pages with your imagination. I was part of that."

"I know. I know," I cut in. "I remember the first time I wrote about you in there. It was after the first day of grade primary and I had hated it. I didn't make any friends, and Tia was in a different class." Memories came back to me.

Clay looked me in the eyes and his began to glow blue. Everything around us turned pitch black. The garage, the truck, the tools—they all just faded away. Suddenly desks and walls lifted from the ground, and the floor below my feet turned into tiles. My jaw dropped. I turned around and everything was…different.

"This was it," I managed to whisper. "My first day of school."

"I know," Clay replied. He crossed his arms, annoyed. "Go on."

"I just remember during recess, I had what felt like a panic attack. I stayed inside and hid under my desk, away from everyone. The only thing I had was my journal. Grampy had given it to me that morning. He told me it was a gift—a good luck charm—and that it used to be his. He wanted me to write about my first day."

I could see a little girl who looked just like me. She was sitting on the floor under a desk, drawing and writing nonsense in her journal. I walked over for a better look: I saw the outline of a person who looked like Clay.

"You're doing it again," I said. "But this time I'm just observing."

I watched my younger self—I looked frightened, scared, and out of place. I remember drawing Clay, but I had had no idea he would actually become real.

I looked over at him now, and his eyes glowed blue again. The classroom around us turned pitch black. A few moments later the darkness faded into what looked like my bedroom, except the walls were brighter and the bed was different. I could see my younger self lying on the bed, face in the pillow, crying. Grampy was patting me on the back. This was after my first day of school. I had locked myself in my room until Grampy finally convinced me to let him in.

"I never wanna go back!"

"Why not?" Grampy asked. "I used to love going to school when I was young! There are so many new and interesting people to meet."

I remember being scared to tell Grampy I didn't want to meet any new people because they all made fun of my name. Earlier that day we all had to write our names on cue cards. I had written my full name: *Annaka*. Bobby, the boy Tia used to have a crush on, picked it out of the hat going around. He read it out loud and then said with a smirk: "What kind of name is Annaka?" Everyone laughed. I felt so embarrassed; I didn't even want to go outside for recess. So I hid under my desk.

But I watched as Grampy patted my back, kissed my cheek, and gently said, "Try to get some sleep. Tomorrow morning I'll make you pancakes, sausages, and eggs. Does that sound better?" He poked me until I heard my younger self giggle. Nobody made pancakes like Grampy could.

After Grampy left, I saw myself get out of bed. He never realized how sneaky I could be. I watched as I went under the bed and grabbed a box—inside were toy airplanes and cars. I watched as I began playing with them. Those were the simpler times; the times I wished could last forever. Before moving, before high school, before everything.

I knew what was coming next. I had gotten so lost in my imagination with the toys that I didn't notice the noise at first. But soon I heard a *creeeak* coming from my closet. It got louder, and louder. I jumped up, and I knew I was remembering what Tia used to tell me:

that she had monsters in her closet and they would come for me too someday. I turned around and jumped back into my bed.

"Who's there?" I called out. There was no reply.

The creaking suddenly stopped, and the closet door opened slowly.

I could see my younger self scramble backwards, eventually freezing against the wall. I had been so scared I couldn't even scream.

For a second, there was nothing but darkness. I waited, too scared to say anything. That was, until a small, round-faced grey figure stepped out. He didn't look like a monster at all.

"Hi," was all he said in a shy voice. He looked scared, out of place, and like he didn't know what to do.

I pulled myself out of the memory for a moment and looked over at Clay, seeing how much he had grown over the years. He was now taller than me. His voice was deeper. Now he had hair, and looked much more, well, human.

"Who are you?" I heard my voice and looked back.

"I don't know," the little grey figure replied. "I'm me, I guess."

Little Anna got on her feet and walked towards the closet. I used to tower over him when I was young. My younger self grabbed his hand and said, "Your hands are soft and grey. Just like…clay. Can I call you Clay?"

Then just like that, everything vanished into darkness.

"How do you do that?" I asked.

"Always could." Clay replied. "Just in different ways. Remember that summer I turned the lake in the backyard into a sheet of ice?"

I nodded.

"I could do that because you wrote about a winter we shared."

As he said that I could feel a chill in the darkness. I shivered and could see my breath in the air.

"What are you doing?" I asked.

The darkness transformed into snow all around us in the distance, and below me I felt ice. I quickly caught my balance and realized that we were outside of my grandparents' house on the lake.

In the distance, I could see myself, looking a bit older than the last memory. I had skates on, and beside me sat a younger version of Clay.

"Lets go!" He pulled me up as he slid backwards holding on to my hand. I could hear us both laughing and it made me feel all warm inside. I loved that memory, even though I didn't share it with anyone else.

Then darkness surrounded us again; the frozen lake transformed into my grandparents' kitchen, and this time it was night.

"Are you sure your nan hid the candy in here?" I could see a younger Clay standing by the sink.

"I'm sure of it!" I heard myself reply as I lifted my head from under the kitchen sink. I was wearing a bright orange cape and a blue domino mask. "Hmm…. Up there! I can see them!"

A jar of mini chocolate bars was sitting on top of the fridge.

I looked around and noticed that the tablecloths and napkins everywhere in the kitchen were orange and black. Close to Halloween. I grinned because I remembered this. Clay had been hungry and I told him I knew where Nan kept the Halloween candy. We weren't going to take all of it, but I remember right around then I….

"Oh no!" I heard my voice followed by a hard *smash*. A pile of dishes fell down and smashed into pieces—Clay had tried climbing the counter beside the fridge.

"What's going on in there?" I heard Nan's voice rush in. "Annaka, what are you doing?!"

I remembered I had been so scared she would see Clay. I watched my young self turn to look for Clay and saw my own jaw drop because he was nowhere in sight.

"Annaka," Nan said, demanding my attention. "Did you drop those dishes?"

"No."

Her eyes bored into mine. "Tell the truth, now."

I *was* telling the truth, but I knew I had to lie for Clay's sake. So I ended up telling Nan, "Yes, ma'am." I was still not completely sure where he had gone.

"What were you doing?" Nan asked, putting her hands on her hips.

"I was…I was trying to get the candy on top of the fridge." I could see my defeated face.

I remember being sent to my room for the rest of the night, and that's when Clay reappeared. I learned two things that evening: that Clay could turn invisible, and that he still owed me one from all those years ago.

"You still owe me for that," I teased, turning my head towards him and hoping for a playful reply.

"I don't owe you anything," he shot back.

Everything went dark again. This time it stayed dark. Longer than it did before. Clay was nowhere to be seen, or heard. "Clay? You still there, buddy? Are you going to leave me trapped in this place forever?"

He didn't reply.

"Clay, where are you?"

Silence.

But then I heard weeping, followed by Clay's small voice echoing in my eardrums: "How long are you going to be gone?"

He was replaying that one again. I knew what he was trying to do.

"Not forever, silly," I heard my voice answer. "We'll be back soon. I want you to stay here—it's safer. The city can be a scary place."

"But I don't wanna stay. I wanna go with you. I don't wanna be alone."

The darkness formed into the front porch, and a younger version of Clay and I appeared on it.

"Do we really have to do—" I tried to say over the scene he was creating. But I was cut off by my own voice.

"I know, Clay. But we'll be back before you know it. Mom said the apartment we're moving into in Halifax could be small. I don't know if you'd be comfortable."

I could see his look of devastation again. It didn't hurt any less seeing it a second time.

"You promise you'll be back soon?" he asked with teary eyes.

"I do." I saw my younger self raise a pinky finger.

Everything faded away into darkness again, only to reemerge with Clay sitting on the doorstep beneath the night sky. He was looking towards the road, waiting. For what I could only assume to be me. That sight faded away to a fall afternoon where leaves were scattered on the ground. Clay just sat there looking towards the road, waiting for the promise I'd never keep. Then I felt a rush of cold air again as the fall faded and snow formed all around me. There he was: still in the same spot. Waiting. It didn't matter what season, he expected me to keep my promise.

"I know what you're trying to do," I said to him now. "I get it. I'm a bad friend."

The seasons began changing faster, but he sat in the same spot, growing older and older and older and older.

"Clay, stop," I tried to say, only to be cut off by my own voice: "We'll be back before you know it." It hurt even more hearing it again. Then that line repeated again, and again, and again. I tried to take a breath but that didn't stop my heart from being overflowed with guilt until I finally screamed, "Stop!"

And everything did.

There was no sound or sight. Clay left me in the darkness and I felt just as alone as he must have.

Shortly, light broke through the darkness and the real world formed around me. I was sitting on the bed of my grandfather's truck again. Clay had waited for me all that time—and I'd rarely ever thought about him. I curled into myself, not wanting to move.

We didn't say anything for a bit. It was awkward but we were there, in it the middle of it. And I finally understood how it worked. Clay spent most of his time reliving those memories, or spending time in that dark place.

God, I wished things hadn't turned out the way they did.

Clay finally spoke. "I know you're back, and I know it wasn't always your choice that you couldn't come visit. But I can't be your best friend right now. I can't pretend that I'm suddenly okay with you…because I'm not."

Without another word, he handed me the journal. I looked at it then closed my eyes.

"Clay, I'm sorr—" I opened my eyes, but he was already gone.

I put the journal back in the glove compartment and made my way to my bedroom. I tossed and turned and couldn't stop thinking about all the people I had let down. Clay, Grampy, Nan. I should have put in more effort to see them all, to stay in touch. There was only one relationship I could fix, and he'd just disappeared before my eyes. I had a lot to own up to.

CHAPTER 7

"**E**ARTH TO ANNA." TIA WAVED HER HAND IN FRONT of my face one afternoon in the school cafeteria.

It was about two weeks since I'd spoken to Clay. Mom got me enrolled into school pretty quickly so I would finish grade eleven on time. I hated it. I was the most popular student in school the first week. Everyone sent their condolences my way. I guess everyone loved my grandfather—or Mr. Brooks, as he was referred to here. There was a large photo of him placed in the lobby, and every morning I had to walk by it. It was heartbreaking. A place where he spent so much time, and I swear it still had his scent. Around Tia and I were Lucy, Laura, and Taylor. We were the crew, before I left Yarmouth. Now they were more Tia's crew, and I kind of felt like her plus-one more than anything else.

"Anna!" Tia cut into my thoughts again.

"Yeah, what's up?" I finally said.

"Dude. You haven't even touched your food. Are you okay?"

I looked down to cold soup, a sandwich, and mucky potato salad. I hadn't had much of an appetite for the last little while.

"I'm not too hungry today."

Tia looked at me. "You've been saying that the last two days. At least try to eat something."

Lucy and Taylor looked over while Laura was studying for the bio quiz.

"To be fair, cafeteria food doesn't make me the hungriest, either," Lucy said with a laugh while eating some homemade biscuits she brought.

"Yeah, well not everyone's mother owns a bakery," Taylor replied.

"Maybe I'll eat something later." I got up from my seat and stretched.

"Where you going?" Tia asked with a concerned look on her face.

"I just need to go for a walk." I let out a breath.

"All right. Well…text me if you need me." Tia seemed worried.

I made my way out of the cafeteria and walked down the main hall of the school. I walked past Grampy's old classroom, room 409. The door was full of sticky notes:

Love you Mr. Brooks. RIP.

Rest in Peace Mr. Brooks ☹

Safe travels to the best teacher I ever had

I couldn't bring myself to step inside. I think I would have burst into tears. I was happy to know he had brought so much joy to so many students—that helped, I guess.

I continued down the hall to where his photo was. He had a big smile on his face, dressed up in a suit. His school board photo. Around it students and staff had placed flowers and notes, just like outside his classroom.

"Hello, Miss Brooks," I heard a soft voice say behind me.

I turned to see a tall black woman. It was Ms. Anderson, the principal. She had introduced herself to me on my first day. She told me Grampy had been one of her favourite teachers, and she was one of the reasons I was squeezed into the school during the spring.

"How has Yarmouth High been treating you thus far?"

"Hey, Ms. Anderson," I greeted. "It's been a change of pace for sure. I went to Citadel High in Halifax, so most of the time I could barely break away from the crowds of students." I laughed.

"Well, I'm glad you're finding the transition comfortable." She smiled.

I wouldn't have used the word "comfortable," but at least I hadn't broken down in public yet.

"Thank you," I replied.

"Are you off to class?" Ms. Anderson asked. "Lunch ends in about five minutes."

Shit. Truth be told, I was planning to ditch school and go on a ride.

"Yeah," I said. "I was just going to grab my textbook from my truck."

"All right. Well move along, young lady," she said, nodding.

Good save on my end. I walked out the front door and made my way to the parking lot.

I hopped inside the truck and put the keys in, but before I could put it in reverse something made me stop. I sighed and opened the glove compartment to look at the journal. I hadn't tried speaking to Clay at all over the last two weeks, but I flipped through the pages. I hoped he would maybe come out and say something. I began looking through old entries and pictures I had drawn of him and me sitting in our tree house pretending it was a lighthouse. I laughed at the thought.

Before I could open my mouth to ask if he would come out, I heard a knock on my window and jumped.

"Holy crap!"

There stood some white boy wearing camo pants, a football jersey, and a goofy baseball cap.

I rolled the window down. "Can I help you?"

"Hey. Uh, hi. You're Annaka, right?"

"The name's Anna. What do you want?"

"Sorry. I don't know if you remember me. I'm Bobby Noah? We went to elementary together."

"Ha," I laughed, remembering that Tia had kicked him in the balls and said she hoped he got kidney stones. Bobby was the guy who had made fun of my name in primary, too, but he was the one with two first names. Idiot.

"Yeah, you were the kid who had two first names."

"Yeah. Double the trouble." He smiled.

What a dumb thing to say, I thought.

"Hey, I just wanted to say that I'm sorry about your grandfather. He was an awesome teacher. Honestly, he should have failed me in grade ten but he passed me with a fifty-two."

Maybe he just didn't want to teach you again.

"But anyways," he continued. "I'm having a party at my grandparents' spot out towards Cape Forchu. They're going to be out of town, and I just wanted to give you an invitation since you're back." He handed me an envelope.

"Wow, an actual old-school paper invitation," I pointed out. *What was he, six?* "Thanks. Anything else?"

"Uh...nope. That's it." He awkwardly moved from the truck and said, "I uh...hope to see you—"

I rolled the window up before he finished his sentence and dropped the invitation in my bag. I couldn't wait to tell Tia that the same douchebag who tried to use her to get back at his ex was trying to get me to go to his party.

I put the truck in reverse and drove away from school just as the class bell rang. I rolled down the window again and could feel the spring air splash across my face. Mom was probably at home grading papers. She had been doing them electronically since we got to Yarmouth, so I knew to stay away from the house. Instead, I went downtown. I heard my phone vibrate and I checked it once I got to a got to a red light.

Tia: *Yo, are you coming back? Bio started and Ms. Clarke is taking attendance.*

I ignored the text and put my phone back in my bag. I wasn't planning on going back. I was just everyone's sympathy case there—just Mr. Brooks's granddaughter.

I parked just off of Main Street and got out to sit on the back of the truck, looking down the hill towards the water. I thought about Clay. I wondered if he had cooled down. I knew he would have to come on his own terms. My heartache kept me awake at night, wishing I could have said or done things differently. I wanted to be accountable, but he had to give me a chance first.

I grabbed the journal and lay in the back of the truck again. I laughed at all the silly drawings. As I flipped through I could see the last memory and entry. It was Clay and me sitting outside of the house together on the front steps. I wanted to avoid that one. There were a lot of blank pages after that, but I flipped through them anyway. I knew Grampy used to write in it a bit—it had been his journal first after all—so I wasn't surprised to see his handwriting. He wrote in cursive so I couldn't quite make it out.

As I flipped back I noticed very clearly that there was a page titled, "Coming to Canada."

When my mind put the pieces together, my heart dropped and I shut the journal immediately. Part of me wanted to respect the fact that Grampy never wanted to talk about any of those things, but another part of me was curious to know more about him. I slid off the bed of the truck and got behind the wheel. I put the journal back in the glove compartment and tried to take my mind off of it.

I knew that before I sought out anything else, there was a bridge I had to rebuild.

As much as I loved my grandfather, his fashion sense wasn't becoming on Clay. He needed something a little more modern. So I decided to drive out to the mall.

I remember there being an old carousel in the centre of the mall when I was a kid. But when I arrived I saw that it was gone, replaced with a wishing well. I could see coins layering the bottom. I took out a quarter that I really should have saved and whispered, "Please let him give me a chance," and tossed it in. I had to start somewhere.

I made my way into a men's clothing store called Wade's Clothing. Not too fancy, or too casual. I looked around, wondering what Clay might like. Turtlenecks? I didn't think so. Casual dress shirt? Sure. Hoodie? I doubted it. Brown jeans? I thought he could rock them. It probably would have helped if I knew Clay's size; I was guessing at best.

I felt weird being one of the only people in the store. I looked around. The men working the floor just pretended I wasn't there, but I didn't want to talk to them anyway. I moved farther into the store and spied a grey mannequin around Clay's size wearing a green hoodie.

Okay, what I did next was pretty embarrassing. I didn't know Clay's size and I wasn't confident I could guess, so I took the green hoodie off the mannequin and wrapped a dress shirt around it, buttoning it up. I couldn't do up the last three buttons, so I grabbed another shirt that was two sizes bigger—it fit perfectly. I stood back and admired the mannequin for a moment, excited to see what Clay would look like.

"Ma'am, what are you doing?" I heard a familiar voice, and I turned.

"Taylor!" I caught myself. "What are you doing here? Shouldn't you be in school?"

She stared at me for a moment, her eyes wide. "Anna? I…work here." She raised an eyebrow. "And it's four o'clock. Where were you for the quiz?"

Ah, shit, I thought to myself. I backed up into the mannequin, knocking it over.

"What were you doing to the mannequin?" she asked, picking it up.

"I—I…I'm working on an art project. With my mom!"

"What kind of project?"

"Oh, y'know…she's building her own mannequin. I mean, better than this one—not that this one isn't great!—I just mean this one is probably mass manufactured, not made with any passion, y'know?" I gestured vaguely. "She made hers from scratch. We're just trying to get clothes, to see if they fit correctly. For the display…." I put my head down, wishing I hadn't said any of it.

"Well, can you not destroy store property in the process?" She dusted the mannequin off. Either Taylor was really concerned with the mannequin's well-being, or she just really didn't care about my "art project" because she added, "Tia was wondering where you went this afternoon. Did you get her text?"

"Oh. Yeah. I got it. I just felt sick. Had to leave, and—"

"And go bully the mannequins at Wade's Clothing?" She waved her arms.

"Yeah, and go bully the mannequins at Wade's Clothing…." I sighed.

I wondered when this would get back to Tia. I knew it would, but this was about Clay. I loved Tia, but the last thing I needed was her looking over my shoulder. Holy shit, this was going to be awkward to explain.

"Well, since I'm working I'll give you the twenty percent discount I can give to pals," Taylor said. "As long as you don't bother any more of these guys, okay?" she grinned.

"Woah, seriously?" I raised my eyebrows. "Thanks, Taylor! I appreciate that a lot."

"No worries." She smiled. "If anyone deserves support right now, it's you." She took the dress shirt off the mannequin, and headed for the cash.

Okay, forty dollars wasn't bad.

Once I got back to the truck I threw the bag of clothes on the passenger seat and hoped Tia wouldn't find out I had skipped class to buy men's clothes.

———

LATER THAT EVENING, I SAT near the firepit in the backyard. It had been a while since I heard the crackling of wood and the warmth of flames, so I grabbed some kindling and started a small fire. I could hear crickets in the distance and I let my lungs fill with the smoke.

I looked in the journal again and skipped past all of my entries to the back, with the older parts that were Grampy's. That's when I noticed there were pages missing. The jagged edges meant they had been torn out, which was weird. Other pages were filled with cursive. I set the book down for a minute and made sure the fire was secure. I walked the short distance to the lake, my mind drifting to Clay.

Clay could recreate whatever was written inside the journal. Maybe that meant he could recreate what Grampy wrote about, too? I hadn't tried speaking to Clay in two weeks, so I wasn't even sure if he still liked me after I let him down big time. I hoped that getting him a new wardrobe would at least be a start.

I skipped a rock and thought about Halifax. I remember at some point I had been sure all the magic had left my heart. I think living in the city surrounded by loud cars, obnoxious people, and light pollution makes you forget there's a whole galaxy above our heads. And it was moments like this—far away from the rest of the world, skipping rocks across water, near crackling flames, with constellations stretching across a dark blue sky—that made me realize the magic never left. I did.

I knew that the only way to make sense of any of this was to dig into it. So I bit my lip and said, "Hey, Clay?"

Nothing.

"Hey, dude. Um, it's been a couple of weeks. Are you still upset?"

Of course he's upset, I thought. *He has every reason to be.* There would be no moving forward in this friendship until Clay and I found some common ground. It was going to be long and difficult, but it had to be done.

"Come on, you gotta give me something. I know you still care, Clay. If you didn't care then you wouldn't have taken me back to that memory in the park. If you didn't care then you wouldn't have given me the journal to take care of."

I took a breath and looked across the lake. I was bad at this. But I knew it was necessary.

"There's so many things I want to say to you, but you know as well as I do that words aren't always my strong suit. Please, come here."

"I'm not your pet." He revealed himself behind me. I jumped, but caught my balance.

"I know," I said.

"So, what? You think I'm just your genie in a bottle? An imaginary friend in your journal? That isn't how this works, Anna."

"Well you're not explaining it well."

"Lets make one thing clear: I don't owe you an explanation," he said. He sounded frustrated. "I don't owe you—"

"You don't owe me anything," I cut him off. "I know that. I know you don't owe me an explanation, a conversation, or even what you did the other night. You *chose* to do that. I'm trying to figure out why, Clay, and I think I know."

"Oh, do you?" Clay crossed his arms.

"Because you still care."

Clay shook his head and started walking towards the firepit. I followed him.

"Where are you going?" I asked.

"Of course I still care about you, Anna," he growled. "Why would I wait if I didn't? Why would I have faith for so long? I knew after the first five years that you weren't coming back. But I stayed, and I grew resentful towards you. I don't know why I stayed—I felt like I had to, I felt like I owed you…and now that you're back, I see clearly that I don't owe you a damn thing."

That hurt. Why hadn't I just taken the damn journal with me?

"I didn't know I would be away for that long," I reasoned feebly. I couldn't bring myself to make eye contact with him. "Mom just…I wanted to stay here. I didn't want to go to Halifax anyways; Mom made me go with her."

"I know it wasn't your choice. But you made me stay here. And that's the part that hurts."

I nodded. "I know. And I can only apologize in so many ways, but sometimes an apology isn't enough. I have to prove it to you."

"And how are you going to do that?"

"You gotta let me try."

We just stood there not saying anything for what felt like forever. I could see Clay cross his arms again. I just wanted him to let me in, let me into his world and let me right my wrongs. He didn't owe me that; it would only happen if he wanted it.

"Okay." He let out a breath. "I waited this long, how much worse can it get?"

So he wasn't optimistic, but it was a start.

"Thank you," I whispered. Then I took a deep breath and changed the subject. "I have something to show you."

"Oh, so now you have a surprise?"

"Just…follow me." I grabbed his hand.

We walked towards the firepit and he grabbed a seat.

"Wait here." I smiled.

He raised an eyebrow. "What're you up to?"

I went to the garage and grabbed the bag of clothes from my truck, hiding them behind my back so he couldn't see. When I walked back towards him, he knew something was up.

"C'mon, what's behind your back? Seriously."

"Close your eyes," I said with a grin. "Do it."

Clay shook his head but did what I told him. I laid the clothes on his lap and said, "I thought you might be tired of wearing clothes that are two sizes too big."

He looked down at the clothes, and then up at me.

"Anna." He picked up the dress shirt. "You didn't have to—"

"I did," I said, cutting him off. "I had to do something. Plus, you deserve more clothes that aren't older than both of us put together," I joked.

I finally got a smile out of him.

"Oh, look! A smile. What timeline is this?"

"I just…." He drew out his words. "Haven't really gotten a gift before."

"Well, why don't you go try them on? There's a mirror in the garage," I said, poking the dying fire.

In the garage, I watched Clay button up his new shirt while looking in the mirror. It fit perfectly—I guess the mannequin situation was worth the trouble to see him in clothing that fit.

"It's a lot more comfortable than your grandfather's scratchy old sweaters, that's for sure," Clay said, throwing the old sweater he had been wearing in my truck. I was glad to see him happy. It wasn't even about me regaining trust; he just looked good with a smile on his face.

I noticed his braids were looking a little soft, and it didn't take long for me to grab a hold of them.

"Hey! What are you doing now?"

"Just sit tight for a minute."

"Oww," he whined. "What are you—"

"Sit tight," I said again. I looked around and spotted an upside-down plastic bucket and pushed him down onto it. "I'm fixing your hair. Don't move." I ran into the house to find a comb, brush, and other supplies.

When I came back, I didn't have to see Clay's face to know he was frowning. I got him to move from the garage to the tree house because he kept whining—it was probably loud enough to wake up Mom and Nan. But the view of the lake wasn't bad, either.

"You know I'm doing you a favour, right?" I laughed.

As I took my seat behind Clay, I was remembering how my grandmother used to braid my hair. It was all muscle memory. Clay's hair was kind of long, and I loved it.

"That doesn't make it fun," he said with a sigh.

"Stop being such a pessimist, you're going to look great."

"If you say so." He looked towards the water. After a minute, he mentioned, "It's been a while since we've both been up here."

"I know," I said, holding a fistful of hair. "You think of it often?"

"It's one of the only things I think about."

I paused, hands full of his dark hair. There was the guilt again, using my heart as a doormat. I'm not saying I didn't deserve to feel it, but it hurt.

"I'm never leaving you again," I said. "I promise."

"Don't promise," Clay said, picking up a mirror I had brought from inside. "Show."

He grinned when he saw his reflection. In the background I caught my half smile as I finished up the braids.

"Look how much better this is!" My half grin became whole.

"It *is* a lot better." Clay admired my handiwork. "Thank you."

"Any time." My eyes drifted away from our reflections, and back to the journal, which was sitting on the floor of the tree house.

"You wanna go back, don't you?" he asked.

"How'd you know?"

"I can feel whenever the journal is open," he said. "You found Rudy's passages, didn't you?"

I nodded. "I did."

"You could always just read them, y'know."

"I...." I was so embarrassed to say. "I never learned cursive."

"Well, luckily you have me." Clay picked up the journal. "Rudy wrote those entries long before you ever wrote about me, but I feel his memories inside of me as much as yours." He paused. "I assume you wanna go back and see for yourself, right?"

"Is that wrong? He never liked talking about his childhood. He always kept quiet about it. I want to respect that. But I also miss him so, so much."

"You know he ripped some of the pages out, right?"

"Yeah, I saw. Why would he do that?" Was he trying to hide something?

"I wish I knew, but they were ripped out well before I came about." Clay turned to another page. "But he has other things in there, not just about himself."

I perked up at that. "Like what?"

"Let me show you." Clay extended his hand in my direction as his eyes turned blue. I hesitated, but I trusted him. I extended my hand....

The starry sky, the tree house, the lake, and the sound of crickets all vanished. We were surrounded by darkness. I looked over at him, and a bright blue energy resonated around us.

The stars reappeared around a half moon. Small buildings rose from the darkness as a street appeared and street lights turned on. Everything was still.

It looked similar to downtown Yarmouth, but was clearly some time ago. The roads had fewer potholes, and the buildings were in better shape. The street lights looked entirely different—not straight and silver, but tall, black, and curly. This was way more than a couple years ago.

"Woah." I looked around. "This is…downtown, isn't it?"

"It is." Clay grinned as he pointed out a tall, slim, dark man in the distance. Everything was frozen, like someone had hit pause on a movie. I couldn't tell who the figure was at first.

"You can go right up," Clay told me. "He can't see you, nor can you change anything."

I took a few steps. The man had a full head of hair and no beard, but I recognized that nose, those eyes, and the smile from cheek to cheek.

"That's…Grampy?" I grinned. He looked a lot slimmer. His face looked smooth and young. He was handsome in his youth.

"Yep." Clay smiled. "I think he told you this story a couple of times—the one where he met your grandmother? But now you can see it first hand."

Clay snapped his fingers and the world began to move. People were walking around, laughing—full of joy. I could hear music in the distance, in the direction Grampy was walking. I followed him as we walked down to what I assumed was Main Street.

"This is amazing!" I said to Clay. "How come you never told me you could do this?"

He shrugged. "I didn't know I could when we were young. Once you left, I spent a lot of time inside the journal, and I figured it out."

I watched Grampy stop outside the door of a small building. The music was loud on the other side of the door. He took a deep breath.

"Come on, Rudy. Let yourself have fun," he said to himself before he walked inside.

I always cringe at men giving themselves pep talks. It just seems so corny, and Grampy wasn't exempt from that.

We followed Grampy inside; the music was too loud and lots of people were sweaty and dancing. Grampy went straight to the bar and ordered a drink. A young black woman passed him a scotch. Ew. I couldn't handle that stuff. He took a sip and I could see the nerves on his face—his eyes were darting around the room. Then he ordered another drink. And another one, and another one. He fiddled with the buttons of his vest, with a look of uneasiness. It was strange; he always came off as overly confident to me. This had to be the night when Grampy met Nan. The dance floor, the bar, being well dressed. It went along with how he used to tell the story. He told me he won her over with his moves, then asked if he could buy her a drink, and next thing he knew they were madly in love. At least that's what he told me when I was a kid.

I watched Grampy edge towards the dance floor. He was awkwardly trying to break through the crowd. Everyone was surrounding a young black woman in the middle of the dance floor who was moving so fluidly and carefree. I assumed this was Nan and my smile extended into something stupid. Eventually Grampy made his way towards her. They made eye contact.

Then Grampy opened his mouth, and instead of a smooth line about buying her a drink, he stuttered, "H-hi…miss!" He tried to get her attention. "I like y-your…h-hair. Can I buy you a beer?"

I groaned and put my head in my hands. "C'mon, Grampy!" I shook my head. "Ask her to dance. Say something sweet. Stop being weird."

"It's all downhill from here." Clay grinned.

"Don't tell me that."

Grampy didn't say anything else. He just kind of moved back and forth, trying to dance with a serious lack of rhythm. I didn't know if this was real life, or if Clay had taken me to an alternate universe. I was flabbergasted at the idea of Grampy being nervous. But I could feel him becoming anxious; he wobbled a bit. I facepalmed, knowing he drank all that scotch way too fast. The dancing woman in the middle took note and asked, "Are you okay?"

"Yeah…I'm fine." Grampy replied. But the next thing I knew he fell backwards, hard.

"How did Nan fall for *that*?" I asked, looking at Clay.

"It'll make sense soon." Clay snapped his fingers and everything sped up, like a movie on fast-forward. The woman on the dance floor left, and two men picked Grampy up and carried him towards the back exit. Clay and I followed. They sat him down against the brick wall outside and the bartender from earlier approached. Clay snapped his fingers again and time resumed normal pace.

"I'll take it from here," the bartender was saying to the bouncers.

She put a wet cloth to Grampy's forehead, and eventually he came to.

"Hey. Woah. Woah." He moved her hand away. "What happened?"

"What happened? What happened is you got drunk and passed out on the dance floor." The woman laughed. "But to be fair, I was the one giving you those drinks."

"I don't believe that," Grampy said. "Did someone hit me?"

"No," she said. "This isn't one of those places. The only thing that hit you was the floor you fell on."

"I don't believe it," Grampy repeated. He shook his head.

"Gosh, you must be a city boy. You got a chip on your shoulder or something?"

"Or something."

He tried to stand up but the woman pushed him back down. "Where do you think you're trying to go?"

"Back inside. I can't go out like that."

The woman laughed. "We are well beyond dance floors right now. You are not going back into that bar."

He sighed with a look of defeat across his face.

"What's your story, anyways?" the woman asked. "You a tourist? We get all kinds men like you in the summer."

"No. This ego grew up here for the most part," Grampy said. "I'm going to university in Halifax right now. Tried to catch a boat down here, missed it, so I thought I'd make the best of my 'vacation' here."

"Huh," she replied, looking at him closer. "You do look familiar now that I think about it. Maybe we've into run into each other in passing."

"I guess I should properly introduce myself," he said with a smile. "My name is Rudy Brooks." He extended a hand.

She shook it. "I'm Tanya Grant."

"What?" I cut in to the moment. "Tanya Grant? That's…that's Nan," I realized. "Holy shit."

"Yep." Clay smiled. "Your grandfather was quite the storyteller."

"You mean he was quite the liar." I laughed.

"You disappointed?" Clay asked.

"Honestly, a little bit. That wasn't smooth at all."

"No. No, it wasn't." Clay laughed.

Clay snapped his fingers and made it all disappear. He brought me back to the tree house. As we came back I could feel my stomach turn. We stared at each other for a few seconds, and then laughed beneath the stars. I wondered what else I could find out about Grampy. It was clear to me that not all of his stories were as he told them, but I guess people aren't always the stories they tell, and sometimes you have to seek out the truth you're after. I wanted to find out more.

"You know a lot more about him, don't you?" I asked.

"I do," Clay confirmed. "But we need to take it slow, you got a little nauseous last time, right?"

"I was," I said. "I'm feeling a bit queasy right now, to be honest."

"Then we should take a break."

He was right. I mean, it didn't look like I was going anywhere for a while. I suppose taking things slow wouldn't be the worst idea in the world, and to be honest I enjoyed the view we were sharing. I thought it was funny I found out the truth about Grampy meeting Nan. I was glad I got to unravel his ego a little bit, and I got to do it with an old friend.

Clay turned to look at me. He didn't say anything at first but looked up towards the stars. "Is it true you can't see the stars in the city?" he asked.

"For the most part, yes."

"Why would anyone want to live there?"

"I asked myself that for ten years."

I sighed. "I missed so much about this place."

"Then why don't you want to stay?" Clay asked.

That was a good question. But admiring your hometown doesn't mean you want to live in it forever.

"I used to love this place—so, so much. But now that I'm back, I feel like I came back to a memory that doesn't really…remember me," I tried to explain. "I've always been a seeker, trying to find meaning in one thing or another." I looked at the journal. "And I always wanted to learn more about my grandfather. Seeing his journal entry labelled 'Coming to Canada' makes me want to figure out more. But knowing that he tore pages out…who knows."

"That could be the next adventure you seek," Clay suggested.

"I remember I spent a lot of time seeking you, out here. Remember our classic hide-and-seek games? They would last hours." I poked him and smiled.

"I always won."

"Oh, sorry. Not everyone can turn invisible." I shook my head and laughed.

"I miss those days." He grinned.

"What's the harm in giving it another go?" I threw that thought into the universe.

"Aren't you too old for that type of thing?"

"Clearly I'm not too old for an imaginary friend."

"Clearly." He grinned. "All right, I'll take you up on that."

Clay and I slid down the ladder of the tree house. Once I got to the bottom I asked, "All right then, who's It?"

I looked over and Clay had already vanished.

"I guess that's me."

I turned to the tree and covered my eyes. Everything felt surreal. I took a breath and began to count.

"One."

The first year away had been the hardest. I thought about Clay every day. I thought about Nan and Grampy every day too. Adjusting was really difficult. I didn't like Halifax. You couldn't see the stars when the moon made its way to the sky. Mom said it was because of the lights all around. But to me, it was because there was nothing magic about that place. There was too much noise. We lived in a small apartment where you could hear people talking and music playing from the bar nearby all night. I just wanted to be home, with a lake and a tree house. We never did visit that summer.

"Two."

The second year we were away, Mom said we would visit Yarmouth that summer instead. I was excited to see Clay, and I remember waiting through the entire winter thinking that the warm weather would bring me home. But once summer hit, Mom was behind—she had been working full time on top of going to school. She ended up doing a summer semester and couldn't get any time off. I was heartbroken, and I think she was too. Not because we couldn't go, but because she broke a promise to me. I remember feeling so awful. I cried for two weeks. I knew Clay would be waiting. I just knew he was. I had told him I would be back soon, and now I was heartbroken because I knew I let him down.

"Three."

I made my first real friend. Her name was Cassie, and for a while she was the only friend I had. I wasn't the most talkative person in class because back in Yarmouth everyone had made fun of my name because it was different. When I started school in Halifax I didn't want to be Annaka anymore. I just wanted to be Anna. Mom was always a bit upset about my name change—she told me the name Annaka meant a lot to her, but I never thought to ask why. I guess I thought maybe I would just...find out some day.

"Four."

It was the first time I ever asked about my father. My family tree was always missing a piece, considering that Mom kept it a mystery. I always thought that time would fill the space but deep down, a part of me felt like we were running from the void. I remember seeing Mom's reaction to the question she wasn't ready for. She was painting a portrait, and she stopped immediately. She brought me to the living room of the apartment and said we don't always need to know about the unknown, and that it's better to focus on the people who are around you. I remember the way she said, "Lingering on those thoughts won't do you good." I couldn't help it; I was still curious, and as Grampy would say, my imagination got the better of me. But I always believed it was the best part of me. I spent so much time wondering if I had my father's face, smile, nose, teeth, or eyes. For a long time I was troubled not knowing the other part of me.

"Five."

Mom graduated university. A part of me was relieved, because I hoped that meant we would return home. Spoiler alert: we didn't. We just moved into a bigger apartment and Mom bought a minivan. There was always so much space in that thing, but Mom used it for art supplies instead of road trips. We didn't end up going home; in fact, Mom just kept getting busier and busier. That summer she started getting commissions for a gallery in Ottawa, so she spent a lot of time creating while I was spending more time wishing on stars I couldn't see. I would spend most nights on the roof of our new place, trying to sketch out the universe in a new journal. It wasn't like back home, back when I could easily look up and draw a night sky full of stars. In Halifax, I was just laying on a rooftop looking into loneliness.

"Six."

Cassie's entire family moved to Toronto because her Dad was offered a government job there. That was a hard year; without Cassie I was basically friendless. Meeting new people always felt overwhelming and I was way too shy to socialize. I thought about Clay a lot, but I had a feeling he was gone. There was no way that he would stick around waiting for me at that point. Each school day felt like a get in, get out scenario. I was good at keeping a low profile, but its not like people cared about what I had to say anyways.

"Seven."

That year Mom managed to make waves across the country. She was shortlisted for a pretentious visual arts award, and actually ended up winning. She was awarded fifteen grand, and I remember our mailbox flooded with fan mail. Mom was getting commission gig after commission gig, which made life pretty easy for a while, even though I didn't get to see her too much. I was getting old enough to hold down the fort while she was away. But of course, that made me feel pretty lonely after a while.

"Eight."

We found out Nan was showing early signs of memory loss. I didn't hit me right away, because, to be honest, I didn't really know what "memory loss" meant. Mom was worried, but she was still busy travelling the country and we couldn't go back home. I spent even more time alone in the apartment. I guess I found a lot of comfort in TV. I came across the old sitcoms Nan and I watched when I was kid, which led me to ask Mom if I could call and talk to Nan. She told me not to. I didn't know why, but now I think she might have been scared that Nan wouldn't remember me.

"Nine."

For the first time ever, I asked about my family's history. Mom said Grampy was from England, and that he came to Canada when he was a boy. His mother died shortly after they arrived, and my heart broke when I heard that, thinking how alone he must have felt. Mom told me that we have a lot of family overseas, but Grampy never figured out how to contact them. I wondered if they ever tried to contact him. It was also my first year of high school, and it didn't take long for people to figure out who my mom was. That's when everything changed. I was no longer Anna; I was now Anna Brooks. Everyone in my high school knew who I was, and every student who wanted to pursue the arts invited me to their parties. But each party I went to, I felt more alone than ever. Then Mom was offered a professor position at NSCAD, which she took in a heartbeat. She was so excited to have a stable income. It made things a lot easier—she no longer had to worry about which commissions would pay rent. But my heart was still aiming to hit back home eventually.

"Ten," I whispered. "I'm home."

Most my life, I've been surrounded by shadows and silhouettes. Smoke, mirrors, stage lights, and sound effects. I always believed it to be magic. I've spent way too long trying to draw a line between reality and fantasy, and for once, I just wanted someone, anyone to

CHAPTER 8

"**W**HY DID YOU SKIP CLASS TO GO KICK OVER mannequins?" I heard Tia's voice as I shut my locker the next morning. She was leaning against the one next to mine with a raised eyebrow.

Shit, I thought. *Of course Taylor told Tia I was at the mall.*

"Oh. Uh," I stammered, not making eye contact. "I, um, left most of my clothes in Halifax…I honestly just needed a bit of a wardrobe update."

Tia narrowed her eyes. "Yeah, with men's dress shirts that are two times your size?" Tia looked me in the eye. "What's going on, Anna? You know you can talk to me. And you could borrow my clothes if you need anything."

"Nothing out of the ordinary, I promise you," I said lightly, trying to play it off.

"Then why were you trying to start a revolution at Wade's Clothing?" Tia asked, half joking, half serious. "You know I'd be down to throw a couple bricks."

"I wasn't 'starting a revolution' at Wade's Clothing," I replied. We started walking towards class. "I'm working on an art project with Mom…and we needed some material."

111

"Uh huh," Tia said, still not buying it. "Whatever's going on, you know you can talk to me, right?"

"Right." I let out a breath while Tia's eyes lingered on me. I couldn't tell her about Clay, and buying him clothes. How safe would that be?

"You know I'm the one who breaks the rules, right?" She grinned. "Because I'm the one who knows how to not get caught."

She was right about that. Tia takes school seriously, but she also knows how to get away with just about anything. I threw my bag over my shoulder and a piece of paper fluttered from it.

Tia bent to pick it up and said, "Wait, what?" She scanned the paper again. "You got an invitation to Bobby Noah's party?" She looked stunned.

"Yeah, he came up to my truck yesterday like a dork," I explained as we walked into the classroom. We sat down at our desks. The bell still hadn't rung, and we had a few minutes before class actually started.

Tia looked at me eagerly. "And? Are you going?" Did getting an invitation from Bobby Noah save me from being interrogated about my shopping habits? Because if so, I was okay with that.

"I don't know...parties aren't really my thing." I sighed.

"What?! No way." Tia's face lit up with excitement. "I'm going to be your plus one!"

That made me laugh. "Why do you even wanna go?"

"To ruin his night, of course. He hasn't invited me to any parties since...the incident."

It was clear that it was Tia's mission to ruin Bobby Noah's life, and girls have to stick together, so I was in. After all, I had never gotten over the irony of a dude with two first names having the nerve to make fun of mine.

"All right, all right." I laughed. "Looks like you'll be my plus one."

"That's the spirit." Tia smiled.

Once the bell rang, the classroom filled with students. I didn't plan to stay, I just wanted to keep my head down long enough to be checked off as present during attendance.

As if she read my mind, Tia asked, "Are you staying the full day today?" She poked me. We were in English and the teacher was new, unprepared, and wasn't coming across well. This was supposed to be Grampy's class; that was reason enough for me to not want to be there.

"Actually, I think I'm going to get out of here," I told her.

"Dude…you can't keep leaving. They'll call your house eventually, I bet you're already on thin ice."

I scoffed. "What are they going to do? Expel me? My grandfather's photo is in the lobby."

Tia didn't reply, but I heard her sigh. I shouldn't have said that. Tia just wanted to help.

The new teacher was a younger-looking white dude named Mr. Davis. I could tell he didn't have much experience. He could barely keep the room under control—students were throwing paper balls back and forth, talking over him, and clowning how high he wore his pants. It wasn't funny but I couldn't help giggling at Travis, the class clown, standing up and pulling his jogging pants up to his chest. There was enough commotion after that for me to sneak out and make my way back to the truck.

Once I got in, I rolled down the window and drove towards the waterfront. I hoped I had been in the classroom long enough to be marked present, but when I heard my phone *ping*, I had a feeling it was a text from Tia. I pulled into a parking lot outside of an empty bar.

Tia: *FYI. Mr. Davis just had a major meltdown and left. Ms. Anderson came to take attendance.*

Shit. That meant the principal was probably going to call home.

113

I hoped it wouldn't be a big deal; I would explain to Mom that it was a mistake.

Tia: *Listen, I know you're going through a lot. But please, if things get heavy you always have me. Never feel like you have to go through this alone.*

I couldn't reply. I didn't want to take advantage of Tia's kindness with my dishonesty. It just didn't feel right. I tossed my phone on the passenger seat and scanned the parking lot.

I had planned on spending the day looking through more of Grampy's journal entries, trying to decipher his handwriting. I still couldn't believe he lied to me about how he met Nan. There had to be more in there. I had put the journal back in the glove compartment and was hoping Clay could show me more of my grandfather's past. I grabbed the old journal and noticed that the cracked leather spine was barely held together.

"This thing really got worn down over the years, didn't it?"

"Yeah." Clay appeared without warning.

I jumped and shouted, "Shit, man! You gotta stop doing things like that!"

"It's the only way I can." He shrugged. "But yeah, the journal is in rough shape. I need you to be gentle with it. Don't be one of those people who breaks the spines of books, please."

"I promise I'll be gentle."

He nodded. "Good."

I put the truck in drive and continued on my way. I hoped no one would see Clay in my passenger seat. I drove down to towards the water and parked out of view behind a bar no one went to during the day.

"Aren't you supposed to be in school right now?" Clay asked.

"You sound like Grampy." I sighed.

"I partly am."

I rolled my eyes and opened the journal. I wonder what had kept Grampy journalling in the later years. For most people, the idea of journalling faded away before they hit the teens, but then, he had always liked keeping track of everything.

I flipped to the back of the journal, skipping to an entry titled "October 2002."

I looked over to Clay, but he didn't look too excited about this one.

"Are you sure?" he asked, a look of hesitation on his face. *What could be so bad about this one?* I wondered. If it was anything like the first couple, I could probably use some popcorn and chocolate along the way.

"Yes, I'm sure. Lets do it!" I was excited.

"All right." Clay shrugged. He extended an open palm in my direction. We touched and everything faded away. The darkness transformed into my grandparents' kitchen. By the time the darkness faded I felt a little dizzy, but it wasn't the dark place that made me feel nauseous; it was the shift in surroundings.

I could see Grampy cooking pancakes while Nan watched television in the living room. She kept tapping the armrest next to the phone, as if she was waiting for a call.

Grampy put the pancakes on a plate and brought them out to her. Nan looked pretty stressed out. I rarely ever saw her like that.

"Did Jayla call this morning?" Grampy asked.

"No. She didn't."

"I can't believe she left like that." He shook his head and placed the pancakes on the coffee table. "It's been three days and not even a phone call. It has to be that damn boy."

"I don't know. It's not like her to pull off a disappearing act," Nan replied. She sighed. "Thank you for breakfast, hon. But I don't think I can stomach any food right now. The stress is eating me."

Grampy kissed Nan on the forehead; it made my heart smile.

"You don't worry about a thing," he said.

Grampy took the plate back to the kitchen. I could see the stress on Nan's face. She stood up and I followed her outside to the deck. She shook her head and slammed her first on the deck railing, over and over again.

"Where is that stupid! stubborn! girl!" she yelled.

Grampy came outside two seconds later with a worried face.

"Hey, hey. Tanya." He wrapped his arms around her. "Shh. She's going to come back soon."

"What if she doesn't come back?" I could see tears coming from Nan's eyes. "What if something happened? I don't know. She hasn't been herself lately. I shouldn't have got into it with her that night. I shouldn't have…." She was weeping now and Grampy just held on tight. I could see his eyes were filled with fear too.

"God," I said aloud. "What happened?"

Clay looked at me, but he didn't reply. He wanted things to play out for me to see.

"I'm going to take a ride downtown," Grampy was saying. "Maybe she's around there. I think you should stay here in case she comes back." He pulled back and looked her in the eyes for a moment. "Let's go inside, okay?"

Grampy led Nan inside, then grabbed his keys—the same keys that were now mine—and made his way to the truck. I followed. Once we were in the garage, I hesitated. Now what?

"This is where you should get in," Clay explained. I opened the passenger door and slid in. It was like I wasn't even there, because I guess, in a way, I wasn't.

Clay knew what I was thinking. "You can't change anything," he assured me. "He can't see or hear you. You're only observing what he wrote." Clay's voice resonated in my ears, but he wasn't anywhere in sight.

"So…how could I talk in the other memory?"

"Because that's the one you wrote. It was your memory. Again, you could say whatever you want. But nothing would really shift how things played out."

Grampy put the truck in reverse and made his way towards the main road. It led him out of the south end. He turned on the radio. He drove down Main Street keeping his eyes to the sidewalk, hoping he would find Mom. He turned and drove towards the water. Then he parked in the same parking lot Clay and I were in now, behind the bar. He got out of the truck and walked to the door.

"This is…weird," I said to Clay, watching Grampy disappear inside.

"Go in," I heard Clay's voice respond.

I got inside just in time to see Grampy go right up to the bartender, who was cleaning glasses.

"Hey, hey, Rudy," the man said. "It's been too long. Can I get you anything?"

"Not today. But have you seen that Morrison boy around?"

"Blake?" the bartender asked, pointing to a booth over to his right. There was a young man with white skin and blond hair, face first into the bar counter with half a glass of beer sitting beside him. "I think I found the treasure you're looking for."

"Yeah. And I'm going to bury it." Grampy moved forward and grabbed the young man by the collar of his jacket, lifting him up.

"Woah, woah, woah!" The young man mumbled, waking up. "Last call isn't until—"

Grampy pulled him off of the chair and let go, dropping him backwards onto the floor. He hit it. Hard.

"Listen, you little shit." Grampy leaned down. "Where. Is. My. Daughter?"

My jaw dropped. It was a mixture of amazement, shock, and

disbelief. I never took Grampy as the type of person to get into bar fights. It felt like a movie.

"Oh, shit," the young man said once he realized who Grampy was. He tried to get up but Grampy sent him back to the floor, harder than before.

"Ow! Stop doing that."

Grampy grabbed him by the face and said, "I'm not playing, boy. I will send you down again. The only reason I passed you was because I was sick of looking at you in my class. And *why*," he squeezed to emphasize his point, "is a twenty-one-year-old dating my seventeen-year-old daughter?"

Ew. Okay, that was weird. I always thought that guys who went after younger girls like that were never mature enough to date people their own age. It was a gross power dynamic issue.

"Okay, okay." The younger man put his hands up in surrender. "She's been staying at my place."

"Where is your place?" Grampy got closer.

"I'll take you there. Let me grab my keys."

"With all the drinks you've had? Don't even play. You ride with me." Grampy shoved him out the door.

Blake got in the passenger side and I managed to jump onto the back of the truck as they drove off. "Jesus. Where was Mom staying?" I asked myself as we made our way out of town.

I never knew Mom had a rebellious side. I remember she mentioned it at the funeral, but I guess I'd get to see it first hand. I couldn't imagine her going after a bad-boy creep who hangs at bars during the day. She was better than that, and she was better than him. I eyed that guy sitting next to Grampy through the back window of the truck. I got bad vibes.

Grampy eventually rolled up to an old rusty trailer near the edge of a forest. I had no idea why this guy lived so far out of town. I don't know if it was the dark, quiet forest, or the lonely trailer at the end of a sketchy road, but the place wasn't exactly welcoming.

They both got out of the truck and made their way towards the trailer. There was a broken window patched with a black garbage bag. Classy. Grampy shoved the young man towards it.

"Okay, okay," the young man said. He let out a breath, and opened the door. "Jayla," he called. "Your fath—"

I saw Mom come out. Her hair was a mess and she was wearing a dirty grey hoodie.

"I seen you pull up," she said. "Let's skip the confrontation." She looked uninterested in the boy and walked past Grampy towards the truck.

"Well, that's that," Grampy said to the boy.

"Wait. Are you going to drive me back to my truck? We left it at the bar."

"The highway is a twenty-minute walk that way." Grampy pointed. "You can sober up while getting your hitchhiking thumb ready."

"Oh, c'mon!"

Grampy laughed and shook his head.

Mom climbed into the passenger seat and sat looking forward, not saying a word. I scrambled up in the back, and noticed when Grampy got in he didn't say a word either. He put the truck in reverse and backed it onto the dirt road.

"Does that guy hit you?" he finally asked, once we were on the highway.

"What? No. Why would you even ask?"

"I have reason to believe he does. Why would you run away to this dirty, old, beat down trailer and—"

"Dad," She cut him off. "Blake is a lot of things. But he doesn't hit me. He never has, and he never will." Mom gave him a serious look. I could tell she was pissed off that he had even asked.

Grampy shook his head and kept his eyes on the road. "Your mother is worried sick."

"Why is she always on my back?" Mom shot back. "Because I broke curfew a few times? Because I hang out with Blake too much? All you guys ever do is nag, belittle, and get mad at me over stupid shit."

"Because we want the best for you!" Grampy spoke over her. "We don't want you hanging out with that loser—"

"He's *not* a loser!"

I cringed when Mom said that. That Blake guy was, in fact, a loser.

"Oh, come on, Jayla. Yes he is. You've been living in a pigsty for three days. Why?"

She didn't reply.

"Are you going to answer me?"

There was nothing.

He sighed loud enough for the entire county to hear.

"I was scared, okay?" Mom finally said. Her frustration turned to weeping. Grampy looked over at her, confused.

"What were you scared of?" he asked.

"Letting you down." The tears kept coming down.

"Jayla, what's going on?"

"I'm so sorry, Dad. I am so, so sorry."

Grampy pulled the truck over on the side of the highway and held Mom's hand.

"Jayla, what are you sorry about?"

Mom composed herself and finally told him. "Three days ago, I was already freaked out by the time I got home. Then Mom started losing her shit at me. I had to leave. I couldn't be around her…or you."

"What were you freaking out about?" Grampy looked concerned.

"Because I'm pregnant."

My heart felt like it fell a thousand feet and hit concrete.

"What the fuck?!" I yelled. The pieces were falling together. Mom was pregnant in October 2002. I was born in June 2003.

That meant....

That Blake....

Blake Morrison.

Is my father.

This was the man I had been so curious about? I felt overwhelmed, heartbroken, and I was chasing each breath that came after.

Grampy sat there, frozen. Not sure how to react. The tears kept coming from Mom while Grampy's face read blank.

"Do you hate me? Do you hate me?" she kept asking. "Say something!"

She pushed his arm but nothing came out of him.

"It's true!" Mom cried. "All I do is let you down. I let everyone down. I am such a fuck-up. I just ruin everything!" She covered her face.

"Shhh." Grampy held her hand. "You could never let me down."

He embraced her while she cried into his sweater. He held on tight, resting his head on hers. Grampy hummed over the crying, and the hums eventually drowned out the sobbing.

Clay made everything fade. My heart was racing so fast I felt like I was going to throw up. I screamed as loud as I could, but all I could hear was Grampy's humming echoing in my head. I kept thinking that I had seen my father, and his name was Blake Morrison. He used to have a trailer just outside of town. That thought kept running through my head.

Again.

And again.

And again.

CHAPTER 9

MY FIRST INSTINCT WAS TO GET ON THE HIGHWAY and drive to the trailer. I could remember the route Grampy took in the memory.

"Anna, that was years ago," Clay said from the passenger seat.

"I know," I said, driving back out onto Main Street. "But I mean, what if it's still there?" Logically, I knew it was a stupid idea. But I did it anyway. I turned onto the highway and sped up.

"Anna, I don't think he's going to be there," Clay cautioned.

"I need optimism right now," I cut him off. "Tell me something positive."

"That's not how friendship works...."

He was right, of course, but I needed to do this. I spent so many nights, holidays, and birthdays wondering who my dad was. I had to find him. I had so many questions. Why did he never call? Why did he never write? Why did he never want me? I was going to find out one way or another. I had to. He owed that to me. The world owed that to me.

I found the dirt road from the memory and floored the truck so it wouldn't get stuck in the mud. I emerged in the big open field where the trailer had been all those years ago.

The funny part was, some small part of me had been convinced it would still be there. I thought that maybe Blake would be there, and maybe, just maybe, he would be happy to see me. Maybe he would invite me in and make me a coffee. Maybe he would tell me that he missed me, and that he had tried to contact me. Maybe we could build some type of relationship. But maybes don't set anything in stone. When I rolled up, I could feel the hope slip between my fingers.

"It's not here." I let out a breath. "Where did he go?"

"It's been years, Anna," Clay replied gently. "He probably moved on."

"Don't say that. He has to be around. I know it. I was so close. He sat exactly where you're sitting." I looked over at Clay sitting in the passenger seat. I wanted to cry.

I got out of the truck and ran to the spot where his trailer had stood. There was nothing there. I fell to my knees. I could see my tears hitting the grass. I could barely catch my breath.

"I saw him, Clay. I saw him with my own two eyes." I was beginning to lose myself. "You saw him too, right?" I was pleading now.

"Yes." Clay knelt down and put a hand on my shoulder. "I saw him too."

I was beginning to get really sweaty and felt super dizzy. It was another anxiety attack.

"I can't catch my—" I couldn't finish my sentence; my throat was beginning to clog.

Clay caught wind of it fast and placed both of his hands on my head and looked me in the eye. His eyes turned blue and he said, "Hold on, Anna. I've got you."

The open field, the grass, the truck, it all faded away seamlessly, and we were surrounded by darkness. A cool breeze blew in my face from the distance, and I finally felt like I could catch my breath again.

"Oh, my God," I gasped, holding on to Clay. "I saw him. I saw him, and he was real. He was real."

"Shhh," Clay soothed. "Let's just rest right now, Anna."

I lay there in the darkness, holding his hand. We stayed in that place for a while. I thought of it as safe place. Somewhere away from the world. It was like a waiting room if life ever got too heavy. Clay motioned his hand and the darkness became peppered with stars.

"Just focus on those, okay?" he said. "It's going to be okay. I promise."

I hoped Clay was better at keeping promises than I was.

IT FELT LIKE HOURS, BUT I honestly had no idea how much time passed. Clay noticed I was breathing at a normal pace again and he said, "You ready to go back home?"

"Not really," I said. "Can we just stay here?"

I was grateful he had taken me away from it all. I still couldn't believe I had seen my dad. Even more, I couldn't believe Mom had never told me any of it.

"You could stay, but your Mom would probably freak out." Clay half grinned.

"She's always freaking out these days." I sighed. "We should go back, I guess."

Clay snapped his fingers, and the darkness began to fade away. The stars fizzed out but once everything was said and done, reality didn't look much different. The moon was resting above us, while stars took over the sky.

"How long were we there?" I asked.

"A while, but it's fine. Are you okay?"

"I don't know." I got to my feet and wiped the grass off my jeans. I turned around and saw the truck still in the same spot. We pulled out and back onto the highway towards Yarmouth. I didn't want the road to end. I wanted to keep driving. At least when I was driving, I was in control. We drove back to the town in silence, and once we got close to my grandparents' house Clay said, "I'm around if you need me."

I looked to my right to reply, but he was gone.

I had a feeling Mom would be waiting for me, and sure enough, there she was, on the front porch in her housecoat.

"Anna!" she whisper-yelled. "Where *were* you?"

When I saw her, I didn't know how to react. I kept thinking about her being the young, scared teenager in the dirty grey hoodie. I knew I couldn't bring that up, since I didn't have any reason to know about any of it. It would only make things worse.

"I was…at Tia's place."

"No. You weren't. I called, and you weren't there." She crossed her arms. "Not only that," she continued, "but I got a call from Ms. Anderson. Why weren't you in class today? Apparently it wasn't the first time either. What's up with that?"

"I… I…."

"Nothing to say? C'mon, Anna. You're better than that. You're better than this."

How dare she say that? After I saw what I saw, those words coming out of her mouth sounded like some sick joke. She was the one who took me away from my hometown and then hauled me back and expected me to pretend everything was normal. This wasn't normal. Grampy dying and her expecting me to finish off grade eleven in the school he taught at wasn't normal. Suddenly moving back to my hometown with no timeline for our stay wasn't normal. Never mentioning my father and pretending he didn't exist wasn't normal. There was nothing normal about any of this.

"Your grandfather worked so hard for everything he accomplished here," Mom was saying now. "He worked so hard for me;

he worked so hard for *you*. I don't want you to go down this road. I don't want you to let him down."

That's when I lost it.

"Hold up!" I yelled. "Me letting *him* down?! You're the one who hasn't visited in years. You never even saw him before he died!" I couldn't contain myself. "Then you have the nerve to hold me to some higher expectation after taking me away from my hometown. Bringing me along to Halifax so you could study. I was fine here, Mom! I would have been fine, but no. You took me along so you could say you did it all by yourself while having a daughter!" I knew that last part wasn't fair, but I was done being nice. "You didn't even take into consideration my feelings when we left. You just *left*, and I never had a say!"

I didn't know where that energy came from, but I wasn't backing down.

"I'm not just some plot device for your story, Mom. I'm my own person. Now we're suddenly back here, and we're supposed to act like everything is normal? Are we supposed to act like Grampy being gone is normal? Am I supposed to pull up my bootstraps and move on? Don't you think it hurts being in the school where he taught? Don't you think it hurts having Nan treat me like a stranger? Is that supposed to be normal? And do you think that I'm supposed to pretend my dad doesn't still live in this town? Or do you just edit him out because it's easier for you, rather than having a real conversation with your daughter?"

I could see the emotions on Mom's face shift: from angry to frustrated to disappointed to just…lost. I had never seen her like that before. I didn't know what else to say, I don't think there was anything else I could say after that. Who did she think she was? How was she acting any different than Nan did when Mom broke curfew in the memory?

"Annaka, that's not a line you cross." Mom crossed her arms.

"No. I'm just supposed to pretend the line isn't even there, right? I'm just supposed to accept things the way they are." I threw my hands up in exasperation. "We've been here for weeks, and you haven't even toyed with the idea of me meeting my dad."

That caused her to pause.

"Some people are better left in the past," Mom said quietly.

"Well he was never in mine to begin with!" I shot back. "Where is he? Where is he, huh?"

Mom shook her head. "I'm not having this conversation with you." She turned to the staircase.

"You never do."

"You're right, I never do." Mom agreed, walking up the stairs. "You do what you want, it's your life after all. If you wanna be a high school dropout, if you wanna fail and tarnish the name of Rudy Brooks, then you do you."

"Oh, that's new," I spat. "You're making it about someone else for once."

That's when she looked back, and I saw she was actually a little choked up. It was then I knew how hard the words hit because she didn't reply, she just continued up the stairs.

Everything was silent. I stood there feeling a mixture of things: regret, anger, but mostly sadness. I didn't want that to go down the way it did, but it did. I walked upstairs to my room and to lay in bed. I was trying to remember when things were easier. Before death, before grief, before loss.

I lay in bed thinking. I couldn't believe I seen my dad. That had to be him, right? His name was Blake Morrison. Could he still be in town? Could he be gone? Of course Mom wouldn't talk about it. I rolled over to look outside through the gap in the curtains; there were a lot of stars in the sky that night. I decided I wanted a better view, so I grabbed my comforter and went outside. I climbed up to the tree house, wrapped myself in the blanket. I placed my head in my hands and closed my eyes.

"Hey," I heard Clay say. When I opened my eyes he was already sitting beside me. "Sounds like you need a friend right now."

"You think?" I said in a sarcastic tone.

"So…you feeling okay?" Clay asked. "After today?"

"Feeling okay? Not really, no. That was a lot for me. That argument with Mom…that was a lot too." I sighed.

"It didn't sound great."

"You heard all that?"

"I'm always around somewhere." Clay looked at me.

"So…is there anything else in the journal about Blake?"

"Unfortunately, that was all I had. I was hesitant to show you at first."

"Why?"

He gave me a small smile. "Because I know how you react to things."

"I don't really think that was an over-the-top reaction, Clay, all things considered."

"Never said it was." Clay continued. "I just know you. You're a seeker. You don't leave any stone unturned if there's anything you can do about it. I knew you would want to find out more. I was hesitant, because that was all I have. I just didn't want to let you down, that's all."

"You're not the one who has to worry about letting anyone down, okay?"

"Noted."

"So, let me get this straight. We can't go back in time, kidnap Blake, go forward, and find him in the same spot?"

"You watch too many movies," Clay said with a laugh. "This isn't time travel. It never was."

"Can you explain? I think I've had enough of these stage lights and magic tricks. I need you to unravel the enigma. The going back in time, it's...?"

"It's the way you wrote it, and how he wrote it too." Clay moved his hand, erasing the reality around us. We were surrounded by darkness again, in the dark place. Clay snapped his fingers, and portals began forming all around us. As I looked around, each portal visualized a memory I had written in the journal. One portal showed Grampy and I at Cape Forchu; another showed all of us sitting around a Christmas tree; another showed the first time I had met Clay. Long buried, they were all coming back to me.

For the first time in my life, something was beginning to make sense. I had never understood Clay's powers as much as I wanted, but something clicked. he created the memories as we remembered them, as they were written. I could talk to Grampy in mine, because it was *my* memory. I could also just observe if I wanted.

"You held on to all of this for so long," I said, as much with wonder as with sympathy.

"You created me to be your friend, but over time I grew into the keeper of these memories. Along that journey, I carried yours, but I also found Rudy's."

"I want to see more." I said. My eyes couldn't stay off the portals. I knew Grampy was a man full of secrets, but I wanted to be selfish. I wanted to know who he really was. I wanted to know it all. I spent so much of my life living in the dark, and these memories brought light to a tangible history I could unravel. One that could make me feel complete. One that could solve my own mysteries.

"This isn't a process we can rush, Anna." Clay's voice filled the air as the portals faded. "We take it slow, and on my terms, okay?"

I knew there wasn't any other way. So I said, "Okay. Your terms. We do this your way."

There had to be more about my father, there had to be more about Grampy...and I felt so close to understanding all of it.

"In the meantime, I just wanted to get you away from all that," Clay continued. "It sounds like you need a friend right now," he repeated as we faded back to the reality of the tree house.

"I do," I agreed. And without hesitation I embraced him in a hug and he hugged me back. I was glad he was around. Clay meant the world to me, and I was never going to let him go again.

CHAPTER 10

TAZ RELAXED ON MY LAP AS I REHASHED THE argument with Tia. It was an in-service day so I was hanging out at her place. I wasn't in the mood to be home.

"It sounds like you and your mom really got into it."

"Yeah, it felt good to say all of it in the moment, but now I'm just down about it. I avoided her this morning." The morning after an argument is always awkward. I wish I could say that it didn't happen a lot, but it did. Maybe not to the degree of the night before, but Mom and I didn't say a word to each other that morning. I tried to get out of the house without her seeing me, but I know she did. I'm pretty sure she gave me the benefit of the doubt, though. I'm sure she didn't have much to say to me either. I was okay with that.

"I think she's trying her hardest." Tia looked up at me. Tia was always good at seeing the other side of the argument. Empathy was her strong suit, but I didn't want to hear that right now. I kinda just wanted my own feelings to be validated.

"Maybe. But I'm done just being someone whose sole purpose is to exist in her world."

"Fair enough." Tia was quiet for a minute and then said, "Listen, you didn't reply to my text."

"I'm sorry," I said. "I just needed to get away."

"No," Tia cut in. "*I'm* sorry, I shouldn't be on your back about school. I know you're going at your own pace, and it shouldn't matter where you go. And I guess being in a building surrounded by pictures of your grandfather doesn't help." She paused. "Sorry—"

"No." It was my turn to cut in. "That's exactly it. Mom doesn't understand that. I'm surrounded by the person I'm trying to grieve. The giant photo of him in the lobby, the notes on his classroom door, the way students and teachers always speak about him, and how they just see me as his granddaughter. "

"That must be…awful. I'm sorry, Anna."

"I learned some things about him, y'know," I said. I knew I shouldn't have said that, but I needed to vent.

"Oh yeah? Like what?"

I guess there wouldn't be any harm in telling her about his journal entries, as long as I didn't mention Clay.

"He had his own set of entries in the journal he gave me. I found some old entries of his; one that really stood out to me was when he found out about my mom being pregnant."

"Oh shit." Tia dropped the CD in her hand. "What did you find out?"

"That Mom ran off for three days. She was scared, worried about my grandparents' reaction."

"Damn." Tia thought for a moment, then continued: "I would be worried too, though. It's kinda weird thinking about our parents being vulnerable, huh?"

It was. Mom always seemed like she had everything together. But seeing her sitting with Grampy in the truck, screaming and crying, made me realize that parents are only human. And, honestly? Seeing that changed me. My memories of Mom were of her always knowing exactly what to do, when to do it, and how to do it. But in that moment she had been lost…just like I feel a lot of the time. Maybe, I thought, she doesn't always have it together. Maybe, like everyone else in this world, she's growing as we spin along with it.

"Did you learn anything else?" Tia asked.

"Yeah…. There was a part where Grampy wrote about my dad. I guess he almost beat him up and everything."

"Oh my gosh, for real?" Tia was stunned.

"Yeah. He used to live little ways outside of town in a trailer. I guess he frequently went to the bar down by the waterfront. That's about it." I shrugged. "I went as far as driving out of town, hoping to find where he lived. Turns out that was just wishful thinking."

"But it's a start, yeah? Are you going to keep looking?"

"I don't know," I admitted. "By the sounds of it, he wasn't exactly a stand-up person. He seemed like a bit of a loser, to be honest."

"Do you think you could get anything out of finding him? Like, I dunno, closure or something?"

Closure was a funny word. It had been almost seventeen years; I didn't think closure was something my father could ever give me.

"I don't know. He would just be a stranger, really," I said, but I knew deep down he was a stranger I still wanted to meet. Was that the worst thing in the world? Just to say, *Hey, I exist?* I knew there wouldn't be much room for a relationship, but I still thought about the what-ifs.

"Do you know his name?"

"Blake Morrison. That was what was written in the journal, at least."

"Can't say the name sounds familiar. But who knows, he could still be in town?"

"Or he could be in Montreal, Toronto, or Vancouver. A lot can change."

"You're right about that." Tia smiled. "But you didn't. You've been a disappearing act lately. A mystery I'm still trying to solve."

Yeah, just like everyone else in my family, I thought.

"I don't think there's much else besides what you see on the surface," I said.

"And I think that's a bold-faced lie," she cut me off. "My childhood best friend had the most beautiful mind on this side of the world. You have more depth than most, Anna, but I think you're just afraid to show the world who you really are. I'm not going to chase you over it, but I just want you to know that you don't have to hide who you are with me."

I smiled. Tia could read me like a book. I *was* hiding something—well, some*one*. I felt a weight of guilt because Clay had always had to hide while I got to explore. I was so scared someone would take him away. I knew no one could ever find out about him.

———

AFTER I HUNG OUT WITH TIA, I got in the truck and drove off. I didn't really feel like going home right away. I didn't really want to see Mom yet. Maybe sightseeing would be a healthy way to let off steam.

"I'm happy to see you're still friends with Tia." Clay faded into the passenger seat.

"Jesus!" I jumped and hit the brakes. "Do you always gotta make an entrance like that?"

"There's no other way to do it." Clay shrugged. "Thanks for not telling Tia about me."

"What could I say?" I laughed as I hit the gas again. "Not like I can just be like, 'I ran into Clay, my imaginary friend from when I was a kid, and we've been spending time together, catching up, jumping back to the past, learning about things I'm not supposed to.'"

"To be fair, she was always the rebellious one." Clay shrugged.

"And how do you know that?"

"You used to write about her." Clay shrugged again. "You wrote an entire entry about her birthday party once, then another about how often you would spend time on the waterfront together." I turned onto the road to downtown.

"Oh, yeah?"

I did remember the time we spent down by the waterfront. Tia's dad, Jonathan, would sometimes buy us ice cream and we'd play on the docks.

"Do you want a refresher?"

I glanced at him to see if he was serious. "Kinda."

I pulled into the parking lot of an abandoned bank that looked like it had been deserted for some time. There was no one around so Clay picked up the journal, flipped through a couple pages close to the beginning, gave me a nod, and extended his hand. We touched, and I closed my eyes. When I opened them again, Clay's hand was Tia's, and she was gripping it hard, spinning round and round and round.

"Woah!" I yelled. "What's going on?"

We both fell down and she laughed out loud. I looked around to see we were on the waterfront, the sun high and boats passing by.

"You were always such a goofball." I smirked.

Tia stuck her tongue out at me and ran across the docks. I got up and followed her.

"Hey!" I yelled. "Where are you going?" That's when I realized I, too, was a kid. I couldn't really pretend to be the adult here. I guess I would just go along with it. I followed Tia as she ran along the edge with her hands extended, which I thought was quite risky, but I remember doing it with her as a kid.

"Girls!" I heard in the distance. I turned to see a stressed-out looking Jonathan running towards us. "Get away from the edge!" he yelled.

Tia laughed, but I was starting to get worried too. Being a kid really is carefree; I could finally see why we stressed that man out so much. I ran up, grabbed Tia's arm, and pulled her back. She fell on top of me in a fit of laughter and fun.

I looked up to see Jonathan's red face let out a sigh of relief. "Tia! What did I tell you yesterday?" He crossed his arms.

She sat up. "No running away anymore."

"And what did you just do?" he scolded.

"Run away!"

Tia got up and ran. I laughed watching her running towards the sidewalk as Jonathan helped me to my feet.

As she ran, I began to remember that day more clearly. We had spent the afternoon on the waterfront, Tia ended up getting lost, Jonathan had a meltdown, and….

"Tia!" Jonathan called. "Tia, where did you go?" He looked left and right, frantically. "Shit, shit, shit!" He gripped my hand, bringing me along as he ran. "Did you see where she went?"

"Towards the sidewalk!" I pointed. It was weird; I knew where she was and that she was okay. I could have told him that Tia had crawled under the small opening of the red warehouse near the waterfront, but a part of me really wanted to see this memory play out again.

Jonathan rushed with me towards the sidewalk. "Tia Evans!" he shouted.

I got my hand free from Jonathan's grip, and looked to my left towards the small opening. I could see a little red shoe.

"Mr. Evans!" I tugged his arm and pointed to the shoe. "She has to be this way."

"Good eye, Annaka." Jonathan ran.

"Tia? Tia!" He yelled. "Are you inside?"

"Dad?" I heard a frightened voice. "Dad? Where are you?"

"Come back the way you went in—I'm here!"

"I'm stuck!" Tia cried.

Jonathan let out a frustrated sigh and tried to force his way in. He was too big.

"Dang it."

"I'll get her!" I volunteered.

"Nope! There's no way I'm losing two kids in one day," Jonathan said, looking around for someone to help. But by the time he looked back, I had already crawled through the hole.

"Annaka!" he called in a defeated voice.

Inside the warehouse was dark, but light filtered in through the cracks. I looked around to see that there were lots of barrels, lobster cages, and fishing equipment in there.

"Tia!" I called "Where are you?"

"I'm over here!" she yelled.

I looked and saw that Tia's foot had gotten caught in a rope holding barrels together.

"Tia!" I called. When I reached her, I asked, "How did you get stuck in there?" That still baffled me. The weird part was, so much of reliving this memory felt organic—some reactions felt automatic. I wasn't in complete control, but I was still participating. "You were always such a rebel." I whispered.

"Just help me!" She looked scared.

"You're gonna be okay." I smiled as I grabbed her hand. "Spin in my direction, just like we were doing outside." I began spinning with her slowly.

"Okay." I could see her eyes were puffy.

As we spun, the rope began to unravel, and her leg eventually came loose. She looked over at me and gave me a hug.

"See?" I told her. "That wasn't so bad, was it?"

"I wanna go home," was all she said.

"Come with me." I pulled her back towards the small hole in the wall. I made sure she exited first, and I saw Jonathan snatch her up quickly.

"There you are!" He embraced her. "You gotta stop running away, Tia." He sounded frustrated.

"You gotta get better at catching me," Tia replied as I wriggled my way out.

"That isn't how it works." Jonathan shook his head, but sounded relieved. He squeezed Tia into a tight hug again and she hugged him back.

"Are you okay, Annaka?" he asked me.

"I'm fine." I got to my feet and wiped the dirt off my pants.

"Good, sounds like you deserve an ice cream." He smiled.

"I want one too!" Tia shouted.

"We'll see about that," Jonathan replied with a wink at me.

Even though Tia could be a troublemaker, Jonathan was such a sucker for her. I smiled at how he hugged her, and rested his head on hers. It was a genuine moment between a father and daughter. It made me kind of sad. I never had that. I mean, I always had my grandfather, but I thought back to the idea of Blake, and I kept thinking about the time that we could have spent together. What if he had grown out of his bullshit? What if he had gone to school? What if he had tried to contact us but never could? Mom always told me not to dwell on those thoughts, but I couldn't help clinging on to them. Why did my entire life have to be a mystery? It wasn't fair.

I stood there, watching Tia and Jonathan, as everything around us faded and the world shifted back into my truck, my hand still gripping Clay's.

"Are you okay? Do you feel nauseous?"

"No." I shook my head. "Okay, maybe a little." I held my stomach. "Okay, maybe a lot." I rolled down the window.

"Oh, lord," Clay said as he held my hair and I barfed out of the window, right in the bank parking lot.

"Luckily no one is around," Clay said as I lay back in the seat.

I looked at Clay and grabbed the journal, flipping through the opposite end.

"What are you doing?" he asked. "Maybe going back again wouldn't be a great idea."

"It's just…." I caught my breath. "Are you sure there isn't anything else in there about my dad?"

"I would know." Clay replied, leaning over. "I'm taking the journal."

"Are you telling the truth?" I asked. I don't know why I implied he was lying, I just remember him saying that he was worried about letting me down and I just wanted to know for sure.

"Why wouldn't I be telling the truth?" He frowned. "No. No, there isn't." He continued. "If there was, I would know."

"So all you know is that his name is Blake Morrison?"

"Why do you want to chase after him?"

"I'm not chasing after anyone. I just want to know."

Seeing Tia and Jonathan, I don't know. Something in me clicked. I knew it was unlikely anything would come of it, but what was the harm in trying?

"I just don't think it's worth the time." Clay shrugged.

Okay, that annoyed me. Clay couldn't relate to what I was feeling.

"That's not fair," I said. "You don't know what its like not having a father."

"I can assume."

"No you can't, you're not even—" I caught myself before finishing that sentence.

"Not even what?" he challenged. "Are you gonna finish that sentence?"

"No." I looked away from him, gripping the steering wheel.

"You have no idea what I've been through. I spent more than half of my life being idle on your behalf, and you're going to say that to me?"

He was right. I shouldn't have said that, it was an awful thing to say. I didn't mean it, but that didn't matter.

"Do you know what it was like? I spent most of my life reliving memories that weren't even mine, instead of creating my own. I never got to live out my own life; instead I had to relive parts of yours. Even then, it was only the parts you decided to record. Do you know how often I observed you and your grandfather going on those trips to Cape Forchu? The times your grandmother braided your hair? I've felt what you felt. I've seen what you've seen. Those memories live in me, just like they are in you. And you sit here and tell me it doesn't matter because I'm not even *real*?!"

"Clay, I—"

But he was already gone. Vanished into thin air.

CHAPTER 11

I DROVE HOME FILLED WITH REGRET. WHY DID I KEEP pushing everyone away? Clay didn't deserve that, and honestly? Maybe I was a little hard on Mom too. I kept wondering if there was anything I could have done differently with Clay...I knew I couldn't have taken him to Halifax when we left; he would've been seen or caught. So instead he spent his time in Yarmouth, waiting. I thought about him watching all of our memories like the reruns of a sitcom. Just like I did when Mom was away. Over and over and over again. It didn't sit well with me. No wonder he was hesitant to let me back into his world. He held the same resentment towards me that I held towards my mom. I wanted him to be more than a character in my story. He deserved more than that.

I could see Mom in the backyard smoking a cigarette when I pulled up. I managed to sneak inside by going through the side door. I tried to get upstairs, but a voice called me down.

"Young lady!" It was directed at me. "Young lady, get off the steps and come see me."

It was Nan's voice. I could have ignored her, but something made me pause and turn around. She was sitting in the living room on a rocking chair. I sat down on the sofa, not really sure what to say. She smiled at me and said, "I see you around. What's your name?" She seemed genuinely curious.

So many emotions filled me: anxiousness, fear, sadness. She had no memory left of the times we sat in this very same room, watching cartoons on Saturday mornings. She helped me grow into the person I am, and yet here she was, asking me what my name was.

"My name is Anna," I said quietly.

"Anna is a pretty name. You from around these parts?"

I didn't want to confuse her, and I knew if I told her I was from Yarmouth she would ask for a backstory, and who my people were. It hurt to lie, but I said, "I'm from Halifax."

"Halifax? My daughter wants to move there. She was always the artistic one of the family." Nan leaned over and gave me a look. "But between you and me, I'd be heartbroken if she left us. I want her close." She sat back in her chair again and said, "If you have family, Anna, stay close to them. Because at the end of the day, that's all we've really got. When the rest of the world falls apart, they will be the only ones who will pick you back up."

I instantly thought about Clay. He had picked me up, even after I left him behind. When he saw me panicking he gave me a place to rest, and after my fight with Mom, he was the first person to let me vent. I thought about that night we both sat in the truck and he held on to me as I bawled. His world fell apart when I decided to leave him behind, but I left him behind with barely a second thought. He had been stuck here, alone and away from me, but when the tables were turned and I needed a shoulder to cry on, he was there. God, now I felt even worse about saying what I said in the truck.

"Thanks for the advice." I stood up to leave.

I went upstairs to hide away in my room to let those thoughts sink in. At least Nan still had her wisdom; if only there was a way we could go back in time and collect the rest of her.

I WAITED UNTIL THE SUN went down to make my way to the truck in the garage. I grabbed the journal from the glove compartment and held it, contemplating my position. I felt like a coward because I knew Clay harboured resentment towards me. The same type of resentment I held against my mom. I realized I wasn't that different from her, and maybe I should have been more empathic, like Clay was to me. I stashed the journal back in the glove compartment and walked down to the lake to skips rocks across the water, hoping it would clear my mind.

But it didn't.

Guilt, shame, and regret filled every part of me, and seeing each rock sink reminded me there was no way this whole Clay thing was going to end with the two of us riding off into the sunset. He couldn't remain a secret forever.

As I threw another rock my surroundings faded into darkness, the sky, trees, and house were replaced with darkness, and as the rock landed it bounced on the sheet of ice that had formed. I wasn't stupid; I knew Clay was playing with the edges of his reality, mixing them with mine.

"Clay," I called out. "I know you're there."

I could see the Milky Way expanding above my head while I stepped onto the ice and slid forward.

"I wanna see you."

"I'm right here," I heard from behind me.

I turned and saw his warm face, grey skin, and dark eyes.

"Hey, Clay—" I began.

"I know," was all he said.

"No, no. Please, I actually have to talk this out."

"That memory about your dad still irking you?"

"It's about you." I let out a breath. "You were mad at me. I didn't put as much thought into that as I should have."

"Oh, Anna—"

"No, Clay. I've been thinking a lot about it. I've been preaching about how I always felt that I was an afterthought on Mom's great journey…but Clay. I left you here. I left you here alone for so long." My eyes welled up as I said aloud what I had been thinking for weeks. "A part of me always assumed you would move on from here—go somewhere else. I should have taken you with us. I know it would have been hard and weird, but I promised you when I was a kid that I would always take care of you. And I didn't."

I could see him left out a breath. He moved past me, sliding on the ice with his back turned.

"That was a hard time," he began. "I stayed up most nights looking down the driveway, wondering when you'd be back." A replica driveway appeared out of the darkness in the direction Clay was looking off to. "I didn't have much human interaction. Most of the time I spent reliving your journal entries, and eventually I went through your grandfather's. I feel like I lived a part of his life as well as yours." He turned back to me and made eye contact. "After a while, I just assumed you had moved on. Thought that you weren't ever going to come back."

"I know, and I feel so guilty because of it," I began. "I mean, I resent Mom for taking me away from everything I love. But I did so much worse to you. I left you here. By yourself. We've been avoiding this conversation, but why don't you resent me the same way?"

Clay let out a breath. "I *did* resent you," he said. "For a long time. I went back to relive the memories we shared over and over and over, hoping one day we would reunite. But that day didn't come. I grew older and got used to a world that was never meant for me." He looked down. "I'm not like you, Anna. I can't go to school,

I can't meet new friends, I can't go shopping. I'm stuck here, in this dark place of reliving nostalgic parts of my short life." Clay looked me dead in the eye and said, "To call me an outsider is an understatement."

"Then why are you giving me a second chance?" I asked, sliding on the ice. I know I begged him for one, but that didn't mean I deserved it. I needed to hear it from him.

Clay closed his eyes, and I knew there was hurt inside him. There was a knot he was having trouble unravelling; a truth he wanted to speak. I was ready. If he wanted to tell me to screw off for the rest of eternity, I would understand.

"That night when I left, and said I couldn't be your best friend right now," Clay let out. "I knew I couldn't navigate through that pain, I couldn't let it flow through me."

"Why?"

"Because I owe it to myself to hold space for something other than pain," he whispered. "Was that the answer you were looking for?"

That wasn't what I expected, but it sent a wave of empathy through my heart. I wished I could be more like that. Like him.

"I...uh...I'm sorry, Clay."

"I know." He looked at me. "I know."

We let silence fill the air between us. There were still so many thoughts and feelings I had, but didn't know how to bring up. I eventually asked, "So, my grandparents never seen you?" it felt silly to ask him that again, but I wanted to know for sure.

"No. At least I don't think," he replied. "I watched over them, like I knew you'd want me to. When your Nan began losing her memory, I picked up on it quick. She kept going to go the grocery store to buy eggs." Clay lifted his hand and a circular portal appeared. I could see the fridge. Grampy opened it to reveal what looked like a dozen cartons of eggs. Concern lined his face instantly.

"That's how it began. When Rudy came home after a weekend away at an English teacher's conference." Clay swiped his hand and the portal disappeared. "Over time it got worse," he continued. "It got pretty bad a year later on their anniversary."

Clay moved his hand to form another portal.

"Grampy wrote about this?"

"No. But somewhere within the ten years I learned how to keep track on my own. I got stronger, learned more about this all while I was alone."

Inside the portal I could see Grampy holding a small box wrapped up with a bow. He handed it to my grandmother, his face tense. Nan opened the box—inside was picture frame with a photo of the four of us, Grampy, Nan, Mom, and me, standing in front of the house. Nan had a warm smile as she observed the photo. Then she asked, "Who's this little girl?"

My heart sank to my stomach; I was the first person she forgot. Now I knew why Mom never wanted me to call her. I began getting teary-eyed as the colour in Grampy's face evaporated.

"Tanya, quit playin'," he said instantly.

"What are you talking about?" Nan frowned, looking back up to Grampy.

"Tanya, that's our granddaughter. Annaka."

"Annaka? But she isn't our granddaughter. I thought you didn't like to talk about her." Nan's eyes were clearly confused, as she looked back up at my grandfather.

That confusion made its way towards me. What did she mean?

"No, I don't mean her." Grampy breathed heavily, when he reached up to wipe the sweat from his forehead, I saw his hands were shaking.

"It's been a while since she left," Nan observed. "Do you still think about her?"

"Clay, who is she talking about?" I asked.

"No idea." Clay waved his hand, making the portal fade away. "Maybe she got her names confused? There's nothing in the journal about another Annaka."

"But Grampy seems to know one? There has to be something." I flipped through the pages of the journal.

"You can look all you want, but I've been through that thing more times than you can count. If anything, it would have to do with the missing pages."

I flipped until I made it to the page titled "Coming to Canada." I turned to the next page but there was nothing there; the pages had been torn out.

"They were torn out a long, long time ago," Clay said. "It's a gap in your grandfather's story."

"You mean torn out before I created you?"

"Yes." He took the journal back into his hands. "I've searched. I've gone to places I shouldn't have, and I still couldn't put the pieces together."

I knew Grampy was secretive about his past, but if that somehow led to what Nan was talking about, I wanted to learn more. I had to unravel it. I just had to unravel something. Maybe this was *my* great journey. And I was happy to have a friend like Clay to guide me along the path.

CHAPTER 12

"**Y**OU CHECKED HIS STUDY?" I ASKED. WE WERE still on the ice in the darkness.

"Yup."

"The basement?"

"Yes."

"Garage? Attic? Bedroom?"

"Anna, I've checked all those places."

"What did Nan mean by 'Annaka is not our granddaughter'?" I paraphrased. "Take me back," I walked away from the ice.

Clay let out a breath and followed. The world around us turned into reality again. I walked into the house but Mom and Nan were nowhere to be found—must have gone to sleep.

I went straight to Grampy's study. I expected to see his desk, his shelves full of books, I expected to see everything that reminded me of him. But I didn't see any of that. His desk was gone, replaced by a canvas facing the back wall. All his books from his shelves were missing, sculptures big and small in their place. The sculptures that had filled the living room back in our apartment in Halifax.

Mom had moved everything.

"She must have come in here when you were gone today," Clay observed.

"I should have figured as much." I clenched my fist. I wanted to break it all. All her sculptures, that stupid canvas. The study had been the last place that had any sign of Grampy left, and at that moment, the world proved to me that he really was gone. I fell to my knees and felt a sudden sadness I couldn't break free from. All of his stuff was gone.

Clay knelt down beside me and placed a hand on my shoulder. "Don't give up yet. His stuff has to be around somewhere. She wouldn't just throw it away. Maybe it just hurt for her to see it all in here."

Maybe it did hurt for Mom to see all of those things, but I didn't even get a say in what happened. She didn't tell me she was moving any of his things. She just packed everything up and put it God knows where. Did she throw it out? Did she donate it? I couldn't always be left in the dark just because some topics were difficult to talk about. I deserved to know.

"Goddammit!" I stormed out of the room and Clay followed. "Who was Annaka? Where is my dad?" I headed for the front porch and put my head down on the journal, feeling defeated.

"I'm sorry that happened, Anna." Clay sat down beside me. "We don't realize how much the little things impact us after losing someone, but we also need to stay focused on what's important here."

"This is important. Finding my dad is important. Finding out about my grandfather is important. And if the world wants to create more mysteries, I'll see them through." I know I was being stubborn, but sometimes I had to be.

I thought coming back home would give me some answers, but it only created more questions. I let out a breath. I looked up to the moon and saw it was almost full. I closed my eyes and took in deep breaths. I walked towards the ladder under the tree house and climbed up. Clay followed. I lay back, hoping the stars would help me feel grounded.

"I always hated my name, y'know? I never liked being called Annaka."

"Why?" Clay asked, lying down beside me.

"Kids used to make fun of me because it was different," I told him. "All through elementary here, they told me my name was stupid, or it was dumb because it was different. It wasn't like other names."

"How come you never told me?"

"I guess…that's why I made you. That day under the desk. I stayed inside at recess because kids were making fun of my name. I was embarrassed, I guess. All my life I just wanted to fit in, but I always felt different. Everyone always seemed to think it was weird that I spent more time writing in my journal than I did playing on playgrounds. Not many people understood. Well, Tia did, but besides her, the rest of the students in school made my life hell," I let out. "It was that dumb idiot Bobby Noah who started it all. Did I tell you he invited me to his party coming up?" I rolled my eyes. "Grampy always loved my name and I never knew why. I kept it for him, despite the bullying. But when I got to Halifax, I wanted to fit in. I just wanted to be Anna. Why are people so awful?" I looked over to Clay.

"I wish I knew." Clay put a hand on my shoulder. "I really do."

"I wish I wasn't so different."

"I don't," he whispered. "I like you for who you are."

I smiled. "I'm glad someone does."

"I'm not the only one."

"Do you think that Annaka was a real person? Grampy must have wrote about her, right?"

"Maybe." Clay stood up. "Maybe she's in the pages he tore out?"

"I wish I understood that man." I got up too.

"We'll figure it out, I promise, but it's getting late. You should probably get some sleep. We can start fresh in the morning." Clay walked towards the ladder.

I stood there for a minute, watching him. Once he noticed I was still there, he looked back. "You gonna get some sleep?"

"I'm not tired." I shrugged. "Not yet."

It was like he could read my mind because he sighed and said, "You want to go back, don't you?"

"I just...I do. Just nothing too heavy."

"Well, the floor is yours." He pointed to the journal in in front of me.

I picked it up and flipped through. I wanted to go to an easier time, not something too complicated. I found one that held a soft place in my heart: a sketch I made years ago of me sitting on the front porch as Nan braided my hair.

By the time I looked over to Clay, his hand was already extended.

"We're getting pretty good at this, aren't we?" I said with a smile.

I extended my hand, and we met half way. Everything around us disappeared. I closed my eyes and took a deep breath. Then suddenly I could feel my hair being pulled.

"Ow!" I yelled.

"Oh, I'm sorry, babe. There was a knot, but you're doing great!" I knew that voice. I looked up to see Nan with a fistful of my hair.

The garden outside was alive, and ants were crawling in every direction towards the steps, but the traps kept them away. I tried to be as still as I could but I still laughed under the warm sun.

"Screaming one second and laughing the next." Nan smiled.

"You do them too tight," I replied.

"That was only one time. I'm a professional now. You have a healthy head of hair, and we're gonna keep it that way." She kissed my head.

I loved having braids. Always did, Mom wasn't as good as Nan when it came to braiding, and Grampy didn't have any idea how to do it at all. But it felt nice to be remembered, and to feel her tightening them again.

"I love you, Nan," I said randomly.

"I love you too, sweetie."

I could feel her breath on the back of my neck. I wished I could stay there forever.

"Anddddd, we are all finished here sweetie." Nan held up a mirror. A little girl looked back at me, sitting with her grandmother on the front porch. Back when life was easy and the occasional knot in my hair was the only thing I had to worry about.

Nan stood up and said, "Well, I'm about to head in and make some coffee, hon."

"I want a coffee too," I said, knowing how she would reply.

"You're too young to be caffeinated. Hot chocolate for you."

It was the middle of summer, but I wanted that hot chocolate.

Inside, I sat and watched Nan put sugar in my hot chocolate, then add an inch of milk, then a piece of dark chocolate from her stash. The secret ingredient.

"Come and get it, sweetie." She put it on a coaster for me.

I remembered this day. Grampy had taken Mom into town to get some shopping done. It was close to Nan's birthday and they wanted to surprise her with a new TV. I peeked under the table and saw a younger Clay sitting beneath. I put my cup below and he took a sip. We always shared.

Nan made herself a cup of coffee and made her way to the living room. She put on the TV. It was mostly just static, but eventually it got to some fuzzy sitcoms. She sat in her rocking chair and I lay on the carpet. I looked to the left and could see Clay under the kitchen table. He could see the TV from that angle. We sat for what felt like hours, not really saying much—but we didn't need to. I missed this version of Nan, the one who was the captain of the ship, gentle, loving, the beating heart of the house. I moved onto her lap, and she wrapped her arms around me and gave me a big kiss on the cheek.

"I miss you, so, so much." I spoke softly.

"Honey, what do you mean? I haven't gone anywhere," she whispered as I closed my eyes.

When I opened them again, I was back in the present, sitting in the tree house with Clay. I let out a breath, wishing the present wasn't so difficult. I noticed one thing though, when I came back to the present this time I didn't feel the motion sickness I had before. Maybe I was getting used to this whole thing. It even put me at ease. I didn't feel angry anymore, I just felt calm for the first time in a while. I thought about Nan again—the present-day version. She was only a shadow of herself. Not the woman who held me tight, braided my hair, and knew how to make the perfect cup of hot chocolate.

But then I had a rush of an idea. My eyes widened.

"Can we bring her back?" I asked.

Clay looked at me as if I was out of my mind. Maybe I was. But it was worth talking about.

"How? What do you mean?"

"Is there a way that we can restore her memories?" I stood up and started pacing the tree house. I was half excited, half scared. But I hadn't thought about it before.

"Are you…asking if I can cure Alzheimer's?" Clay frowned.

I stopped pacing and looked at him. "I think it's worth a shot." I shrugged. Why not give it a chance?

"You barely know how any of this works."

"Well, I think I'm getting the hang of it," I replied.

"I don't know if it would work, Anna. You know much it drains you."

"But I feel fine this time! I don't have any body aches or anything!" I waved my arms to show him.

"Yes, but unlike you, your grandmother isn't sixteen years old." Clay shook his head. "Who knows what would happen when I bring her back."

That was true. But maybe, just maybe, taking Nan back would restore some of her memories? Maybe reliving them would help her remember in the present.

"I just want my grandmother back." I thought for a moment. "Is there another way you can take people back?"

"What do you mean?" Clay raised an eyebrow.

"Your hand." I grabbed it. "When we touch, the memories extend all around us. What if you condense it? What if you condense it in such a way that it doesn't impact the body as hard as it impacted me?"

"I've never tried that before."

"You've never had anyone to try that on," I corrected. "Why don't you let me be that test subject?"

Clay took his hand back. "That sounds dangerous."

"Nothing's dangerous if you're in control." I grinned. "Why don't we give it a try?"

Clay turned and walked away from me. I don't think he knew the full extent of his powers. But the way I saw it, the only way to find out was to challenge what he already knew. I wondered why Clay wasn't as eager as I was; he spent most of his life here with that power. It's clear he was comfortable, but if you get too comfortable you'll never move forward.

"So…is that a yes, or a no?"

"It's a maybe." Clay turned back to look. "If we do this—and that is a big if—I need some time to see if I can actually pull it off. Give me a week?" Clay put his hands in front of his face. "I'd hate to mess this up."

"Okay."

I had no idea if this would work, but I knew we had to try. If there was a way we could restore Nan's memory, we had to.

CHAPTER 13

CLAY DISTANCED HIMSELF FOR THE NEXT WEEK. I HAD no idea what his process was, so instead of prying I tried to respect his boundary. I spent most of that week—when I wasn't at school or avoiding Mom—searching the house, hoping to find my grandfather's torn-out journal pages. I went to the basement one night and ended up discovering all the things Mom had moved from his study. I was thankful none of it had been thrown out. I went through file after file after file. No luck. I kept thinking about what Nan had said in that memory about the other Annaka, and Grampy not wanting to talk about it. Maybe if the plan to bring Nan's memory back worked, I could even ask her? But that was thinking too far ahead.

As I looked through a box of papers, I could hear creaking from the ceiling. When I looked up, dust hit me on the forehead. It must have been Mom or Nan moving around upstairs—it was getting close to her bedtime. Maybe I should touch base with Clay to see where he was at regarding our plan.

"Hey."

I startled and fell back onto the floor, only to see his silhouette. "Goddammit, dude. We spoke about you not doing that, remember?"

"I do," Clay said with a laugh. "I didn't make any promises."

"Clearly." He helped me to my feet.

"Have you found anything?"

"Old assignments, lesson plans, a syllabus...no journal entries."

"I could have told you that."

"Yeah, yeah, yeah," I said, a bit embarrassed. "Have you come to a conclusion on your end?" I hoped Clay could pull this off.

"I *think* I know how."

My heart skipped a beat. *Yes!* "All right, well Mom's taking Nan to bed, and she'll probably go to sleep herself shortly after. Why don't we get started?"

Clay seemed hesitant. "Are you sure you want to do this?"

"Yes." There was no room for doubt if we planned to move forward.

Clay sighed. "You know there are...risks."

I knew the risks more than anyone else. I knew this process would put Nan in physical and mental danger. It might worsen what she was already going through, or it might cause her harm in other ways. But we had an opportunity to bring her back. My heart told me we needed to try.

"We'll cross that bridge when we get to it," I said.

I walked upstairs with the journal in my hand. I knew Clay would follow. I headed to the backyard to see the moon reflected on the lake. The spring night was calm.

"So...how are you going do it?" I asked.

"I'll pick a page in the journal, and focus my energy on your *mind* instead of your surroundings. The memories should fall into place like puzzle pieces."

"So...you need to pick something I don't remember?"

"Yes," Clay said, looking straight into my eyes. "Are you ready?"

"I should be asking you that," I said as he took the journal from me.

Clay stepped back and flipped through a bunch of pages. He finally asked, "What were you thinking about the day you and Tia had a sleepover and she almost found me?"

"Ohhh…I half remember that." I was putting the pieces back together. "We were in my room, and she opened my closet. She saw your measurements on the wall next to mine, and thought it was weird I took measurements of an imaginary friend. Then I explained that I *did* have an imaginary friend, but I remember you refusing to show yourself. So she just thought I was being a dork."

"At least I was being consistent." Clay shrugged. "So we're clearly not going to go with that one." Clay flipped to another page. "Okay, okay," he said. "What about Tia's birthday party. Ring any bells?"

"Probably eating cake or playing video games at Tia's?" I couldn't remember specifics; I've been to a lot of Tia's birthdays.

"So you don't remember too much, then?"

"Can't say I do." I shrugged.

"Then this is the one."

Clay closed the book. He looked nervous. Ultimately, he had no idea if this would actually work. He extended a hand, and instead of his eyes glowing blue, the air around him glowed. And then the glow began to extend in my direction. I looked directly into it. I felt the energy focus like wind; I could feel my braids lift into the air.

"Close your eyes," Clay said in a soft voice.

When I did, I was in Tia's living room. There were snacks everywhere, and Lucy was playing pin the tail on the donkey. I could see it all so clearly, and it was happening all so fast, my head filled with thoughts so quickly. Everything I was feeling was rushing through me all at once. I felt anxious, excited, and nervous. I had always been shy, and being around other kids wasn't always ideal for me. Tia understood that, though. I stood in the corner of her living room, away from the rest of the party.

"Hey, Annaka, get over here!" I heard her voice as she grabbed my hand, pulling me towards the game.

"What's going on?" I could hear Clay's voice from the real world.

"I'm thinking how silly you would look playing pin the tail on the donkey," I replied.

"Focus," he said nervously.

Clay was all business with this task. I knew he was scared that I might get hurt, but everything was going fine. I could see everything so seamlessly.

As I stood in line for my turn at pin the tail on the donkey, time suddenly sped up. It felt like everything was on fast-forward. From Tia's birthday cake, to the gifts, to the games, it all entered my mind at high speed, connecting dots that had become disconnected a long time ago.

"I think I got it," I finally said.

Clay closed his grip, and when he did it felt like all the wind was sucked out of me. I fell to my knees but caught myself before I face-planted. It felt like waking up from a dream, when you're temporarily disoriented by the sudden changes in time and space.

He ran over and immediately demanded, "Anna! Are you okay?!"

"I'm fine, it just…it felt kind of like I was dreaming."

That was when the pounding headache started.

"Owww," I said, clutching my head. "I didn't expect the massive headache."

"Yeah, I kind of figured that might happen." Clay crossed his arms and regarded me closely. "Too much activity in your head at once. Instead of your entire body experiencing it, it's focused in one spot. I guess it's replacing the body aches. Can you stand?"

I got to my feet. "It isn't as bad as the body aches, but it still sucks."

"So…," Clay ventured.

"So what?"

"What did you give Tia for her birthday?"

Right. There was this part. I closed my eyes. What did I remember? I tried not to think too hard, to let the thoughts come to me organically.

"I got her…I got her a slingshot! And her dad took it away instantly." I smiled at the memory. "I remember that clear as day now."

Clay handed me the journal, and said, "See for yourself."

I grabbed it and read aloud:

"February third. Today Grampy drove me over to Tia's place for her birthday. There were a lot of other girls from school there, Laura, Lucy, Taylor. We all sat in the living room and tried pin the tail on the donkey. I thought it would have been nice to bring Clay, I couldn't stop thinking about how silly he would look playing with all of us. I'm sure he would love it. I gave Tia a slingshot for her birthday but Jonathan took it away as soon as he seen it. He was no fun, but there was a lot of cake and ice cream. Tia wasn't too sad about the slingshot but I really wanted her to have it. Maybe she could have it again when she gets older."

Above the entry there was a sketch of the living room. It showed Tia blindfolded while the other girls and I looked on.

"Wow," I said, scanning the page again. I looked back up at Clay. "It worked!"

If that had worked, then we could try the same thing with Nan. Of course, not all entries could apply to her, but what if we brought her to the memories she was in? Like braiding my hair? Or watching TV with me? Or an entry of Grampy's, like when he found out Mom was pregnant with me? We were onto something, and we were going to get her back.

"Lets do another."

"You should get some rest," Clay said firmly. "This is still new to both of us. I don't want to overdo it."

"You always take things slow," I said with a sigh.

"No. I always take things safe."

I knew he was right. "Do you really think it'll work?" I asked.

"It's hard to say. Definitely risky to say the least." Clay walked towards the lake and I followed.

"That…doesn't say much."

"No. But I want to be honest with you."

"Have faith," I replied.

"I thought you and your grandfather didn't believe in that kind of thing."

"I'm talking about faith in ourselves, fool," I said as my phone buzzed. It was a text from Tia.

Tia: *Earth to Anna. Where have you been? Can you answer me, please? You were only at school twice this week.*

I put my phone back in my pocket.

"Was that Tia?"

I nodded.

"Aren't you going to reply?"

"I will later."

"She's just checking on you, Anna. She's a good friend."

"I know, I know," I said. "Can we just do one more? My head doesn't hurt as much as it did. I just want to see if this works for sure."

I was lying; my head felt like it was on fire.

"We're done for the night. Get some sleep. Maybe we can pick this up in the morning. Key word is *maybe*. Depending on how you feel."

"You're the worst." I smiled and looked away.

"You know that isn't true."

"I know." When I looked back he was already gone. "That's no better than ghosting, man."

———

I WOKE UP THE NEXT morning to the smell of bacon wafting from the kitchen, so I made my way down and found Mom and Nan sitting at the dining room table.

Mom didn't say a word to me, but I grabbed a plate and decided to eat on the front porch. I wanted to keep trying this new method with Clay, but we couldn't do it with people around. Maybe we could drive somewhere a little ways out of town. Before I could continue that thought, I heard the front door open.

"Anna," said Mom. "I need to talk to you."

I sighed. I had been wondering when Mom was going to give me another one of her "stay in school" talks. I thought she was done with that. Ever since we had our argument, we'd been avoiding each other like the plague. I knew she was hurt by what I had said, but I wasn't backing down. I had a point that she didn't want to see. I wasn't going to allow her to invalidate my own feelings, because they were anything but invalid. Most days were me just coming inside and heading straight to my room, or me leaving the house and hitting the road. But I sat there and listened to what she had to say.

"Listen, the school called three times this week saying you skipped class." She gave me a hard look, but I remained silent. She rubbed her eyes. "Don't think we're not going to talk about this. But right now, I need your help with something. I gotta head back to Halifax and pick up some supplies from my classroom. It looks like I'll have to do a lot of my grading and teaching online for now."

"Meaning?"

"Meaning I need you to watch your grandmother while I'm gone."

My eyes widened and everything inside felt kind of fuzzy. "What? Mom, you can't be—"

"Anna, I need you to do this one thing for me."

"Why can't Ben and Lillian do it?"

"They left for a trip to Lunenburg two days ago. While you went on a road trip, alone." Mom raised an eyebrow. "Have you spoken to Tia lately?"

"No. I've been busy."

"Doing what?"

"Can we stop? I don't know if I can do this. I don't know if I can look after her. It makes me anxious."

I wanted Nan back, but being a stranger to her, that was the worst feeling in the world. She was a shell of herself and if I was being honest, it scared the shit out of me. I didn't know how to interact with her. How could I pretend that we didn't have history? In a way, it felt like I'd already lost Nan. The only thing I wanted to do was try to find a way to bring her back.

"I understand," Mom said. "I do. But I promise, it won't be so bad. You've barely spoken to her since you've been here. I know what happened on our first day spooked you, and it's an awful thing to go through. But your grandmother still has fight in her, and you can't let her go. Not yet."

I wasn't letting her go; I was doing the exact opposite. If only she knew.

"I need help," Mom continued. "I need a co-pilot for this, and you're it." She sat beside me. Mom and I had been pretty distant since our fight. I knew she was struggling to balance everything, and it was no easy task. If I said no it would leave her stuck here, unable to do any of the grading she needed to finish. It was lose–lose.

"Fine," I replied. "I can do it."

"I know you can. But please, if you need anything, text me or Tia's parents, okay?"

I nodded. "Okay."

Maybe it wouldn't be as bad as I thought. I at least had to attempt to convince myself that it wouldn't be.

LATER THAT DAY I HELPED Mom clear out stuff from the back of her minivan; it was mostly just supplies she hadn't had the chance to bring inside yet.

"You got everything you need?" Mom asked when we were done.

"You're the one going on the trip," I replied.

"Sorry. I'm just nervous." She closed the trunk. "Are you sure you're going to be all right doing this?"

I wasn't, but I knew there was no one else.

"Mom, I'll be fine. It's…whatever. I'll get over it. You should hit the road."

"The schedule is on the kitchen table. Take care." She gave me an awkward side hug. I gave her one back. Moms are still moms even if you get in an argument once in a while.

And just like that, she got in the van and I watched her drive off.

I went inside and checked the schedule.

6pm – dinner + meds

8pm – bath

9pm – TV

It didn't seem too difficult, and Mom was going to be back in the morning. I set reminders in my phone in case I lost track of time. I could see Nan sitting in front of the TV in the next room. When I saw her it felt like my heart was on fire. I began feeling anxious and wasn't sure how to approach her, so I ended up circling the kitchen only to open and close drawers. I wasn't the best at managing stress.

"Hey, you in the kitchen!" Nan's voice called from the living room. "I can hear you pacing in here. You might as well pull up a seat."

I slowly made my way into the living room.

Nan looked at me. "Miss, sorry, but have we met before? I don't recall."

"It's Anna," I replied shyly. "Yes, we've met a couple of times."

"Well, come here, Anna," she said as she turned up the TV.

Nan still remembered Mom, but she didn't remember me, and I was scared to confuse her by saying, *Hey, I'm your granddaughter who you don't remember.* So I didn't say anything. I just stood there as she explained: "My daughter's out for the evening it looks like, so you're stuck here with me." I could see her smile. Even after everything, her smile could still light up a room. I remembered her smile well.

I smiled back, God I missed the woman she was. Well, the one I knew.

"You're shy, aren't you?" she asked.

"A little bit," I admitted, too afraid to make eye contact.

"If you're gonna be in my home, I'm someone you're gonna have to get used to."

Nan flipped through the channels until we got to a sitcom called *Harry's House.* I remembered the episode we watched. It was the one where Harry's stepdaughter, Kelly, went through a breakup and she was in her room crying into her pillow.

Harry kept trying to comfort Kelly, but eventually Kelly went on this huge rant about how men are pigs, trash, and not welcome in her room. Kelly shoved Harry out of her room and slammed the door. This was the part where Harry looked into the camera, sighed, and said, "I'm trying, universe. Be patient with me." Nan and I said the famous catchphrase in tandem, then caught eyes and smiled.

She asked, "You know this show too?"

"I do," I replied. I hesitated, then I said, "My grandmother and I used to watch it all the time."

"Who's your grandmother?" Nan asked, and everything seemed to pause when she asked that. Even my heart felt like it stopped. But I knew right then, in that moment I had to be brave.

"I'm trying to find her again. I think my biggest fear is her being gone."

"You think?"

"Yeah. Time created distance between us, and I haven't heard from her in a long, long time." I glanced at her. There was no flicker of recognition in her eyes, but she glanced back at me and smiled.

"Time is a battle no one can beat, but it seems to me like your grandmother has a lovely granddaughter."

I smiled at that. My phone's alarm startled me as it buzzed. Six o'clock: dinnertime.

"It's time for dinner, I'll be right back." I got up and went to the fridge. There was already a pre-made meal for Nan: a lasagna wrapped in tinfoil, some garlic bread, and a salad. Her pills were all organized in a little container labelled with the days of the week. I heated the pasta and bread in the microwave, then placed it on a plate with the salad, her medication in a little paper cup on the side. I set everything in front of her.

"Thank you, ma'am," Nan said with a smile. "Looks delicious!"

I felt a bit too young to be called ma'am, but I smiled nonetheless.

She ate in silence for a few minutes, watching the TV. Then she turned to me. "So how do you know Jayla?" she asked.

God, I hated that. I hated that so, so much. I could feel a lump in my throat but I managed to say, "Oh, I met her at an installation once. She was showing off some artwork at the museum." I didn't know what else to say.

Nan nodded. "That sounds like my daughter. Showing the world she has a universe inside of her."

In a way, Mom did show the world the universe inside of her. Her creations came from the heart. I loved the painting she had left in Grampy's study. I felt bad about what I had said to her, but that didn't mean it shouldn't have been said, and sure, I think she knew where

I was coming from. Just as I knew it wasn't an easy thing for her to talk about. But we had to. That was the only way to move forward.

After Nan finished eating it was time for her bath. I drew the water, making sure it wasn't too warm or too cold, and poured in the soap. I inhaled the scent she always smelled like: strawberry lemon. Nan was capable of bathing herself, so I waited down on the steps, holding the journal. I thought about Clay and our plan. Would tonight be the right night? Mom was gone, and it might be the only chance we would get.

"Clay, I need you."

He walked out of the living room, leaned against the wall, and crossed his arms.

"I know what you're thinking," he said.

"Then you know this might be our only chance."

"Anna, no."

"Clay, come on. We've practiced, it worked."

"On you, a sixteen year old. Not a senior citizen."

"I believe in you."

"And that's the problem, Anna. This is all on me. What if I mess up? It may cause damage that might not be fixable." He looked at me seriously. "This could be more than just nausea or headaches. She is a senior with memory loss, and I don't know what's going to happen. That's what scares me about this!"

"I'll take the blame," I said. "If anything goes wrong, it's on me not you."

"That's not how that works." Clay shook his head.

I knew making him budge would be difficult. His concern was real, but the more I thought about it, the more I was convinced this was the only time we could do it.

"Clay, we might not get this chance again for a long, long time. Mom is gone. We just do it—we just bring her back."

"It's more complex than that, plus she's not as strong as you. She's old."

"Yes, but she's strong. She always was, and always will be."

Clay sighed and shook his head.

"Clay, please. You know I know the risks. And if you were in her shoes, what would you want me to do? This is dangerous, yes. I'm not denying that. But you have a power—it's more than rewinding time and creating nostalgia. You can cure whatever is going on inside of her, I know it, and that power is a gift." I pointed my finger at him, touching his chest.

Clay looked around for a minute, and then looked to the floor. He seemed conflicted but I knew I could reason with him.

"Clay, I know you can do this. I know you're scared, but sometimes we have to take a risk. We have to face our fears head on. That's what being brave is about." I paused and tried to catch his eye. "Can you save my grandmother? Not for me, but for her."

Clay looked directed in my eyes, and I could see they were not as frustrated as before. I knew he genuinely wanted to help.

"I just want my grandmother back," I whispered. That was the truth of the matter. If I couldn't have my grandfather back, this was the next best thing. Clay knew how much it meant to me, and deep down, he knew it might work.

"Okay. I'm going invisible," Clay said, annoyed. "Bring her down when she's done her bath, and make sure she sits in the rocking chair."

"Thank you, Clay."

"Don't thank me yet."

I ran upstairs and saw Nan had already gotten out of the tub and put on her pajamas and housecoat.

"Hey, Tanya," I said. "We've got a bit of time before bed…do you wanna watch some more TV?"

"That's not even a question, hon. Let's head down."

Nan and I went back into the living room. I made sure she was comfortable in her rocking chair, and I turned on the TV. By this time, it was mostly nighttime talk shows so I left it on for her and went into the hall outside of the living room to pick up the journal. I couldn't see him, but I felt Clay grab my hand.

"Right behind you," he whispered, still invisible.

This whole situation stressed Clay out. I knew because of how hard he was breathing on the back of my neck. I entered the living room and opened up the journal to the later pages—the ones Grampy had written. There were a few memories I knew we could choose from, but I opened up to the night they first met.

"You there?" I whispered.

I felt Clay's hand wrap around mine, and I moved forward towards Nan. I stood in front of her and held out my hand.

"What are you doing, Anna?" Nan asked.

Clay put his hand in front of mine. A blue energy formed between them.

"What in the...? How are you doing that?" Nan's eyes widened as she stood up and moved around behind the chair. I knew she was a little scared, and so was I.

"Clay," I said. "Take her back to the night she met Rudy."

"Rudy? Who's Clay? What's happening?"

"Tanya," I said to Nan, "I just need you to close your eyes, all right?"

"Close my eyes? What's going on?"

"Please, Tanya. Trust me. This is going to help you, I promise."

Nan looked confused, but she could see the eagerness in my eyes. She sat back down, took a deep breath, and closed her eyes. The blue energy extended to Nan's face, and her jaw dropped open.

"Wait, what is this?" she said. "This is...I think I know this bar."

"Just relax," I spoke calmly.

Nan's shoulders relaxed. I hoped that reliving this memory would be somewhat relaxing for her. Besides the whole having to take care of a passed-out Grampy aspect.

"You still there?" I asked Nan. There was no reply, but she had a grin across her face, and was breathing rhythmically—almost as if she was asleep.

"You think she's okay?" I asked Clay. I stepped aside to see him fade into the living room.

"I think so. I think she's just hyper focused."

"We are well beyond dance floors right now. You are not going back into that bar," Nan said aloud. She laughed.

"That's exactly what she said to Grampy," I said, remembering the scene. The memories must be coming back to her. It seemed to be working!

"All right, what do you wanna do now?" Clay asked.

"We've got to do another memory," I said.

I flipped the pages until I got to the one where Grampy had written about Mom running away.

"This one," I said.

"Okay."

Clay closed his fist to open it again. Nan leaned back and sunk into the rocking chair a little more. I hoped she was okay. She was quiet for a few moments—then I heard her yell.

"Where is that Stupid! Stubborn! Girl! Rudy, what if she doesn't come back?" I noticed a few tears rolling down her cheeks. "What if something happened? She hasn't been herself lately. I shouldn't have got into it with her that night. I shouldn't have…I shouldn't have…."

Oh shit, I thought, *this was setting the wrong tone.*

"Clay," I cut in, as I flipped through entries. I found the one where Grampy had written about me being born. "This one."

"Okay." Clay opened and closed his hand again. Nan's tears turned into a smile as she said out loud: "Rudy! Rudy, pick up the damn phone and come meet your granddaughter. And dress nicely. She's healthy, she's fine, and her name is Annaka, Rudy."

"All right, Clay," I said after a few minutes. "Go to the entry when she braided my hair."

"Sure thing," he replied. The glow on his hand grew wider than it was before, and her eyes changed colour with them.

"You have a healthy head of hair, and we're gonna keep it that way." Nan's voice in the living room was playing out what I remembered. I let her speak it, the whole thing. I smiled through the stress, and crossed my fingers. As the memory went on, she drifted off—she wasn't talking anymore.

"Wait, what happened?" I demanded, suddenly nervous.

Clay closed his fist. "I don't know. She shouldn't have fallen asleep." I could hear worry in his voice. "I don't know why she did that."

I grabbed her wrist and felt a pulse, thank God. My heart didn't feel like it was in the pit of my stomach anymore.

"She's...she still has a pulse."

"Of course I have a pulse," Nan replied. She gently pulled her wrist out of my grip. "Who are you talking to?"

I looked back and Clay was gone. I let out a sigh of relief.

"No one. No one at all." My eyes welled up. I was so glad we didn't lose her. "How are you feeling?"

"Watching reruns of *Harry's House* with my granddaughter? I'm feeling pretty great."

Everything was silent. Did that...did that really work? She knew who I was. She wasn't showing any symptoms, which must be a good thing.

"Nan, you're here." I let out a gasp and gave her a hug. She squeezed back, real tight.

"I didn't go anywhere, sweetie. You did, remember?"

"I remember." I laughed.

My brain worked a mile a minute. Could she really be back? Did my plan actually work? How was I going to explain this to Mom?

In that moment I didn't care. All I cared about was Nan being back.

"Hon, I haven't seen you in years." Nan pulled back and studied my face.

"It's been way too long," I agreed while she squeezed my cheeks. "Way too long."

I pulled up a chair and held on to her hand. "Do you remember anything that had just happened?"

"We were just watching TV...why, did I doze off?"

Clay must have blocked Nan from remembering what happened; she just thought I'd been there all along.

"Yeah, you must've dozed off," I lied.

"Guess that nap got the better of me," she said as she got up. "I think I need a coffee." She started towards the kitchen.

"I think I could use one too," I said, standing up as well.

"I guess you're not too young for caffeine anymore."

Before Nan reached the coffee maker, I stopped her and said, "Why don't I do it this time? You just take a seat."

"You can't be a guest *and* make me coffee!" Nan grinned.

"I'm not a guest," I said. "I'm here to stay."

Clay has nothing to worry about, I thought. The plan had worked perfectly. Better, even. I couldn't believe she was back—it was like nothing had happened.

"How's school been treating you?" Nan asked.

"It's been fine," I lied again while starting the machine. The smell of brewing coffee filled the air. Sure, it was almost bedtime, but Nan and I had a lot to catch up on. A coffee would do us just fine.

"You're going to be heading to your first year of high school in September, won't you?" Nan raised an eyebrow at me.

"I'm sixteen, Nan," I said with a laugh. I picked out some mugs while I waited for the coffee to finish up.

"*Sixteen*?" She laughed. "Sorry, love. Time flies at my age. Wait until your grandfather gets home. He'll be so happy to see you."

Oh, my God.

She didn't know.

She didn't know he was dead.

She didn't know about the funeral.

Did her old memories block it out? Were there too many things going on in her mind at once? I didn't know. Suddenly I felt anxious to the point of throwing up.

"I'll be right back," I said, trying to keep my composure. "I…have to use the washroom."

I grabbed the journal from the living room and went upstairs to my bedroom.

"Clay! Clay, did you hear that?"

He made himself visible to me. "Yes."

I glanced up at him and had to do a double take. He looked paler than normal—not grey, but white. I could see his fists were clenched tightly, like he was having a difficult time keeping them shut.

"What's going on?" I asked him.

"Um, a couple things," he said. "It seems like bringing her back jiggled some things."

"You think? She doesn't even know Grampy is dead!"

"I told you this wouldn't be easy," Clay said, gripping his hands even harder.

"What's going on with you? Are you okay?" I reached for him.

"Anna. If I let go, it's going to hit her like a pile of bricks."

I took a step back. "What do you mean?"

173

"It's the same thing that happened with your headache, but it was easier with you. You still had a healthy grasp of your memories. But with her—" he paused and grimaced. "There's too much going on. There's too much to sort out. She isn't young. Her memories didn't just come back neat and orderly—they spun, shifted." He looked at me. "Anna, I'm afraid she's going to crumble."

His fists gripped harder and blue energy leaked through his fingers. My heart fell to my stomach. I couldn't believe I pushed Clay to go through with this. I should have just listened to him, but I had to go and fuck everything up. Again.

"Anna," Clay said, bringing me back. "You wanted to find out more about Rudy's past. This might be your only chance. I can't hold much longer and when I let go, she might be…."

"She might be what?" Anxiety filled me to the brim.

"She might be gone," Clay whispered.

I didn't pause to let that sink in, I just ran down the stairs.

Nan was sipping her coffee, smiling to herself and humming a nostalgic rhythm. Everything felt so perfect, calm, and normal. This was exactly how I remembered her. And that is what made everything hurt so much more.

"Nan," I started. "Can I ask you something?"

"Sure, sweetie. You can ask me anything."

Everything inside of me shook. I didn't have a lot of time. I wanted to ask Nan so many questions. I wanted to sit with her and watch TV one more time. I wanted to stay up all night and catch the sunrise with her.

Then it hit me like a brick wall: I hadn't thought about the after, I had only focused on the now, and it wasn't something we could maintain. The way Clay held his fists shut made it look like he was using every fiber of his being, and I couldn't have him hurt himself in this process. I'd already hurt him so badly.

"I overheard you say something once...," I began, trying to catch my words before I broke out into tears.

"Nosy girl." Nan smiled.

"I know." I cleared my throat. "But I think this is important. Nan, am I named after someone?"

She raised an eyebrow. "What makes you ask that?"

She knew I knew there was a secret, I could see it in her face, but she didn't answer me.

"Nan," I pressed, "is there another Annaka?"

She looked at me hard. She had the "you ain't grown enough for grown-up talk" look on her face. But I was sixteen, and not a little girl any more.

"I think that's a conversation for you and your granddaddy."

"He's not here. And he's not coming back," I said, and then caught myself. "He's...going to be...gone for a few days."

Nan frowned. Shit, I shouldn't have said anything. I thought about Clay holding everything together. Time was running out. I asked again.

"Nan, who is Annaka?"

"You are! The one and only," Nan answered with a falsely bright smile. I knew she was lying. I wanted something, anything. I opened my mouth again, but before the words could come out I heard Clay yell.

Nan's head whipped around. "Who's that?" Nan asked, standing up. "Rudy? Rudy, are you there?"

I knew Clay must have been in the hall, and I knew I couldn't let Nan see him.

"Sit down," I told her. "I'll go check it out." I made my way to the hall. I could see Clay trying his hardest to hold his fists shut. He was leaning against the wall, his teeth clenched.

"Are you hurt?" I whispered.

"You need to hurry," he replied. "I can't go invisible, this is taking too much out of me." He was struggling with every ounce of his will. I turned to see Nan coming towards the hall.

"Everything is fine!" I said, putting my hands up to stop her. But she was determined to see around the corner; she moved me out of the way, and that's when my heart dropped.

Nan turned the corner, and I couldn't see Clay's reaction but I'll never forget the way Nan screamed when she saw him. And I think that's when Clay let go. Nan fell back and hit the floor. I ran over and put my hand under her head. She was shaking.

"Nan! Oh my God, Nan!"

I looked over at Clay and his face did all the talking. He was traumatized. He was slumped against the wall, completely frozen.

"Nan, stay with me," I cried. She was still shaking. I couldn't believe what we'd done. It was such a stupid idea, and we had caused so much damage. I rolled Nan onto her side. Then the doorbell rang.

"Anyone home?" a familiar voice called. "Anna, I seen your truck outside. How come you haven't replied to my texts?"

Tia turned the corner, and her jaw dropped when she saw all of us.

I looked back at Clay and he looked at me.

"I'm so sorry, Anna," he said before he faded away.

"What the *fuck*?" Tia shouted. "Wh—What…was that?! What…Oh my God, Tanya. Tanya! Anna, we need to take her to the hospital *now*!"

It felt like everything around me went silent. The only thing I could hear was my heartbeat. I couldn't catch my breath no matter how hard I tried to chase after it. I kept blacking in and out.

Vaguely, I was aware of Tia sitting with me until Nan stopped shaking. That's when she lifted Nan off the floor, and she pulled my arm too. Together, we carried her to the truck. Tia made sure Nan was secure in the middle seat. Then she turned to me and yelled, "What the hell *was* that thing?"

I didn't reply. I kept thinking I couldn't lose Nan. Even if a part of her was already lost.

"Anna!" Tia shouted.

"I... I...."

"Save it," Tia said as she went to the driver's side. "Get in."

I got in and passed Tia the keys. She hit the gas. Nan was sitting between us, unconscious.

Clay had been right. We should've been more patient. No, *I* should have been more patient. Tia sped down the path and made a sharp turn onto the main road. She was still hitting the gas pretty hard, and I sat there dazed. I felt dizzy, and had to chase after every breath I took. I couldn't speak because of the knot in my throat and I closed my eyes, wanting to go anywhere but there. But Clay wasn't around. He was gone, and I was stuck in the moment. I closed my eyes and pretended I was in the dark place. I wanted to be away from all of this.

"Anna! Is she still breathing?" Tia's voice cut into my thoughts.

I looked over to Nan sitting beside me, her eyes closed. Tia gripped the steering wheel with both hands.

I grabbed Nan's wrist and felt for a pulse. I could feel it, thank God.

"Yeah. Yeah she has a pulse."

Tia turned onto a small bridge and drove through an intersection. "We're almost to the hospital."

I didn't say anything for the rest of the ride. I held on to Nan's hand, wishing upon every star I could see that she would be okay.

Tia pulled up to the entrance and together we carried Nan inside. We didn't even have to say anything. A few nurses immediately put Nan onto a bed and rolled her into an examination room, calling for a doctor. I put my head down, still chasing the breaths, tears running down my face. What had I done to her? How had I let this happen?

I looked up to see Tia looking deep into my eyes.

"Anna," she said seriously. "What was that?"

CHAPTER 14

MY HANDS COULDN'T STOP SHAKING IN THE WAITING room. I kept thinking, how could I have hurt one of the people I loved most? Was it too selfish to want my grandmother back? I don't know, but sitting in that waiting room, I felt helpless, and frozen. It felt like a few hours had gone by and nobody had come out to speak to us yet. Tia sat with me, rubbing my back. I was freezing, and my stomach was in a knot. The lighting was way too bright. The constant ticking of the giant clock was mind numbing. I wanted to keep my eyes closed so badly. I wanted to be anywhere but there, but I knew I was stuck in the moment.

"Do you think she's going to be okay?" I finally asked. I hadn't said anything since Tia and I had gotten to the hospital.

"She's the strongest person I know," Tia replied.

I nodded, and was silent for a few more moments. Then: "Tia?"

"Yeah?"

"You can't tell anyone what you seen."

I heard a sigh from Tia. She sounded frustrated. "I don't even *know* what it was that I seen."

"Please."

She sat there, crossed her legs, and gave me a look. She always said I was a mystery. Now she had solved a part of it.

"Okay." She let out a breath. "But you're going to tell me everything. Got it?"

"All right," I agreed. I really had no idea what I was getting myself into. But it didn't make sense to hide the truth from Tia any longer.

"Are you going to text your mom?" she asked.

That was a loaded question. Mom had trusted me, and I let her down. What was I going to tell her? *Yeah, Mom? By the way, I know you trusted me to take care of Nan while you were gone, but she's in the hospital.* I didn't want to think about it.

"You have to tell her," Tia said.

"I know. I just…don't know how."

Tia wrapped her hand around mine. She knew this was hard on me, even if she didn't completely understand it.

"It's better to do it now, than later," she whispered.

She was right. I pulled out my phone and began typing.

Me: *Mom. I'm so so sorry. I didn't mean for this to happen. Nan is in the hospital. She just started shaking uncontrollably and I froze. Tia came though, and she drove us to the hospital. We've been here for a couple of hours. Text me back when you see this, please.*

After I pressed send, I started bawling. Everything started coming out of me. I hated crying and I especially hated being vulnerable in public, but I couldn't stop. I was so full of guilt. I let Mom down. I let Nan down. I let Clay down. Tia put her hand on my shoulder, and I hugged her tight.

I didn't hear back from Mom, which made me even more anxious every moment. I thought about Clay, how he must be feeling. He had told me not to do it. I hoped he was okay, and wondered if he was angry with me. I remembered seeing his face and that terrified look he had.

"Oh, Clay," I whispered to myself.

"Anna," Tia whispered. "What are you talking about?"

I didn't reply right away, I just looked at her and took a few deep breaths while she sat with that thought for a few moments.

"His name is Clay," I finally replied. "And you have a drawing of him in your room."

I watched her try to piece together what I was saying. Finally, Tia tensed up, and recognition dawned on her face. "Oh my God. How? You can't be serious?"

"I'll explain later. I promise I'll explain everything." I would; I owed her that. I hadn't been a good friend to Tia, but she had always been there for me. Every time. The least I could do in return was be honest.

It felt like another hour before a doctor walked into the waiting room. He was an older man, balding with glasses. He wore a nametag that said Dr. MacDonald. I didn't say anything, I didn't know what to say or what to ask.

Tia took the lead and said, "Hey, sir."

"Hello," Dr. MacDonald said. "I'm assuming you're the granddaughters?"

"Just her." Tia pointed at me. "I'm a family friend."

"I see. Your grandmother is in stable condition," he said to me. "It was a seizure, though she stayed unconscious for a couple hours." *That's not normal.* Was that our doing? "We did a CT scan, which showed an unusual amount of electrical activity in her brain. Even though she doesn't have a history of seizures, the Alzheimer's can put her at risk."

The electrical activity must have been Clay.

"Is she awake?" I asked.

"Yes, she woke up about twenty minutes ago. However, with her having been unconscious for quite some time, we ask that only one visitor goes in at a time. We don't want to overwhelm her."

"Anna, you go. I'll be here, okay?" Tia said. "I'll call my parents and tell them what happened."

"Okay." I was glad Tia had my back.

"Follow me," the doctor said. The once-white walls were stained yellow, and the fluorescent lights were buzzing, bringing on a headache. Dr. MacDonald led me through a series of doors and down a hall to the very last room on the left. He opened it up and I noticed the lights were off, moonlight splashing the walls. Nan was sitting up in her bed, looking out the window. She didn't acknowledge us.

"...Nan?"

She didn't reply. I looked back at Dr. MacDonald and he only shrugged and said, "I guess I'll leave you two alone." And he left.

I was so scared. What did she remember? How much damage had we done in the hopes of fixing her mind? What if she hated me? Could she even speak? Questions filled me to the brim, turning my anxiety into a whirlpool. At least she was alive.

"Nan, I am so, so sorry about what happened," I began. "I didn't mean for that to go down. I was so scared. I freaked out, I froze, and I didn't know what to do."

She didn't respond. She just looked out the window at the stars above the lake. I let out a breath and as my shoulders dropped, she turned to me

"I keep seeing you in the strangest places."

She didn't remember any of it.

As much of a relief as it was, it only made coming to terms with my grandmother being gone even harder. I closed my eyes and took a breath. *Don't cry, don't cry, don't cry,* I kept thinking to myself. But then I remembered what Clay had said: Nan didn't have a healthy grasp of her memories. Maybe he was the one holding them together like a bridge and when he let go, it all collapsed...and so did her memory. It never would have been a permanent fix. Magic isn't medicine.

"Look at you, always looking upset. Come over here," Nan said as she pointed towards the chair beside her bed. I walked over and sat down. She grabbed hold of my hand and spoke softly.

"Young lady, I believe you told me that your name was Anna last time we spoke." She remembered my name. But how? "My memory isn't what it used to be," she continued. "That's what they keep telling me anyways. Now, if I had to put money on this, the reason why I think I keep seeing you is because you used to be a part of my life to some degree. Is that correct?"

Wait. She wouldn't have been able to piece that together before. Something had changed, shifted. Maybe reliving the memories didn't work the way I thought it would, but she had held on to something. It seemed like she at least remembered me from the last little while.

But I didn't speak on it; I just nodded, still feeling awful about the entire situation. What changed? I knew if I spoke I would burst into tears. I just sat there. I just sat there and I listened.

"I see, hon." She nodded as she held on to my hand. "I feel like I met you before, but I fear that was a lifetime ago."

It was a lifetime ago, but I still felt awful after she said that.

"Those memories we shared, I'm afraid they're too far gone from me," she continued. I looked away—I didn't want her to see me cry anymore. Before I could get up and turn, I felt her squeeze my hand and she said to me, "I think the biggest problem we have is being too afraid to let go. We're so afraid about what happens when we release our grip. We're afraid that we'll be left in the dark, we're afraid that we'll be alone. But dear, believe me when I say it isn't the end. Things only end so we can start something else. Do you want to create something new with me?"

She didn't remember our past, but she remembered me here, now, in this moment. That wasn't possible until Clay did...whatever he did. I could hear the genuine warmth in Nan's voice. It was warmth that put me at ease. I didn't want to let Nan go. I didn't want to just leave her behind. Being around her hurt a lot at first. But she was right. We could create new memories together, if the old ones were too far out of her reach. She still had so much fight in her, and I had to hold on. That's the only thing I could do. Hold on.

She smiled. "My name is Tanya."

"I know your name." I cracked a smile.

"Then how were we connected, Anna?"

"Because I'm your granddaughter." I smiled through tears.

"Ahh, I always wondered when Jayla would give me one of those." She gripped my hand even tighter.

"You always had one." I laughed. She laughed too.

She held on to my hand for a while, and I gripped hers back. Sure, she didn't have the same memories from the time we shared together, but I would create more with the time she had left. I didn't think that would be a hard task; she was the most timeless woman I'd ever known.

CHAPTER 15

I DIDN'T REMEMBER FALLING ASLEEP, BUT I AWOKE TO someone poking me.

"Woah, cut it out!"

"Shhh! Anna, it's me. Tia." She put a hand on my shoulder.

I looked over to see Nan still asleep. She looked comfortable. "What time is it?"

"Three thirty in the morning."

I rubbed my eyes and sat up straight. "Why did you wake me up?"

"Because I got tired of waiting, duh."

"Oh." I wasn't thinking straight. I reached for my phone. "Oh, *shit*." I had ten text messages and six missed calls from Mom.

"Oh no. Oh no. Oh no."

"Don't worry. I called her," Tia assured me. "I told her Tanya was okay, but she's still coming. She should be here soon."

Thank God for Tia. I felt like I could catch my breath. But then I thought of Clay. Was he okay? I had to get back home, fast. Once I got to my feet, Tia locked eyes with me.

"Anna, I think it's time to talk." She crossed her arms.

She was right. I must have broken the "how long can you hide your imaginary friend" record. I always thought I could keep Clay a secret forever. But eventually, forever ends. Forever ended now.

"Okay," I said.

Tia followed me out of the room and closed the door. I turned around to face her.

"I don't even know where to start."

"Dude, what *was* that thing at your grandparents' place?!" Tia was trying to piece everything together. "You said that was Clay? Clay isn't real, he's just some imaginary friend you made up when you were a kid."

"To be fair, I did tell you about him when we were kids. You didn't believe me."

"Of course I didn't. Everyone had an imaginary friend. And that's exactly what they were—imaginary!"

"He's more than that," I replied. "He always was."

"What does that even mean?" Tia raised her arms in the air.

"It means…Clay was never just an imaginary friend. Clay was always real. He always ate too many of Nan's cookies, and I blamed it on Grampy. He was always afraid to sleep alone, so we shared the bed in my room. He always thought you sounded really cool, and wanted to meet you someday," I told her. "But he was afraid. He was afraid of being caught because he was afraid of being taken away."

"Taken away?" I had never seen Tia's eyes wider than they were right then. "I…I don't even know what to say right now."

"Neither do I." I put a hand on her shoulder. "But this is where we are."

Tia looked like she was about to say something, but then we heard footsteps from down the hall. I looked to see Mom. Her eyes were wide open and her hair was falling out of her elastic.

"Mom!" I ran towards her. She wrapped me in a hug and held on tight. "I'm so sorry. I'm so so so sorry," I said.

"Shhh," she cut in. "None of this is your fault."

If she only knew.

I looked back at Tia, and wondered if she was going to tell Mom. We locked eyes and I could see the tension, confusion, and distrust in hers. But eventually Tia sighed, which was somewhat reassuring.

"Where is she?" Mom let go.

"She's in there." I pointed to the door.

"I'm gonna go in, you coming?"

"No. I was in there all night, I think Tia and I have to talk."

"It can wait, really, Anna," Tia cut in.

"No. I don't think it should," I replied.

"All right," Mom said. "Be safe."

"Always."

Mom gave me a big hug and a kiss on the cheek then slipped into Nan's room.

I grabbed Tia's hand, and rushed to the lobby and out of the hospital. I took a big gulp of fresh, nighttime air. I was happy to get out of there.

I rushed towards the truck when we got outside. I had to show Clay to Tia, and explain everything. She was going to think I was out of my mind...and maybe I was. But she wanted to solve my mystery, and this was it.

"Anna, slow down." Tia grabbed her hand back. "Where are we going?"

"I have to show you how it works."

"How *what* works?"

"Clay, the time travel, the memories—"

"Okay, we're going a mile a minute here," Tia cut me off. "Time travel?" She sounded worried.

I didn't know how to explain it, so I had to show her. "Tia, just trust me, okay? You said it yourself: I am a mystery you want to solve."

The ride back was a bit awkward. We didn't say a word, but I knew once we got back to the house then I wouldn't have to say a thing. Clay would reveal himself. Hopefully Tia wouldn't freak out, and we could reassess everything from that point. I counted the street lights we drove by to break away from the anxiety. I pretended that I was a kid walking from Tia's house to mine, if only it were still that easy. I put on music to cut the tension, but for once in her life, Tia didn't want music to fill the lack of conversation.

"Anna…," she eventually said. "I don't even know what's going on."

"I know, but I need you to trust me."

"I think we're beyond that, honestly. This is something you've never told me about, ever."

"I know, and from here on out, I won't be keeping any more secrets. I promise you."

She didn't say anything. I didn't blame her; promises from me didn't seem to hold much weight as of late.

"Thank you," I spoke over the silence. "If you didn't show up when you did, I—"

"Don't mention it," Tia replied. "You saved me one time. Not sure if you remember, but when we were kids, I ran off from dad and ended up—"

"—getting your leg caught in the warehouse just off the waterfront," I finished. "Yeah, I remember that like it was yesterday."

"Keeping score?" Tia laughed.

I smiled. "No. Just keeping the memories close."

"Guess we're even," Tia replied as I turned up the path towards the house. The lights were still on, but I could feel the emptiness. I parked outside of the garage, turned to her, and said, "Come on."

She didn't move, and it was clear she still wasn't completely convinced I wasn't having a nervous breakdown.

"He…should still be inside." I tore the key out of the truck and made my way towards the house. Tia followed.

I walked inside and everything was the same as we'd left it: lights were on, the TV was static, and an eerie calm settled over everything. I could see the journal on the floor, so I picked it up gently and flipped through. *Poor Clay*, I thought. He didn't deserve any of that. He had been so scared, and being seen by Tia must have only added to the dumpster fire of this night.

"This is my journal," I explained. "Clay lives in here."

"That's the journal your grandfather gave you, right?"

"Right. I used to write in it a lot. It's where I first wrote about Clay, on our first day of school. You were in a different class so I created my own friend, I guess. Then after some time he, well, walked out of my closet. And the rest is history."

"I guess…. Where is he?"

"I'll show you." I held on to the journal with both hands, and spoke softy. "Clay? Clay, it's me. Please come out." I paused. "It's safe, I promise. Everything is okay."

There was no reply, and I looked back to see a frown on Tia's face. I let out a nervous cough and tried again.

"Hey, Clay. Everything will be okay. Nan is going to be fine. Tia is here, and she wants to meet you." I looked at Tia and smiled. "It's okay, she won't tell anyone. Remember when you told me that you always wanted to meet her? Well, here's your chance."

There was still no reply. I let out a nervous laugh when I looked at Tia and her arms were crossed.

"Okay, Clay. You're making me look a bit silly here, you're supposed to have my back, remember?"

I opened up the journal, and flipped through for a bit. I found the page that would make Tia believe, and I whispered softly to the book. Tia couldn't hear me. I didn't want her to.

"Take her back," I whispered as I pointed to the page. I could see the blue energy manifest around the book, then near my hands. I could feel his hand against mine, but he was invisible. He didn't want to be seen, not yet.

I looked over to Tia—her jaw had dropped open.

I smiled. I knew Clay was nervous, and that was okay. I extended my hand with Clay's in front of mine. Tentatively, Tia extended hers, and as our hands touched everything disappeared. We were surrounded by darkness.

"Woah! Anna, what's going on?" Tia looked around in shock.

"You'll see."

The darkness began to fade away as a table lifted from the ground, and walls with decorations appeared. A banner across one of the walls read, "Happy Birthday Tia!"

I could see the shock in Tia's face as she began to age backwards. She was a little girl again, and so was I.

"Breathe, Tia," I reminded her.

She took a deep breath and said, "Dude, you look like a kid again!"

"So do you."

She looked at her hands and her eyes widened. "Dude!"

Before she could say anything, Jonathan's voice overshadowed everything.

"Hey, birthday girl!" he called as he brought in the cake.

"Dad?!" Tia screamed.

"Aha, who else, Tia?" he replied as he set the cake on the table.

Other girls ran towards the table.

"Taylor, Lucy, and Laura," Tia said in shock. Then she looked at me. "Anna, what's going on?"

"Come on." I grabbed her hand and ran towards the table.

There was no better way to show Tia how all of this worked. Maybe if she could relive something she remembered, she would understand.

"This is so surreal!" Tia said, once we were seated at the table.

"Not that surreal." Jonathan cut a piece of cake and put it on Tia plate. "Birthdays happen once a year...at least!" He smiled.

I laughed, and so did everyone else at the table.

I leaned over and whispered to Tia: "Do you remember what I got you for this birthday?"

Tia froze for a second, thinking. "Yeah," she said with a smile. "You got me a slingshot."

"That you're not going to use until you're at least eighteen." Clare walked into the room and crossed her arms.

"She's right," Jonathan agreed. "We know you'll accidentally take someone's eye out with that thing." He shrugged.

"Wow. I remember this," Tia whispered at me.

Tia grabbed her fork, and dug deep into a piece of her cake. But before she could take a bite, it all faded into nothing. Darkness surrounded us again. She stood up, looking her age again, and stared at me, dumbfounded. Then she asked, "Is this what you've been doing? How do you do that?"

"It's not me," I replied as our surroundings reverted back to my grandmother's house.

"It's me," a shy voice said.

Tia and I both looked left, and Clay approached us; tall and grey, with a soft face.

Tia froze.

Clay extended a hand to shake Tia's. "I've...heard a lot about you over the years," he said to her. "It's nice to finally meet you."

Tia gulped, and eventually replied, "What the hell is going on? And why do I feel so dizzy?" She stumbled and almost lost her footing, but I caught her.

Clay lowered his hand. "Nice to meet you too," he said in a low voice.

"Tia, this is him. This is Clay."

"What did he *do*? Suddenly you just took me to a birthday party from my childhood?"

"Yes, it's a memory Anna wrote about in her journal years ago," Clay explained.

"Why were you writing about my birthday party?" Tia looked my direction.

"I was a journal kid, okay?" I shrugged. "Grampy made me. It was a memorable time at least. And Clay can…recreate what was written inside the journal."

Tia's eyes darted to the journal in my hands, then back to Clay. I couldn't tell if she was shocked, scared, worried, or angry. Maybe a mixture of it all, but I could tell she was connecting the dots, because she finally said, "Oh my gosh…this whole time. You've been the mystery I wanted to solve. I…I don't know what to say."

"I guess this explains me not returning your texts."

She rolled her eyes at me. "Explains, doesn't excuse."

I looked over at Clay, he let out a breath and nodded his head. It was time we told Tia the truth.

About everything.

CHAPTER 16

"DAMN. SO, YOU REALLY SAW YOUR DAD IN THERE, huh?" Tia said, sitting on the couch in my grandmother's living room, a coffee in hand. It was almost four thirty in the morning, but we were just getting started.

I nodded. "I did."

"And you were curious because your grandmother mentioned another Annaka?"

"Yes."

"Do you think that it was maybe just…rambling?"

"No…I think it has something to do with Grampy. He used to write in it, and Clay can recreate his memories too. I can view them like a movie. I mean, it's just a hunch, but maybe it has something to do with my Grampy's past. He wrote about it, but I don't know where those pages are; they were torn out a long time ago." I sighed and looked at Tia. "I was hoping somehow Nan could bring some clarity. That's part of the reason why we did that stupid thing." I clenched a fist. I was so mad at myself.

"I wish it never happened." Clay faded into the room.

Tia jumped back in her seat, spilling coffee on the floor. "Jesus! I hate that."

"Yeah, it's kind of his thing," I replied.

Clay didn't say anything. It must have been weird for him to suddenly have someone new know of his existence. I thought it was about time he met Tia, and I knew it was weird for him, so I wanted him to adjust at his own pace.

"You're not going to tell anyone about me, are you?" Clay asked Tia.

"I don't think that would be the best idea." Tia wiped up the coffee on the floor. She seemed to be taking it pretty well, all things considered.

"So, what happens now?" she asked . "Will you two try to find those pages? Are you going to try to find your dad? Are you going to try...that...again?"

"We are not trying *that* again," I said with confidence. "It was a stupid idea to begin with."

"You're not the only one who took part." Clay rested a hand on my shoulder.

"Yeah, but I should have been smart enough to listen to you. You know yourself more than I do, and I took advantage of that." I looked him in the eye. "I'm sorry."

Clay sat down beside me. "We all have some learning to do."

We all sat there silently and watched as the sun began to break through the stars. It had been the longest night of my life, but at least I could say I was in good company.

"Do you think they'll be home soon?" Clay asked.

"I don't know," I replied. "They might keep her for a bit longer."

Tia looked at me. "So you're looking for those missing pages, eh? You're hoping those pages could solve a mystery."

"It's not about a mystery; I guess I'm just looking for clarity." I picked at a loose thread on my grandmother's couch. "All my life I feel like I've been aimless. You know what my grandmother said to me in the hospital?" I looked at Tia and she shook her head. "She didn't remember me as a kid. I told her I was her granddaughter. She told me she always wanted one of those. Well, I always wanted a dad." I shrugged. "I always wanted to know what Grampy went through when he came to Canada. I wanted something. Everything has always been so far out of my reach, but I can feel it close, and I want to latch on to it." I spoke softly.

I always felt alone in my journey. Even though most of the time it was by my doing; I always held a barrier between me and my friends. From Tia, from Clay, even from Mom. I don't know why I was so afraid to let everyone enter my world. Maybe it was because everyone in my world wouldn't let me into theirs. There was so much I didn't know about Mom, there was so much I didn't know about Grampy, and then there was my dad.

"Clarity isn't a journey you have to go on alone." Tia put a hand on my shoulder. "Anna, you were always so distant, but now I see why. Our experiences—the good, the bad—they form us and make us who we are. You've been living alongside mystery your entire life, and somewhere along the line you became one. But we're your friends, and we'll walk with you every step of the way."

Tia embraced me.

"She's right." Clay put a hand on my shoulder. "However we move forward, we can do it together. Maybe the worlds colliding isn't such a bad thing." Clay sat down, and rested his head on my shoulder.

They were right. Having my worlds collide wasn't the worst thing. We were just there, holding onto each other. I think that's what I needed most. The reassurance, the love, and the support. I thought my worlds would collapse when they met, but now I felt stronger than ever.

I was ready to move forward.

I was ready for clarity.

CHAPTER 17

"WHERE ARE THOSE DAMN PAGES?" I ASKED, navigating through the basement again. We were still deep into the night, and I wasn't ready to stop.

"There's a lot of clutter down here," Tia observed. "Who knows if they're still here."

"They have to be," I said, opening boxes of books and taking everything out.

Tia was looking through Grampy's desk for stray papers.

"Score!" I heard her yell.

"You find them?" I looked back.

"Oh. Uh, no." She raised a paper to show me what she was holding. "I just saw I passed my essay."

I shook my head and smiled. "Weirdo." I looked around. "Clay, a little help would be nice?"

"It would," he said. "If they were here. You already searched this place for a week."

"They have to be here," I said, wiping dust off my face. "Unless Mom threw them out."

"I doubt that," Clay replied. "And besides, if they were here, you know I would have found them by now. I think if he tore them out, he wouldn't leave them for someone to find. If your grandfather wanted you to find them, you would have."

"He's right," Tia said. "Something about this sounds too easy. And Anna, we've been up all night. You should get some rest."

"I can't, we're so close. I can feel it," I pleaded.

"We can always come back to it," Clay said gently.

As much as I didn't want to admit it, they were right. I was exhausted and should have gotten rest hours ago.

"We can come back to this later, I promise," Tia said.

Tia went home shortly after that; took off into the sunrise. I was still wide awake even though we had been up all night.

I texted Mom looking for an update, but I didn't expect to hear back until later that morning. I went upstairs to my bed, and when I laid down it felt like gravity kicked in full force. God, that felt good.

Clay tucked me in as Grampy usually did.

"What's this about?" I laughed.

"Oh, uh," Clay stammered. "I'm sorry, it—"

"Feels like routine, doesn't it?"

"Yeah, yeah it does."

"Maybe it's part of him living inside of you."

"Maybe." Clay sat down on the chair beside my bed. "Are you gonna go to school tomorrow?"

"It's like six A.M.," I said with a laugh. "We've been up all night. Was that him, too?"

"No, I can assure you it was me."

"Why do you care, anyways?"

"Because it's important," Clay said. "It was important to you in Halifax, it should be important to you here. Besides, you need to get out of the house."

"That last part was him."

"I'll give you that."

I laughed, and Clay laughed too.

My phone buzzed and I saw Mom's name.

Mom: *They want to keep her for a bit longer*

Me: *How is she doing?*

Mom: *She's asked me when I planned on telling her she had a granddaughter. I don't know, what's going on, but she seems to remember your name, says she sees you around the house. What happened? That wasn't the situation before.*

Me: *A lot, Mom, we had a talk.* ☺

Mom: *I can see that. I'm glad you did.*

Me: *When will you be home?*

Mom: *Not for a while. Are you with Tia?*

Me: *No, she went home.*

Mom: *Are you good staying by yourself?*

Me: *I'll be fine, really.* ☺

I wasn't alone. I had my best friend sitting at my bedside.

"How is she?" Clay's voice filled up the room.

"She's fine," I replied. I waited a beat and then said, "You know, a part of it worked."

"What do you mean?" Clay asked, surprised.

"She remembers my name. Says she seen me at the house, told me she wants to create something new with me. I don't know how it happened, but maybe what you did somehow repair a piece of her mind? Not completely, but enough to make her realize we need to start something new."

"Wow," Clay replied. He looked relieved, glad it wasn't completely for nothing.

"How are *you* feeling?" I asked him. "This has all been rough on you, too."

"I never felt that kind of fear before." He let out a breath. "I guess when it happened, I didn't know what to do." He looked at me and shook his head. "I just froze, and I'm sorry I didn't do more. When Tia saw me, it felt like I couldn't breathe. It felt like I was trying to catch my breath, so I disappeared."

"I think that's the me in you." I sat up. "It's called an anxiety attack."

"Ahh, so that's what it feels like."

"Yeah."

"I'm sorry, I let you down."

"You never let me down."

He smiled, and so did I. It didn't take long for me to fall asleep after that.

CHAPTER 18

MANAGED TO WAKE UP BY ELEVEN, AND DIDN'T FEEL like waiting around the house all day for an update. I knew Clay was there, but he wanted me out of the house too. I needed to keep myself busy. Tia wanted me to go to school, so I ended up meeting her in the cafeteria during lunch.

"They home yet?" she asked me.

"They should be home this afternoon," I replied, then bit into a burger. "Apparently Nan is excited to meet her granddaughter. They're doing some tests, but her memory seems to be holding onto new things."

"Is that because of…him?" Tia's eyes lit up.

"I think so." I smiled. She smiled back.

"Bobby's party is tonight, are you going?" Tia followed up.

I sighed. "I don't know. Parties were never really my thing."

"Oh, c'mon. You said I could be your plus one."

"I know, I know. But I might just want to chill."

"Big city girl doesn't want to hit up Yarmouth parties? They're a different kind of animal."

"You're not doing the best at selling this," I said with a giggle.

"You could bring your friend." Tia raised an eyebrow.

I shook my head. "That's an awful idea."

"I think he would be a great party trick."

"Tia, Clay isn't a trick."

"I know, I know," she said. "But he must be bored staying inside all day."

I paused to consider how well Tia was taking the whole 'Oh my God you have a real life imaginary friend' thing. That didn't mean I was ready—more specifically, it didn't mean *he* was ready—to be broadcasted to the rest of the world. But I thought about it. Would taking Clay to a party be a terrible mistake? Probably, but it did give me an idea. Maybe he didn't have to physically be there in order to enjoy it.

Tia went to her class and I made my way to my locker. I walked past room 409. Grampy's classroom. It had been weeks, but still the sticky notes papered his door. I approached them but couldn't read any of them. It would be too much. Something inside me wanted to open the door, walk around the room, get a scent of him, and see where he had spent most of his time away from home. I wanted to sit in the chair at his desk. Before I knew it, my hand was on the doorknob.

"Hey, Anna."

I turned around. Bobby. He had his hair slicked back and was wearing a button-up shirt.

"Hi, Bobby." I sighed, letting go of the doorknob.

He looked shy, and I could tell he had a crush on me, but he was way too dude-bro to be my type. Besides, he had made me miserable about my name. I couldn't get past that.

"Are you still down to come to my party tonight?"

"I'm not sure, I might be—"

"You won't want to miss it!" he cut me off. "It's gonna be LIT!" He really empathized on the lit part. "Everyone is gonna be there."

"I don't really know many people here." I shrugged. "I don't think I'll be missing much."

"It'll be a good way to meet some folks." He smiled.

I sighed. "Okay, I might go—on one condition: I can bring a guest."

"Sure, bring whoever you want."

I smiled sweetly. I couldn't wait to see his face when he saw my guest would be Tia. She had told me that Bobby had made it a point to keep his distance from her. But hopefully bringing her would be double payback, not only for making me hate my own name, but also for using Tia to get back at his dumb ex.

"All right, I might be there." I tried to contain my laughter.

He blushed for all the wrong reasons and said, "See you there!" and walked off.

I grabbed my phone and shot Tia a text.

Me: *K, you win. We're going.*

Tia: *Yes!!!!*

I still owed her big time for everything she'd done for me, and maybe this was a start.

WHEN I DROVE HOME AFTER school I could see Mom's van parked out front. She and Nan must be home. To say I was nervous would be an understatement. I sat in my truck for a few minutes gathering my courage. When I made my way inside, Nan was sitting in the rocking chair. Mom was sitting on the steps getting some marking done.

"I was surprised to not see you here," Mom said, looking up from her papers.

"I went to school."

"Ahh, that's new." Mom smiled at me. "How was it?"

"Not too bad." I paused. "Tia's dragging me to a party tonight."

"That might be good for you, to get out there and socialize." Mom always held out hope that I would break out of my cocoon and turn into the social butterfly she was. I was doubtful, but at least one of us held faith.

"How's Nan doing?" I looked over to the living room.

"Excited to be home!" she shouted from the living room. "Hospital food is a lot of things, but tasty is not one of them."

I laughed and made my way into the living room. I was glad she'd kept her sense of humour; I shouldn't have stayed away for so long. I guess after everything was said and done, she wasn't a scary shell of herself. She was still her, I just had to adjust.

"Are you okay?" I asked, placing my hand on hers.

"I feel great now that you're here," she said. She patted my hand and smiled.

"The feeling is mutual." My heart melted.

I was glad she was home, and I was glad we would create something new to remember.

"Strangely enough, I didn't have to remind her that she had a granddaughter," Mom said to me under her breath.

"I didn't hear you, what was that?" Nan asked.

"Oh, it was nothing." Mom laughed.

I grinned and went upstairs to my room. When I opened the door I could see the journal on top of my bed.

"Clay," I called. "Did you keep looking in the basement today?"

"No." He walked out of the closet. "The pages aren't there." He sighed. "We'll find them, Anna. We will. He had his reasons."

"I'm just thinking, like, where?" I shrugged.

It seemed so silly to take those pages away. It seemed silly to me, anyway. But we had time to focus on that, I guess now it was time to head to Tia's place.

"You got any plans tonight?" I grinned at Clay.

"What are you getting at?" he asked.

IT WAS CLAY'S FIRST TIME at Tia's house. He looked super uncomfortable as he and Taz eyeballed each other.

"Your first time seeing a real dog?" I asked Clay.

"Yeah, it's…a lot to wrap my head around."

"He's really not that complex," Tia said. "Not like meeting your childhood best friend's imaginary friend." Tia grinned at him. "You ready to head out?" she said to me.

"Ugh, I don't know. House parties are a lot." I sank into her bean-bag chair.

"Don't get cold feet on me now." Tia sank down beside me and nudged my shoulder. "C'mon, what's the worst that can happen? I'll be there with you."

"She's right," Clay said. "You've been stressing a lot lately. Maybe letting loose isn't such a bad idea."

"Yeah, yeah, yeah," I said. "The faster this party is over, the faster I'm in bed."

"That's the spirit!" Tia laughed.

"Who's all going to be there?" I asked, knowing I wouldn't know any of them, and most of them probably wouldn't remember me.

"No way, Taylor and the girls will be there, they love you."

"Whatever." I laughed. "Taylor probably thinks I'm the biggest dork after seeing me at Wades, but I guess now you know why I was there." I pointed at Clay's shirt.

"I kinda figured." Tia grinned. "But I'm still down for the revolution. You know that, right?"

"Stop it!" I laughed.

"Taylor, she was one of the girls at your birthday party, right?" Clay asked Tia.

"Yeah...yeah, that's right." Tia said. "Normally I would think it was creepy you knew, but I'm sure you must be familiar with a lot of folks from Anna's past, right?"

Clay nodded. "I am. I replay the memories a lot, usually whenever I'm alone."

Tia's smile turned to a frown when she heard that. Clay didn't live a very exciting life, and there we were getting ready to go to a party right in front of him.

"Oh, Clay...." Tia put her hands on her head.

"I didn't mean for it to sound like that!" Clay said. His grey cheeks began to turn warm pink; it was the cutest blush I'd ever seen. "I'm not saying I'm not lonely...."

"We can fix that." I smiled.

"Wait, what do you mean?" He asked.

"It'll be a surprise." I put the journal in my bag.

"I'm not sure I like where this is going."

"Time to go," I said, ignoring Clay. Tia and I walked out the door. I had offered to be DD, since I wasn't a big drinker anyway. Tia took the passenger seat and I put Grampy's truck in drive.

Bobby's grandparents lived somewhere along the way to Cape Forchu. I drove slowly down the dark road, but it wasn't too hard to find. There was one house that looked super small, but had lots of cars parked in the driveway and along the road. The lights were on and music was blasting.

"My intuition says this is the spot," I said, trying to find a place to park.

"Your intuition is right," Tia replied. "So, what's your plan with the journal?"

"I'm gonna give Clay something new to remember." I put the

truck in park and got out, knowing the journal was in my bag. When we reached the house I could hear people cheering and loud music bumping.

When we got through the front door there were shoes all over the place. I felt like I had to watch every step as Tia pulled me through a crowd of people cheering and yelling. The music was a mixture of hip-hop and new country. And no, it was not a good mix.

"Tia!" I heard a voice float above the crowd.

"Look, there's Laura!" Tia said to me.

"Hey, girl." Laura pushed past everyone and pulled Tia into a hug. "And you brought Annaka!" My new-name memo must not have stuck. "I've been trying to find you at school but you've haven't been around too much." She slid over and gave me a hug that was a little too tight.

"Hi there." I let out a breath. "It's just Anna now. It's good to see you, Laura."

"Why haven't I been able to find you at school?" Laura asked.

"Because she's a rebel now," Tia intervened. "Got a big old truck and everything. Starting revolutions at Wade's Clothing too."

I shook my head and couldn't help but grin.

"I feel like we never really got to touch base yet." Laura was saying. "Again, I'm sorry about your granddad. I lost mine a couple years ago, and it's hard. It really is. But trust me when I say it gets easier in time."

I nodded and tried to smile. I felt like the party was going to be a lot of that. And it was.

Taylor and Lucy eventually came over, and they all began taking about memories I was never a part of. I wasn't sad because of it, I just wanted to explore a bit. I made my way to the basement to find a bunch of white boys crushing cans and playing beer pong. As I counted how many cups were left, I looked up to see Bobby gulping one of them down, then crushing the red cup and throwing it in the air.

"Yeahh!" he shouted as everyone cheered.

Ugh, I couldn't believe this was the guy Tia had a crush on. I couldn't believe this was the dude who flirted with me in the school parking lot and in the hallway. I went upstairs before he caught sight of me. When I got back up there I couldn't find Tia in the crowd, and no one was talking to me.

"Let's go the party, Anna. It'll be fun, Anna," I muttered to myself. I shook my head. But I wasn't there just for me. I took the journal out of my bag and walked outside to the back deck. Thankfully everyone was busy inside, so there was no one around. I fished around for a pen and started writing everything I could see, hear, and smell.

"This is for you, buddy." I smiled as I wrote it all in. From the shoe field, to the sour smell of spilled liquor. From the boisterous game of beer pong, to the overly long hugs and the warm temperature making everyone sweaty. I described the people I could see dancing through the window and the loud hip-hop blasting through the speakers in the living room. I made sure to include the sight of crushed paper cups and beer cans. The last party Clay had "been to" was Tia's childhood birthday. I wanted him to know what a real party felt like, even if I knew he would hate it.

"There you are!" Tia found me outside.

"Hey, hey." I looked up from the journal. "How you doing?"

"Girl, I'm feeling—"

"Tipsy?" I caught her elbow to help her walk straight. We both broke into laughter. "I'm glad you're having fun."

"What are you doing with the journal? Are you trying to go back again?" Tia asked, concerned.

"No. I'm just writing down what's going on in the party. I want Clay to enjoy it like we are."

"That's the cutest gift ever." Tia smiled. "He's lucky to have some-one like you."

"Blah, blah, blah." I blushed and put the journal away.

"Wanna go inside?" She grabbed my hand and pulled me in with-out waiting for an answer.

Suddenly Travis barged up from the basement and screamed at the top of his lungs: "Everyone out! The cops are coming to break the party up!"

Before I had the chance to look back, Tia grabbed my hand and pulled me towards the front door.

"Can we go home now?" I asked as we made it to the front deck.

"No!" Tia replied. "This always happens. It just means we're going the field. It's called a field party in case you haven't heard of it," she laughed with a hint of drunken sarcasm.

I rolled my eyes as she climbed into the truck. I got into the driv-er's side and as I backed up, Bobby came running out the front door shouting, "We're going to the field!"

"What? You're leaving? Isn't this your grandparents' house?" I yelled at him.

"They don't get home until next week!" Bobby yelled back as he and some pals jumped on their bikes and darted down the highway.

I shook my head and rolled up my window. "These boys are too much."

"Girls, get in the back!" Tia said as Taylor, Lucy, and Laura ran down the steps and climbed into the bed of the truck.

"Who's the chauffeur now?" I grinned.

"Lets go before they get here!" Tia squealed.

I made sure not to speed, considering there were three more people in the back of my truck. Once we got to the field I could see everyone else pull up, some in cars, others on bikes.

"You guys go enjoy the fun; I'm gonna stay here and give the journal a bit of an update." I smiled.

"Whatever you say." Tia jumped out. "Come on!" she called to the girls in the back as they hopped off and ran into the field.

I sat, describing what a field party looks like. I had a feeling Clay would hate it as much as I did, but I found humour in how ridiculous all of it was. When I finished I made my way out to the field. I expected to see more beer pong and shenanigans, but to my surprise a lot of people were just lying in the grass, looking into the sky, talking and laughing. It looked calming. Tia and Laura were leaning against a tree taking selfies with the flash on, sticking their tongues out with funny faces, while Lucy and Taylor pointed to the sky, deep in conversation.

"Hey, you found us!" Laura used her phone flashlight to call me over.

"I guess so." I sat down by them. "So this is a field party, huh?"

"This is it." Tia sat up and leaned on my shoulder.

"Maybe this isn't all that bad."

"Oh, yeah? Not macho men crushing beer cans on their heads?" Taylor laughed. "I can do without the toxic masculinity."

I laughed at that.

"Speaking of toxic masculinity, here comes dude-bro one-oh-one." Tia pointed to Bobby, who was walking towards us.

"Anna!" he called. "I saw you walking over and I just wanted to say hi."

"I'm sure you did," I replied. "Can we help you?"

"Yeah, Bobby. Can we?" Tia looked up directly at him.

"Shit! Why are *you* here?" Bobby took a few steps back.

"I'm Anna's plus one, dummy."

Bobby looked at me with a face of full of betrayal. His jaw dropped and his eyes looked almost tearful. I shrugged; I wasn't sorry to be the ultimate disappointment for dude-bros. He looked back at Tia and said, "I would have declined if I knew she was going to bring you."

"Yeah, well, we're in a public park now, asshat." Tia stood up and walked towards Bobby. He backed away.

"Okay, okay!" he said. "Just…don't do what you did last time."

Tia narrowed her eyes. "Don't give me a reason to."

I was really enjoying what I was witnessing. It's not every day your badass best pal gets to actually be a badass.

"I just…ah, forget it." Bobby walked away.

"We probably will," Tia said with a snarky laugh.

"Look at you, being a badass!" Laura said to Tia.

"I had to give it to him." Tia shrugged and sat back down.

After that, we just lay in the grass trying to make sense of the universe. The stars were like a big game of connect-the-dots. I rested my head by the journal and thought about Clay looking at the stars with us.

"Hey, what's with the diary?" Taylor asked.

"Oh, this?" I sat up. "I uh, journal a lot, I guess."

"What do you journal about?" Laura wanted to know.

"It's…personal."

"Fair enough," Taylor replied. "Hey, that reminds me, when I didn't pass grade ten English, I had to retake it in the summer. Mr. Brooks was the teacher. He had us journal all summer long. It was a really reflective experience that I appreciated a lot."

"He had you journal too? What did you journal about?" I sat up.

"He had us write about experiences from our past. Y'know, like where we grew up, and why certain things influenced us the way that they did. I wrote a lot about my older sister, and how important our relationship was for me while our parents went through a divorce"

"Did he ever mention anything about his past?" I was eager.

Tia raised an eyebrow.

Taylor thought for a moment before she said, "Not really. He did talk about the little things, like coming to Canada from England, and starting a new life here."

At that moment something clicked. What if Grampy left those entries in his classroom? I had felt so drawn to the room earlier that day—something had been pulling me in before Bobby interrupted.

"Hey, I think I'm gonna head out." I stood up.

"You okay?" Tia got to her feet slowly. She was a little tipsy, but she definitely noticed how jumpy I was all of a sudden.

"I'm fine, I just…I'm just tired, I guess. Do you need a lift home?"

"Uh. Yeah, sure," Tia said sounding a bit disappointed. "Do y'all wanna crash at my place tonight?" she asked the girls. "There's room."

"I'm down," Laura said, and she got to her feet.

We all got back into the truck and made our way to the main road. Tia was up front with me again, the other three girls in the bed.

I didn't say much on the ride back. What Taylor had said kept going back and forth in my mind. *Of course Grampy made other students journal.* I don't know why I hadn't thought of that before, and I couldn't believe it had taken going to a house party to get that information.

"Everything okay, Anna?" Tia asked.

"Everything is fine. I think I just wanna get home and lay down."

"I see. Well, if you need anything, let me know…." Her eyes lingered on me.

"I know," I said with my eyes on the road. I couldn't take Tia with me, she was drunk and I needed to focus. I would tell her all about it once she sobered up.

I parked in front of her driveway and she gave me a huge hug.

"Thanks for everything, Tia." I hugged her back. "You being there when everything went down…it means a lot."

"Any time," she said. "I always got your back, Anna. And I always will."

"Likewise." I let go. "Though, I think right now what you need is some water and a bit of sleep."

"You right." She laughed as she got out of the truck. "Girls, let's go!" she called. Then she turned back to me. "I'll text you tomorrow, and if I don't hear back, I'll come find you."

"Pffft, I'll bring you a cheeseburger to work tomorrow, my treat." I closed her door, waved to the girls, and hit the gas.

"You lied to her." Clay faded into the passenger seat.

"She was only going to hold us back," I replied.

"Maybe she could have helped when she, well, sobered up."

"Maybe. But I want answers sooner rather than later."

"What's your plan, then?"

"We get Grampy's keys to the school. We go to his classroom, and find those missing entries."

"If they're even there." Clay shrugged.

"They're there, I can feel it." They had to be there. Where else would Grampy put them? I was running out of ideas.

"Anna, we're talking about breaking and entering."

"Whatever." I turned onto the path and drove up towards my grandparents' house. I didn't need Clay second-guessing me every time we had to do something different. He was too innocent, always wanted to play safe. He wanted to follow a set of rules, but when had that ever gotten anything done?

When I got into the house I checked key rack, and found Grampy's school keys at the very end. Before I could grab them, Clay reappeared beside them.

"You know if this goes south, if we get caught, bad things could happen."

"We won't get caught. We'll be in and out. Nothing bad will happen"

"Just like nothing bad happened last time?"

I froze. I couldn't believe he would use that as leverage. Of all the things.

He saw my face. "I didn't mean it like—"

"I know what you meant," I said, walking back out to the truck. He got in the passenger side. It was deep into the night, and no sign of Mom, so that meant Clay didn't have to vanish, but that didn't mean I wanted to talk to him.

Our ride to the school was silent.

CHAPTER 19

WHEN WE ROLLED UP TO THE SCHOOL, CLAY FADED and I stuck the journal in my bag. The moon was still high above our heads, so I knew there would be no one around. I walked up towards the entrance, trying to avoid the street lights. Who knew if there was a security camera or something? I looked through the glass front doors but couldn't see a thing. It was too dark inside. I reached for Grampy's key and stuck it in the lock, and immediately pulled it back out.

"What if an alarm goes off when we open the door?" I thought out loud.

"Hmm, you're right," Clay said, appearing by my side. "Any ideas?"

I looked around the outside of the school, and saw the main office window. There would definitely be some type of alarm system in there.

"Something tells me we need to get in there," I said, pointing to the office.

"Not a bad assumption, we just need to open this window somehow."

I used my phone's flashlight to see it was double locked, but luckily for us, I noticed the left side wasn't fully in place.

"Think we can force it?"

"Seems risky," Clay observed. "But why not?"

Clay and I placed our hands side by side on the window and tried to force it open. It was heavier than it looked, but we managed to lift it a few inches. Clay slipped his hands beneath and held it up.

"Oh God. This is heavy. I don't think we can get it up any higher than that." Clay was struggling to keep it open, and I had to find something to wedge it. "Hurry!" he yelled.

I thought about sticking a rock in between, but then I had an idea. If I threw the journal inside, Clay could fade out, then fade in beside it. I grabbed it from my bag and tossed it through the opening.

"What are you doing?" Clay said as he let go. The window slammed down.

"Think for a minute." I poked his head. "Just fade to it."

Clay's frown melted away once he realized what I was thinking. "Oh! Yeah, I'll be right back." He faded away.

I saw him reappear on the other side of the window. He switched on a desk lamp and looked around the office. He finally noticed a security monitor.

"The buttons! Try to see which button is the alarm!" I called, but he couldn't hear a thing. He just looked at me and shrugged. I kept pointing to the button board beside the monitor, but he wasn't understanding any of it. It got to the point where I just shrugged and he tore the plug from the wall, making the entire room go dark.

"Clay! Clay!" I tapped the window but couldn't see anything. "Dammit," I said under my breath.

He didn't open the window and there was no point waiting around, so I made my way back to the entrance of the school and tried sticking Grampy's key in the lock again.

"Please, please don't let an alarm go off," I murmured while twisting the key and pulling forward.

Thankfully nothing happened when the door opened, just a loud creak. Moonlight washed the giant picture of Grampy in the entrance. Clay must've turned the alarm off, if there even was one.

"Clay? Clay, where are you?" I called out.

Nothing.

I eventually made my way to the main office where I'd thrown the journal to see the door opened, no sign of Clay.

"You're starting to creep me out, dude."

I made my way back to the hall. I couldn't worry about Clay; I knew he'd be okay, so I just followed the classroom numbers.

I walked past classrooms 389, 390, 391—409 was a little ways away.

On the way there, I reflected on the past week. It had been non-stop. One minute, Clay and I had restored Nan's memory. The next, we were rushing to the hospital, only to find out Nan's short-term memory was partially repaired. Then Tia met Clay, I went to a party, and now I was breaking into my new school. It was the weirdest time of my life but I had a feeling it was only going to spiral from there.

I squinted down the hall and could just make out 409. And there was Clay, staring at the door.

"Clay! There you are."

He didn't reply right away. He was focused on the door. He reached out and placed a hand on the number—409. All around those numbers were all the sticky notes. It was a nice reminder of the impact he had left on this place.

"So this is where Rudy taught," Clay observed.

"Yeah, what about it?"

"It's just that I spent most of my life trying to understand that man. Replaying the memories he felt were worth sharing. He wrote a lot about going to university, about the struggles he had faced. But he never really wrote about this part of his life. He never wrote about the great teacher so many saw him as."

That surprised me. "He always seemed like the kind of guy who wanted the spotlight. He was always after attention one way or another."

"That's what you told me," Clay replied. "You told me about how the story of him and Nan meeting didn't align with the one he wrote in the journal. Maybe looking for attention was a way he hid a part of himself. Maybe he was more honest in his private moments."

"I still have my suspicions about that one," I replied. "Which one can we really know is true?"

"I'd go for the one without the audience." Clay grinned.

"There was an audience of one," I shot back.

"True, but one he didn't know would watch."

As we stood outside Grampy's classroom, I began to feel anxious. What if we *did* find something? And what if it was something I didn't want to find? There had to be a reason those pages were torn out, after all.

"You think we might find something heavy?" I asked Clay.

"There's only one way to find out, I guess." He shrugged. "What do you think we'll find?"

"I dunno…maybe something about his childhood? It was the one thing he was never really open about. Mom didn't know much about it, and Nan didn't want to tell me about it." I squared my shoulders and faced the door. "I'm just hoping we find something. Anything. What was it like when he first got to Canada? What was his family like? I'd love to know. His past was a secret."

"Well, I hope the only thing keeping you away from the secret is this door." Clay pointed at the numbers.

409.

I grabbed the doorknob and turned. The classroom was cold and dark. Grampy's desk was still there, topped with a nameplate that read *Mr. Brooks*. Papers were stacked on one end of the desk, along with a framed picture of Mom, Nan, Grampy, and me. I choked up.

"How come no one took any of it down?" I managed to ask.

"They must have cherished him here."

Clay approached the desk. He picked up the family portrait, examined it with a smile, and passed it to me. My emotions were mixed. That classroom was the place Grampy spent most of his time away from home. I could smell the same lemon air freshener he used in the attic. It was so weird; I could almost feel him there.

I put the photo aside and tore apart his desk. The pages had to be here. I opened drawers and found loose papers, unmarked tests, and stacks of writing supplies.

"You have to be here, you have to be here, you have to be here," I kept saying out loud, trying to convince myself.

Inside one of the drawers was a wooden box with a lock.

"What do you think this is?" I picked it up to show Clay.

He grabbed hold of it, observing each side. "I don't know. Do you think the pages would be in there?"

"Must be, but I can't find a key." I kept searching in the other drawers. "Where else could it be?"

Clay could tell I was anxious. "Anna, let's step back for a minute. Breathe."

"I can't step back!" I looked up. "Do you know how long I've been waiting for this? We're so close." I kept looking, not realizing the box was slipping between my fingers. I lost my grip and heard a loud *crack*. The box had broke open, spilling papers all over the floor. My heart skipped a beat. But when I looked closer I saw they weren't journal entries; they were cards. I picked them up one after another. That's when tears began to fall. They were the Father's Day cards I had written to Grampy from Halifax. I'd sent one every year, and I just assumed he had thrown them out. But he had kept them. All of them. I sank onto the floor and began to weep.

"I'm sorry, Anna." Clay leaned down. "He loved you very much."

"I know."

Clay held on to me, and I could feel him, you know. I could feel both of them. I cried for all the times I had wanted to come home. I wished I could have done more. I wished I could have done things differently. But we can't change the past, all we can do is live it, learn it, and try to do better.

And I was trying. I was trying my hardest and I hoped he understood that.

Clay stood up and picked up the photo frame. He looked at it for a good minute. He squeezed his eyes shut. Then all of a sudden, he smashed the frame on the ground.

"What are you doing?" I was shocked.

Clay knelt down, picked away the glass, carefully took the photo out of the frame, and picked up a stack of papers that had been nestled in behind it.

"I had a feeling," he said. "I think like him, y'know."

He went through the papers for a minute. I was still too shocked to move a muscle. Clay's reaction went from intrigued to interested and then to sad.

"Oh, Rudy," was all he said.

"What is it?" I asked, finding the strength to stand up.

"We found it, Anna. I think we found what you've been looking for." He held out the pages to me.

I grabbed the papers, and noticed there was a lot of text. It was all in cursive, messy, and I was frustrated because I couldn't make out his handwriting. I began breathing heavy because of the anxiety, and I could feel my throat begin to clog.

That was when I felt Clay wrap his hand around my free one. He put his other hand on my shoulder, and we faded into darkness.

"What happened?" I asked. I was exhausted.

"There's only one way to find out," Clay said as the world around me began to shift. The darkness faded and a dusty floor expanded around our feet. A bed rose from the ground and there was a young woman lying in it. Her face looked familiar.

"Where are we?" I asked.

"We're in a hospice," Clay replied.

"Why are we in a hospice?" I asked as a small black child—he couldn't be any more than ten years old—entered the room. I didn't recognize him at first, but it all clicked when the woman in the bed said, "Rudy, Rudy come here."

All the warmth in my heart began to fade away, and I could feel intensity in the air; the boy looked scared. He reminded me of…me. I didn't have a good feeling.

As he walked closer to the bed I could see tears in his eyes. I didn't know who the woman in the bed was.

"Why do you have to be sick?" young Rudy asked, choking back a sob. The way he spoke was different—he spoke with an English accent. That must have faded with age. The woman held on to him. She was young, but her face was very weak. Though I could hear her humming, a similar tune to one Grampy used to hum to me.

"Why did Mom have to get sick? And how come Dad never made it to Canada?" he cried.

I was witnessing one of my grandfather's earliest memories. Then I looked closer at the woman in the bed. She was the woman in the photo album I had found at Grampy and Nan's house. But who was she?

"I don't know what I'll do without you." Young Rudy was holding on to the woman's hand.

"You'll find a way," she said to him kindly. "You always do. You were always the most resourceful one of us." She tried to smile.

I looked back to see Clay and he had a sad look on his face.

"How old was he?" I asked Clay.

"He was seven. The same age you were when you left."

I could hear my grandfather crying. I grew up seeing him so confident, so strong, so ready for whatever the world threw at him. But this was one of his most vulnerable moments, and it was heartbreaking."I don't want to be alone," he managed to say through his tears.

"You won't be. I'll always be with you, I promise." She squeezed her hand around his. "I need you to be strong, Rudy. The world is a hard place, but it's the only thing you got." She coughed.

The young woman's face looked sunken and pale, as if she had been sick for a long time. Each breath she took was long, raising the bedsheets. She closed her eyes. I could see her smile took more energy than it should have. Just like Grampy, she was smiling when the world was trying to take it away.

"Who is she?" I asked.

Clay didn't answer me. He only looked on.

"Rudy," the woman was saying now, "I need you to keep going. I need you to stay strong, and true. I'll always be with you, no matter how lonely you feel. I'll be above rooting for you like I always have been." A tear came to her eye. "I love you, so, so much. You're the best little brother anyone could ask for. You're smart and funny, and you're wise in your own weird way. You're going to change so many lives, I just know you will. Someday we're going to meet again, and I promise we'll be together. All of us." She rested a hand on his cheek and he pressed her hand against it.

"I'll never forget you."

After she heard that, her eyes closed for the last time, and Grampy's face crumpled.

"Annaka, come back!" He was sobbing uncontrollably, gasping for breath. "Come back…."

I looked over at Clay. His eyes were teary. He gave me a hug, and I held on.

"I wanna go home," I whispered.

"Then that's where we'll go."

It all faded away—Grampy, the woman, the hospice—but the pain stayed. When I opened my eyes, we were back in the classroom.

"She was my aunt, wasn't she?"

Clay nodded. That's why Mom named me Annaka. That's why Nan was confused and said, "Annaka's not our granddaughter." That's why Grampy was emotional when he found out what my name was.

"He carried that pain for so long, Anna." Clay spoke softy. "But he always seen you as his light."

"Mom named me after her," I said. "And I threw that name away. That's why she was so upset when I told her I wanted to be Anna." I looked up at Clay. "Why didn't he ever tell me?" Tears began rolling down my cheeks.

Clay didn't know the answer.

All I could do was sweep up the broken glass, pick up the Father's Day cards, and stuff them back in the box. I was taking it with me. I was taking the portrait and the pages too.

"Lets go home," I told Clay.

Although things were now clear, I still felt lost.

———

THERE WAS SO MUCH ON my mind on the ride home. I guess the only thing I wanted to focus on was the road, and to let what I witnessed settle in my soul a little bit. I thought back to when Grampy told me about the first time he heard my voice. He didn't just cry because he heard my voice. He cried because Mom named me after his sister. Mom named me after my aunt Annaka.

"He didn't know Mom would name me that, did he?"

"He didn't have a clue," Clay replied.

"There's not much in there about my great-grandmother, is there? His mom?"

"I don't think he remembers too much about her."

It made sense. He was so young, and so lost. He meant so much to so many people but for the longest time he was alone and surrounded by grief. He was resilient, but before any of that, there was so much pain that I finally understood. I understood why he didn't want to talk about it. I understood why he only focused on the future. The past can be a painful place, and there I was, chasing history hoping to find clarity. And what I found wasn't a happy ending; it was a sad beginning. I didn't open a door and find a solution; I opened a closet and found where he hid his trauma and despair.

When we drove up the path towards home, it was late, and I saw some house lights on. That couldn't be a good sign.

"You know the drill," I said to Clay. But by the time I glanced over, he was already gone. The front door was open, and I could smell cigarette smoke drifting from the living room.

"Anna, is that you?" Mom called. She was sitting in Nan's rocking chair, smoking.

"Hey, Mom. What's up?"

"Nothing," she replied. Her eyes looked a little red. "How was the party? You get Tia home safe?"

"Yeah, I drove a whole gang of girls to Tia's place. They're probably still wide awake."

"Good." Mom smiled.

"Nan sleeping?"

"Yeah, she's sleeping like a pile of bricks. That woman can snore."

Mom took a puff. "Listen, we haven't really had a chance to really speak in a while."

"I know."

Things between Mom and I had been sideways ever since we had the argument. We had given each other a hug after the hospital incident, but after that it didn't seem like there was much else to talk about. We were both navigating feelings neither of us knew how to translate; we were both hurt in different ways. It made communication tough.

"I think we should talk," she continued. "Come pull up a seat."

What I wanted most was to get some sleep. My eyes were burning, my head was aching from the noise of the party, and I finally felt like I was breathing right again. But deep down, I knew talking to Mom was the right thing to do. I sat down across from her.

"What's on your mind?" I asked.

"A lot. Are you okay? After everything that happened with Nan?"

She didn't even know the other half of the story, and I wasn't about to tell her.

"I think I'll be fine. Tia helped me a lot when all of it went down. She's a life saver."

"Keep that one close." Mom stuck her cigarette face down into the arm of the chair. "You know, your grandmother said something to me today."

"Oh, yeah? And what was that?"

"She told me that the only way to let go of the past is to not hide from it. The only way to let go of the past is to face it. To not fear it, not let it bother you anymore. Then I thought about how your grandfather spent so much of his life running. Not from any of us, but from himself. He was never open about any of it. I had to pry his past from him. That man didn't have an easy life, y'know."

"I know," I replied. "I found out some things."

Mom looked at me. "Like what?"

"He had a sister, didn't he?"

"He did," Mom confirmed. "And he loved her so much. He didn't talk about her often, but she was never far away from his mind. As brave as he was, he was mainly brave about moving forward. He was afraid to dwell on the past, because it hurt him—it hurt him real bad. He hid that part of himself because he was scared, and all he ever wanted to do was be brave." She let out a breath. "He knew you were brave, and he always wanted you to move forward, even when we were away. He knew there was more out there for you." She sighed and lit another cigarette. She inhaled and paused for a moment, looking up at the ceiling. "Nan told me the story of him coming to Canada," she continued. "His mother was already older, and she died of pneumonia shortly after arriving from England. A couple years later, his sister was diagnosed with cancer. Grampy was so young, and they never really told him the details.

"We assumed his father passed away somewhere overseas. He wasn't the type of man who would abandon his children. Your grandfather never had anything in this world, so he took it into his own hands. When he found out you were named after his sister, he cried. He let it out."

She smiled at the bittersweet memory. "Aunt Annaka sounded like a strong young woman. I knew you could carry her name. I knew you could do it justice."

I didn't know what to say, so I didn't say anything.

"He lost everything at such a young age," she went on. "And the only way he knew how to deal with it was to hide it. He hid his past so deep inside him and it pushed people away. I always thought I'd be different—do better. But I ended up doing the same thing. I also hid a part of myself so deep inside that it pushed you away, Anna." Mom paused. I could see a tear racing down her cheek. "You just wanted to know about your dad. That's more than a reasonable request."

"Mom, we don't have to—"

"I owe you that, Anna," Mom cut me off. "Your father. He's still here. He wasn't a good man. In fact, your grandfather despised him. So did your grandmother. But I learned he wasn't a good man the hard way."

Maybe, I thought, the seeking part was done. Maybe it was my turn to sit and listen, so I kept quiet, waiting for Mom to continue at her pace. From what I'd learned about my dad, he didn't seem like that great of a guy. I guess my suspicions were now confirmed.

Mom took another drag on her cigarette before she started in on the next part. "He wanted me to move with him to Halifax, then Toronto. He wanted to start a family business. At least, that's what he told me when I was pregnant with you." She rolled her eyes. "He was broke, couldn't keep a job or stable income. I told him I couldn't rely on that. Not with you on the way. I couldn't trust it. But he was determined to go. He didn't have the money to go on his own, so he was relying on me to for money. One night he tried to break into the house. He wanted to steal as much stuff as he could to sell it. Grampy found him outside after he heard a window break. He had armfuls of their belongings, and he was trying to start up the truck that's now yours."

I was shocked. He *broke into* my grandparents' house and tried to steal Grampy's truck?

"Grampy went out to confront him, only to be sucker-punched." Mom shook her head and stubbed out her cigarette. "But it didn't end there. Your father hated Grampy. He kept punching him over and over and over. I remember I came out screaming at him to stop, but he wouldn't. He pushed me to the ground when I got close."

I couldn't believe it. "What happened?"

"Well, your grandmother came up from behind and hit him so hard on the back of the head that he went limp. Grampy called the police, your father went to jail, and eventually prison. It turned out we weren't the only ones who had been robbed; he had already stolen a car he was trying to sell, and had broken into Ms. Layton's shop a week prior. You were born shortly after all that." She looked at me in anguish. "I carried guilt for so long. Not because of you, but because I trusted someone who hurt the people I love. I trusted someone who hurt me, someone who would eventually let you down. I had to live with that guilt, and I was so ashamed that I buried it deep inside of myself." She shook her head. "He sent me so many letters saying he wanted me back and he was sorry, and this and that, and he had changed. I never believed a word of it. But I knew when he got out of prison he would come looking for you. That's why I decided to take you to Halifax with me. I wanted to keep you safe no matter what. Because of that, I ended up pushing you away, and I am so, so sorry, Anna. I am so sorry I hurt you."

The entire time, Mom just wanted to protect me.

"That's why we never came back?" I asked, choking up. "You were afraid he might try to find us?"

"I was afraid of a lot of things. But I also knew this town was one I wanted to leave behind—I never wanted to come back. But life throws you curveballs, and one day you accept a job as a professor, and it doesn't take long before you get a phone call saying your mother is showing signs of Alzheimer's. Then you get a call saying your father had a heart attack." She reached out and took my hand. "I knew it wasn't an option to stay away any longer. I had to come back and help Nan for the little time we have left with her."

Mom let out a breath and cried. Her hands covered her eyes, tears running down her cheeks.

"Mom, I—"

"I just want to tell you I'm sorry, Anna. I'm so sorry." She wept.

"You don't have to be sorry over anything." I darted over and

CHAPTER 20

I WOKE UP THE NEXT MORNING KNOWING IT WAS A NEW world. The dots were connected and I could see the universe for what it really was. Trying. I walked downstairs to an empty kitchen and living room. Mom and Nan must have been asleep. It was still pretty early, but I went out to the truck. When I approached the garage I felt a sudden wave of uneasiness, knowing my father had beaten my grandfather where I was now standing. I hopped in the truck and drove.

"How are you feeling, after everything?" I heard Clay ask. I didn't even look over at him in the passenger seat; I knew he was there.

"Complicated, I guess," I replied. "Well, maybe it's not that complicated. As much as I said I didn't have expectations, a part of me always did. A part of me wanted a father who was smart, and kind, and gentle. Not one who was...awful."

"I know," Clay said. "I can only imagine how hard this must be. But one thing I learned through all of this is that clarity doesn't always fix things; it only helps make sense of why people are the way that they are." He looked at me and smiled. "You're all trying your hardest, and because of that, it creates distance. You've been shortening that distance as of late, Anna, but shortening it doesn't necessarily make it easier."

He was right. Not much felt easier—I just felt more guilt, fuelled by grief.

"I guess, on the bright side," Clay continued, "having our worlds colliding isn't so bad."

That made me smile. This hadn't been the easiest homecoming for a lot of reasons, but I was glad Clay was with me.

"Can I tell you a secret?" I asked.

"Of course."

"There's no one else I'd rather have as my co-pilot."

He didn't reply, but I knew he was smiling too.

———

I FOUND A PARKING SPOT at the edge of the waterfront. The sun was still rising and seagulls were making their presence heard, but no humans were around quite yet. I was feeling brave and told Clay he could sit on the back of the truck with me. We sat quietly for a few minutes and just watched the water lapping at the shore. It felt like the calm after a storm.

"So," Clay eventually said, "I noticed you added something in the journal." He paused. "Are parties really like that?"

I snorted. "Yes."

"That's horrible." Clay put his hands on his head. I laughed; he was so innocent. "Why would anyone want to go to one of those?"

"You're asking the wrong person, friend." I grinned and put a hand on his shoulder. Eventually I rested my head on it, and he rested his on mine. Our relationship wasn't always perfect, but he was my best friend, my co-pilot. I'd never leave Clay behind again.

"Are you still thinking about finding him?" he asked after a few more moments of comfortable silence.

"My dad?"

"Yeah."

"I don't know." I sat up. Everything was still kind of a lot. Would it be worth it? What if he was still just as awful now as he had been in the past? I know people can change, but how much faith could I place in a man who had tried to steal from the people I loved most? I didn't know. A part of me was still curious if there would be anything worth salvaging.

"What do you think?" I asked Clay.

"I don't think he's a dream worth chasing."

I raised my eyebrows. "Yeah?"

"Yeah." He nodded.

"What about your whole world-colliding monologue?"

"I just think there are some things we shouldn't allow. I don't think you're chasing clarity with him. I think you're chasing hurt."

"I appreciate that," I replied. "But I think whatever I choose has to be my choice, and my choice alone."

"Okay," Clay said "Just…just don't end up hurting yourself along the way, okay?"

"With you as my co-pilot, I think I'm going to be just fine." I smiled then checked my phone. "It's almost nine. Folks will be around soon, you should probably—" When I looked up I was alone. "—disappear."

I didn't know if finding my dad would help, but something inside me wanted to see him, hear him, speak to him. I wanted to ask why he did what he did, and I wanted an answer. I wanted an answer to everything.

I took one last look out at the water and climbed back in my truck. I went to a greasy diner called Joe's and ordered two cheeseburgers.

The man at the counter said, "We don't usually get anyone buying cheeseburgers this early—mostly breakfast wraps. What's the occasion?"

"Sometimes your friends are hungover, and you gotta look out for them," I replied, grabbing the brown paper bag.

The man laughed. "That's real friendship."

I grinned. "I lead by example."

I left and got back in the truck. I had a feeling Tia would be working the early morning shift. When I opened the door of the corner store I could see her sitting on a stool with her head down on the counter.

She grunted until she sat up and saw me.

"Anna...hi!" she said.

"With medicine." I handed her a cheeseburger, and kept the other one for myself.

"You're a goddess." Tia smiled. She still had last night's mascara smudged under her eyes. She jumped into the burger.

"I know. How are you feeling?"

"Like someone who embodies bad decisions."

"You didn't drink too much, though, did you?"

"When we got home we finished my parents' wine, and we continued to dance all night with Taz."

I laughed uncontrollably at the image of the girls hopping around, holding paws with Taz.

"Laugh all you want, but he's the only man that's not trash." She spoke with half a burger in her mouth.

"I believe you, I really do." I giggled.

"What did you do after the party?" Tia asked.

"Things I shouldn't have."

"I knew you had other plans." Tia sat back on the stool, her back touching the wall. "So what's up?"

"My mom told me about my dad last night."

Tia bolted upright. "What did she say?"

"He wasn't a great man," I explained. "He tried robbing my

grandparents, got in a fight with my grampy, went to prison. Mom moved to Halifax when he got out. She didn't want me to come back here and see him."

"Was she in danger?"

"He pushed her to the ground once." I sighed. "Sounds like he was the type of guy who would just use me as a way to leech off of Mom. And Mom wanted better for me, and herself. So she went to Halifax."

"I see." Tia took another bite of the burger and chewed thoughtfully. "How are you feeling about it?"

"I don't know. A part of me is still curious. People can change, right? A part of me wants to know if he is still the same person. I want to see if he has my laugh, my smile, I don't know, maybe it's selfish but I just...I just have to see."

"I can understand that." Tia took a breath. "I think that makes a lot of sense actually. Did you talk to your ghost friend...?"

I shrugged, and shook my head. "He doesn't think I should."

"Why not?"

"He thinks I'm chasing hurt."

Tia polished off her cheeseburger and said, "There's more to it than that. I mean sure, it sounds like he's a man full of faults, but if you think meeting him can bring any type of fulfillment then I think you should." She shrugged and balled up the burger wrapper. "It's important to be honest with yourself, even if it is hurtful. What are you thinking?"

"I'm still thinking." I shrugged and took a bite of my burger. "He's here, and that's all I know."

I had no clue where he would be. I also didn't know what I would say to Mom. If I decided to search for him, maybe she didn't need to know. It would only hurt her. Just like he did.

"What are you doing tonight?" Tia asked.

"Nothing planned. Not yet, anyways."

"Well my parents are gonna be out for a bit. The house is ours if you want. We can vent and just shoot the shit."

"Thanks, I'll let you know," I said, polishing off my burger. "I'm gonna head back home. Text me if you need anything."

When I got back into the truck I saw the box of Father's Day cards I had taken from Grampy's classroom. Grampy was the father figure who always had my back, and who looked out for me. Not Blake. I had trouble even referring to Blake as "Dad." He never had been a dad to me, and if I were being honest, he probably never would be. He spent most of my life being a ghost story.

―――――

BY THE TIME I GOT back to the house, I could smell bacon and spied Mom flipping a bunch in the frying pan.

"There she is!" my grandmother said as I walked through the door, "my granddaughter." It made me chuckle. At least now she was holding on to a part of me.

"Hey, Nan." I pulled up a seat at the table.

Mom smiled from the stove. "You hungry, babes?"

"Nah, I had a burger with Tia this morning."

"Burgers for breakfast?" Mom laughed.

"Someone needs to bring their best friend hangover food."

"Oh. It was one of *those* parties. Wait, you didn't—"

"I was driving, Mom. Of course I didn't drink."

Mom nodded and turned back to the bacon. "Good."

I spent the rest of the morning sitting with them. Laughing with them. Telling stories with them. I didn't really feel afraid anymore when I spent time with Nan. We were creating something new.

After that I spent the rest of the day thinking about Blake and reflecting on what Mom told me. I opened up the journal and began drawing a portrait. I drew the mannequin I had seen in Wade's

Clothing. I didn't even need to say anything for Clay to know I wanted to go to the dark place. Everything in my room faded away into darkness and a mannequin stood in the middle of it. Clay could read the room enough to know I wanted to be alone, so he didn't bother revealing himself. I started drawing Blake's facial features as I remembered them, and they were formed on the mannequin. His dirty blonde hair, blue eyes, long face. I remembered he had been wearing a plaid shirt and blue jeans. As I drew, the mannequin turned into him. I walked closer, looking at his facial features and comparing them to mine. I didn't have his eyes, or his cheeks, or his hair, or his lips, or his nose, or his chin. I must have something of his, but I didn't know what.

Part of me was wondering if any of this was even worth finding out. I lay back on my bed, trying to figure out what I was going to do.

———

LATER THAT EVENING TIA TEXTED; I had been watching videos on my phone, trying to take my mind off everything, but there are only so many videos of creepy stories on YouTube you can watch before you recognize the same old formula.

Tia: *Hey, wanna come over?*

Me: *Sure.*

Tia: *Okay, but lets just keep it a girls night?*

Me: *You don't want Clay to come?*

Tia: *I think maybe we should talk more about what you brought up today. Without…the baggage.*

Me: *Okay.*

I pressed send. I felt weird about leaving Clay, but if I was going over I guess I had to respect her rules.

"You're staying here, grey boy." I smiled at him in my bedroom.

"Aww, and I was just starting to like dogs," Clay said sarcastically.

"I'm sure you were." I shook my head. "I'll be back tonight, and you got a party waiting for you." I pointed to the journal. Clay didn't look too impressed.

When I got to Tia's, most of the lights were off. I knew her parents were gone, so I went straight to the basement door and Taz greeted me.

"Hey, you." I patted his head.

"There you are." Tia was putting on some music.

The basement was a bit of a mess—blankets, glasses, and pillows were strewn everywhere.

"Well…you guys partied last night."

"What else is there to do?" She sat down in a beanbag chair.

"Feeling any better?"

"I feel like my head exploded." She popped a painkiller.

"Yeah, well, at least you got memories from it, right?"

"I can't remember a thing."

I laughed as I sat down in the other beanbag chair beside her. Tia was a lot of things, but she was one of my favourites. That's for sure.

"Be honest with me, Anna. Did you break into the school last night?"

I shied away from eye contact. "I did."

"I knew it! And you didn't bring me?"

"You were in no shape for that."

"Oh, shut up," she said with a laugh. "Did you find what you were looking for?"

"Yes."

"Shit, no way!" Tia looked at me. "That means you found…."

"The pages. Yup, I found them. They were hidden in the picture frame on his desk."

"What did they say?" Tia's eyes were wide.

"It was actually really tragic." I paused. "It was about an aunt I didn't know I had."

Tia was hanging on to my every word. "Oh yeah? What did he write about her?"

"He wrote about her dying when he was seven years old."

"Oh my God." Tia put her hands on her head. "What was her name?"

"This is the freaky part." I looked over at her. "Her name was Annaka."

Tia sat up straight. "Seriously? That's...."

"Unexpected. I know." I nodded. "I was named after her. It's a weird feeling, but I guess Mom thought I could honour her in some weird way?"

"I wouldn't call it weird." Tia put a hand on my knee. "If you were named after her, she must have been special. And clearly that rubbed off on you."

"Why do you say that?" I smirked.

"Well, for starters, you're the first person I've ever met with a real-life imaginary friend."

I shook my head. Maybe Annaka was special, and I hoped that I would someday understand why. Until then, I'd stick with Anna. I looked back to Tia and her eyes were locked on me.

"Have you done any more thinking about your dad?"

"First of all, let's not call him Dad. His name is Blake," I replied. I had decided to let that word go—it was a dream that was never going to happen. "And I'm feeling a lot of things...not all good."

"Well, do you still wanna find him?"

"Would you?" I didn't mean to sound harsh, I was honestly curious. I wasn't sure if what I was feeling was valid.

Tia thought for a moment before replying. "I think I would," she said. "As much as Clay doesn't think you should, I think it's normal to feel that curiosity. And it's not you betraying your mom—it's being honest to yourself."

There was too much pain he had caused my family already. But maybe if I did want to find him, nobody had to know. It could be a secret.

"Where would you start?" I asked.

CHAPTER 21

TIA BROUGHT DOWN THE PHONE BOOK AND BEGAN looking for leads.

"This is pretty old school," I teased her as she flipped through the pages.

"Better than nothing," Tia replied, not looking up.

I had already tried searching Blake Morrison on social media, but there was no one by that name living in Yarmouth. Maybe he wasn't tech savvy.

"My Mom said he wanted to start a business," I mentioned. "I never asked what kind, though."

"Do you think you could follow up with her?"

I shook my head. "I don't think it's a good idea. It took her almost seventeen years to finally bring him up. I think it'll be a little while until she wants to talk about him again."

"That's real," Tia said, keeping her eyes on the book.

I wondered what Clay would think of all this. Then I realized: I knew. He would think it was stupid. But he was wrong. I wanted Blake to be accountable, and I wanted him to know that I existed, and that Mom and I had made it without him.

As those thoughts lingered my mind, the front door opened upstairs.

"The 'rents must be home." Tia closed the phone book.

Then I had an idea. "Do you think your parents know about him?"

"That's…a good question." Tia put the book down. "But if you ask, they'd probably tell your Mom."

She was right. Jonathan and Clare were always so by the books. Let's be honest: Tia's parents were narcs. I always found it bizarre they had a kid like Tia. She broke rules as if it was her life's mission.

"You might wanna ask my dad. Mom's probably heading to bed, you know how she is." Tia pointed to the stairs. "But try to be subtle. You don't want him telling your mom."

"All right," I said, making my way to the stairs. How hard could it be?

I could hear what I assumed to be a football game playing from the living room. Jonathan's feet were up on the coffee table. Nan would have used the spray bottle on any of us if we dared try that.

"Oh, come on! Three more yards!" He sighed.

"Hey, hey Jonathan?" I said as I entered the room.

"Anna! Hi, come have a seat." He smiled. "I didn't see you come in."

"Oh, I came in through the back door." I sat down. "You were out."

"Figures. Tia had guests over last night." He looked at me and rolled his eyes. "God, they were making a lot of noise. You're lucky you weren't here."

"No, but I was the one who dropped them off." I laughed. "I remember those girls from Tia's birthday party years ago."

"I do too. They're good kids, but they never focused on anything. Never had any hobbies. Growing up, I always had sports—football, hockey, baseball. You, you always had your journal. I remember you always carrying that thing around." Johnathan smiled.

Jonathan always used to say that he couldn't wait until I grew up to be an author, and to read a book by Annaka Brooks. But writing fiction wasn't exactly my thing. I only wrote from the heart, for the heart.

"I still have that journal, actually," I said.

"Hold on to it as long as you can," he said. "One day when you look back, you'll see all the magic you wrote it in."

If only he knew how far back I'd been looking.

"But between you and me," he whispered, leaning in. "You should stick with school too." Then he sat back and said, "I know, I know, I'm just an old guy. But I know you, Anna. You have so much drive when you put your mind to it. School isn't perfect, but you're so close. Finish strong, please." Of course Jonathan went there.

"I'll try to do better," I said with a sigh. "I'm trying."

"That's the first step!" Jonathan raised a finger in the air, as if this was some eureka moment. "And once that's accomplished—"

"Can I ask you something?" I cut him off.

"Oh. Yes, of course. You can ask me anything."

I didn't know what he would say or how he would react. It's not like I had ever had the opportunity to ask anyone this question before. There was so much that could go wrong in theory...but it could also lead me to exactly what I was seeking. And I was the seeker, after all.

There was no subtle way around this. I decided to face it head on. "Listen, my mom told me about my dad the other night, for the first time. Like, ever."

"Oh." Jonathan froze. "Did she...tell you what he did?"

"Yes. And he's awful for doing that. He is so, so awful."

"I know." Jonathan turned off the TV and gave me his full attention. "I never liked him," he admitted. "And I was so angry when I found out what he did to your grandparents—especially what he did to your grandfather."

I nodded in agreement. "He's still around, isn't he?"

Jonathan looked at me closely. "Are you trying to find him?"

I paused. I could tell by the tone of his voice that he was hesitant, but I had to decide. No more teetering. "Yeah," I said eventually. "Yeah, I'm trying to find him."

"Anna, he's not the type of person you seek out. He's the type of person you leave in the past."

"But he was never in *my* past," I cut in. "He was only ever in other people's past. I never got that chance."

"Your mother left him behind," Jonathan said. "And for a good reason: so he wouldn't cause you hurt. I knew him; he wasn't a good man. He only ever wanted to hurt other people. He wasn't—"

"What would you do in my shoes?" I interrupted. "You have to understand. What if you never had your parents? I'm not asking for a relationship. I'm just asking for a little bit of clarity. To make sense of all of this."

His facial expression changed; I could see the empathy making its way into him.

"God. That must have been so hard on you." He shook his head.

"It was. I grew up looking at you and Tia, and wished I could have had something like that. But I never did. I just know if he's here, I need to talk to him. I don't want a father–daughter relationship. Not with him. Not with Blake."

"Blake…." Jonathan looked up at me. "Last I heard, he hangs out regularly at a bar just outside of town. I seen him there while I was at a staff get-together a little while ago. I haven't been back since."

"What's the name of the bar?"

"The North Crow. But it's not like you could get in—nor should you even try!"

He didn't know how resourceful I could be. "Thank you,

Jonathan." I gave him a hug. "This means the world to me."

"I can't stop you from whatever you're doing. But please be careful." He looked at me. "If you got hurt, your grandfather would jump out of his grave to find me."

I grinned. "I'm sure he would. You have nothing to worry about."

I knew he regretted telling me, but I had to take what I could get. I ran back downstairs to see Tia on the last page of the phone book.

"Nothing here," she said, putting it down.

"You must have known that at some point." I crossed my arms.

"I did. This thing is basically an artifact."

"Even by Yarmouth standards?"

"Shut up." She laughed. "What did you hear?"

"Apparently Blake hangs out at The North Crow outside of town. Do you know where that is?"

"Huh, I do," Tia said. "How would we know if he's there, though?"

"Your dad said he's a regular."

"Okay, okay. We can go by that. But how do we get in?"

I didn't want this to be a "we" thing. As much as I loved Tia for everything, I knew this could be messy. I thought about how badly I had messed things up just a few days ago. If I brought Tia into the mix, she could get into shit with her parents. I didn't want to drag anyone else farther down this path with me.

"I don't know, Tia. I think this is something I gotta do on my own."

She rolled her eyes. "Don't be dramatic."

"I'm not! I'm being honest. I think this is something I have to do. Alone."

"Why do you say that? I thought we were a team?"

"I know what I said. But if I'm going to go into it, I gotta see him on my own terms. Remember what you said about boundaries?"

She started to reply, but her face showed that she did remember.

"Okay. But that doesn't mean I'm not going to blow up your phone. You text me immediately, okay, Anna Brooks?" She stood up and pulled me into a tight hug.

"You got it, Tia Evans." I hugged her back. "I appreciate you more than you know."

"I'm pretty great, aren't I?"

"Yeah, yeah, yeah." I laughed. "I'll text you soon, okay?"

I made my way to my truck, and knew I should at least tell Clay my plan. I wasn't going to bring him along, but I owed it to him to at least let him know.

CHAPTER 22

C LAY SHOOK HIS HEAD. "ANNA, YOU CAN'T BE SERIOUS."
"You remember what I told you?"

"I know, but—"

"But you thought I wouldn't go through with it, did you?"

"If I'm being honest, no. No I didn't."

"You know how stubborn I am," I said as I sat down on my bed. "And you know I'm a seeker. I have a thread, and you know—"

"You're gonna pull it. I know." Clay sighed. "At least let me come with you. It's getting late"

"No," I said firmly. "I have to go alone."

"What?!" Clay was beginning to get upset. "What happened to all the co-pilot talk?"

I put my hands up like I was surrendering. "I know what I said, but please. You have to know where I'm coming from with this stuff."

"Are you going tonight?"

"I thought I'd check it out." I shrugged, trying to look casual.

"What happens when he tries to hurt you, just like he hurts everyone else?"

"Oh, cut it out, Clay. You're too much sometimes."

"Too much of him?"

I didn't reply. I wasn't going to go there now. I went to grab my keys, but couldn't find my bag.

"Here." Clay handed it to me. "Don't stay out too late, and be—"

"Be safe. Yeah, yeah. I got it, Grandpa," I said with a smirk.

I left the house feeling brave, but as soon as I sat in the driver's seat, my anxiety erupted. I kept taking breaths to bring myself back to the real world. I had a horrible feeling something bad was going to happen. It was hard to explain, but I could feel it inside of me.

I looked up at the stars, took a deep breath, and hit the gas. Was I really going to find Blake? I didn't know. Mom could never find out what I was doing. She would lose it. I wondered what Grampy might have thought. He might have been disappointed to some degree, but I knew ultimately he would understand.

I eventually found the North Crow; I remembered seeing it when Mom and I had first driven in to town. It was old and run down, with flickering lights in the parking lot and grimy windows that were hard to see in. The "O" in the word "North" was falling off the sign. It didn't exactly make me feel hopeful.

I put the truck in park, grabbed my bag, and walked up to the entrance. The doorman was too distracted by drunken men on the deck. They were drinking and laughing loudly, and it was like I wasn't even there. I made my way inside to see folks playing pool, drinking, and chatting. I knew better than to walk straight to the bar, so I slid into a booth. I looked around, trying to scope it out.

I didn't even know if Blake was there. I wondered if he still looked the same almost seventeen years later. Maybe he'd aged poorly, or maybe he'd moved on altogether. I had no idea.

A bartender finally caught wind of me and approached the booth. "Can I help you?"

"Uh…no. I'm just waiting for someone," I said shyly.

He narrowed his eyes. "Can I see some ID, please?"

Okay, maybe I wasn't as resourceful as I thought. My plan wasn't perfect after all. The bartender showed me the door.

Ahh, Anna. Why are you like this? I facepalmed on the way out. But I wasn't about to give up—not that easily.

I snuck around to the back, where more people were sitting on a deck overlooking the water. I knew I wasn't getting back inside, but I made my way up the steps leading to the deck. Eventually an older man looked over at me.

"Hey, you. You're new here. What's your name?"

"Anna," I replied without thinking. "My name is Anna."

The man was older, white, and had a gross patchy beard. I totally should have brought Tia or Clay; it was dumb of me to come here alone.

"Are you even old enough to be here?" he asked.

"It doesn't matter, I'm here to find someone."

"Who?"

"His name is Blake. Blake Morrison."

"Blake? Whaddaya want with that bag of bones?" The man laughed.

"Ah, shut the hell up, John," said a voice that sent a shockwave down my spine. A man emerged from the shadows; he looked almost exactly as he had in my grandfather's memory. He had a beard, blond like his hair, but I could see it was beginning to grey. His eyes were still blue, and his face was still long. His eyes were tired; just by looking at them I had a feeling he didn't smile a lot.

"What do you want?" he asked me. He was wearing a leather jacket and had a chain around his neck.

"Are...are you—"

"Yeah, I'm Blake. What the hell do you want, little girl? What did you say your name was, Anna?"

I composed myself. "Yes. Anna. My name is Anna. I, uh...I'm—" My throat was starting to clog up. Why was I doing this? Why couldn't I just let it go? What the hell was wrong with me?

"Spit it out, little girl."

"I'm not a little girl," I growled at him. I'm a lot of things, but I'm not a little girl. He didn't get to minimize me. Not then. Not ever.

"Then what do you want?"

Was this really him? I knew the answer. But as soon as he approached me I regretted coming to this shady bar, with its gross men. But I was here now, and I knew I had to see it through.

"I'm...I'm Jayla Brooks's daughter."

Everything about his body language changed when he heard that. He went from being edgy, suspicious, and rude to having his shoulders relax, his jaw fall wide open, and his eyes light up. "You're *what*?"

"I'm, um, your daughter." I stepped back slowly, unsure of what his reaction was going to be.

"What's going on here, Blake?" the man named John asked, looking up from his beer.

"What? Holy shit." Blake shook his head, staring at me. "No you're not."

"Yes I am."

"Then prove it."

"My grandfather is Rudy Brooks, my grandmother is Tanya. Her maiden name is Grant. My grandfather left you stranded at your RV seventeen years ago after he found you drunk at a bar on the waterfront. My mom was in there."

"Holy shit." Blake put his hands on his head. He was breathing heavily, like he couldn't catch his breath. I thought about how I had drawn him earlier that day in my journal. It turned out I didn't share any of his features—not his hair, chin, eyes, or nose. But the way he was trying to chase his breath, that was me. *So that's where I got it from.*

He waved me over when he finally regained his composure. "Come here, sit down."

I walked over, and past everyone on the deck. All eyes were look-ing at us in a "what the hell?" way, but I tried to ignore it. I was where I needed to be to find answers.

"This way." Blake sat down and pulled a seat out for me at the other end of the deck. "So you're Jayla's daughter. My daughter," he said. I just stayed quiet while he had his moment. "Holy. I thought I would never meet you."

I put my bag down and sat in the chair. This whole encounter felt uncomfortable, but I knew this was probably one of the only shots I would ever have to meet my father.

"Can I give you a hug?" He got up without waiting for an answer and made his way towards me.

"No." I paused him with my hand. "I don't think I'm into hugs."

"Okay." He sat down. "That's reasonable. I get it. It's not every day something like this happens."

"No. It isn't," I agreed. If only he knew what my return home had been like.

"So, why did you come?" he asked me. "Last I heard, you and Jayla took off somewhere. What brought you back to these parts?"

"My grandfather, Rudy. He passed away."

Blake slumped when those words came out of my mouth. "Rudy…," he murmured. "Oh, oh no." He put his head in his hands. "I'm sorry, Anna," he said sincerely. "I know he meant a lot to a lot of people."

I couldn't believe he was showing sympathy towards the man he beat up in his own driveway. He had hated Grampy. He had tried to steal his truck, along with a bunch of valuables from the house I grew up in.

"Rudy was a good man," Blake continued. "I loved him, very much."

I cringed. That's not how it went down in the journal, and that's definitely not what Mom told me.

I decided to call him out. "Don't pretend to grieve him. You hated him. And I know what you did."

Blake's tone changed quickly. "Hated him? You should have seen how he treated me! That man was nasty to me. Awful."

"Just like how you were 'nasty' to my mom? And just like how it was 'awful' of you to break into their house and try to steal everything they had?"

Blake gave me a long stare. It was like he was looking through me.

"They fed you that lie, huh? I can assure you, that's not how it went down. People can change, y'know."

"It wasn't a lie," I said. "Even Jonathan told me about you."

"Jonathan Evans? Ha, that fucking narcissist. What's he up to nowadays? Still showing people the football trophies he won in high school?"

"He's clearly doing more than you."

"Don't talk to me like that, girl. You might not know me but I'm still your—"

"You're still my what?" I challenged. "You're still my father? That role was taken a long time ago by a man named Rudy Brooks."

Blake tensed up, resentment forming in his eyes. He didn't like that, not at all. But that was the kind of response he'd earned. I wasn't going to pretend this loser in front of me was my father. How did he go from wanting to start his own business to being a regular at some shady bar just north of Yarmouth? The entire situation made me feel gross.

He looked frustrated. "I guess I should ask: why did you come here tonight?"

That was a question I should have considered in more depth. But I already felt like depth was something Blake was lacking.

"Was it money? 'Cause I ain't rich, sweetheart."

"I figured." I rolled my eyes. "I don't know why I came here. I guess I just wanted you to know that I exist, and that I'm fine." I looked at our sad surroundings. "And I want to know why you did what you did. Why did you hurt Grampy? Why did you hurt Mom?"

"Hurt them? They're the ones who always second-guessed me. They took you away from me, and have the nerve to make *me* the bad guy!"

I stood my ground. "You took yourself away from me," I said. "You chose to try and rob them, and you chose to not reach out to me after you were out of jail. You chose to be a ghost story, and now you're choosing to victimize yourself."

"I'm tired of this shit. You talk just the way Jayla does. Thinks she's too good for everyone else. I can see I didn't miss out on much."

"I could say the same thing." I stood up. "I don't even know why I thought this would change anything. All it did was confirm that Mom was right to leave."

I was so fucking done with this man. To know what I knew, see what I have seen, and then have him try to justify it all made me feel sick to my stomach. What did he ever do with his life? Mom raised me on her own, in a city that is always pushing people who look like us away. To have him trying to be the voice of reason was astounding. I turned to go.

"Wait, sit down." He waved and added in a soft voice, "I'm sorry, okay?" His face had a pained expression. "I always regretted not being in your life. I didn't mean to come off as a dick." He was beginning to breathe heavily again.

I paused. I had come this far—why not give him another minute? "All right. What do you wanna say?" I asked, taking my seat again.

"I don't know if saying sorry will really mean anything, especially from someone like me. I don't expect you to forgive me for doing what I did, or for not stepping up to be the father a kid needed. I regret that every day, believe it or not." He looked down at his hands and then back up at me. "You think I never thought about having a daughter? Or all the things we could have done together? It haunts me." He shook his head. "But that's what I gotta live with."

Hearing those words caused a storm to stir inside my heart. Blake thought about the same things I did?

I hadn't expected to hear that. I was more surprised than anything else. "I…think about those things too." I looked down. Had I been too mean? I kind of regretted going off on him like that.

"I'm glad I'm not the only one." He looked up at me, tears in his eyes, a half grin on his face. Maybe time really could change people.

"What happens now, then?" I was almost afraid to ask.

"Sit right here. There's something I want to show you." He got up. "I keep it in my car. I'll be right back." He walked off around the building, I was guessing to the parking lot out front. What did he want to show me?

I glanced around the deck and noticed all the men staring at me. I couldn't handle their eyes, so I grabbed my phone to check the time. It was past midnight and I had a few messages from Tia.

Tia: *Did you go? What happened?*

Tia: *Keep me in the loop. I'm half tempted to drive out there myself.*

Tia: *???*

I put my phone down when I heard John laughing.

"What's so funny?" I asked him.

"Blake, that daddy of yours? The reason he comes all the way out here is because he's banned from most bars in town."

I didn't reply. I just looked at him, confused. Why would he tell me that?

"Never pays his tabs. He's a thief. And as you can see, he's made off with your bag."

I looked down—my bag was gone.

"What the fuck!"

Blake was a compulsive liar, and I should have known better than to trust him. It must have been the same manipulative shit he'd used on Mom. I made my way around the building to see Blake running. But not towards a car...he was running away from something. He had my bag in his hands.

"What the hell *are* you?!" He was screaming like a baby.

I didn't see who it was, but I could hear someone yelling back, "Give me that damn bag!"

"Holy shit," I whispered. I knew that voice.

"Clay!" I yelled. What was he doing there? How was he there? I thought I'd left the journal in my bedroom.

Oh, shit.

I remembered that I hadn't been able find my bag, and Clay had handed it to me. He must have stuck the journal in there. I couldn't believe I'd missed that. Goddammit, he was sneaky.

I chased after them and I could see Clay grab Blake's arm only to be punched in the face. Clay didn't look too fazed, and reacted by head-butting Blake, knocking him back a few feet. Blake still had the bag as he retreated towards the road. Cars were zooming by.

"Give me my bag!" I yelled, running towards Blake. He couldn't take the journal, and he couldn't damage it. I didn't care about anything else in that bag; I just had to get the journal back.

"Anna, what *is* that thing?" Blake kept walking backwards, barely able to keep his composure.

I didn't reply. I just walked forward. Blake was trying to make a quick buck off of me, just like he had with Mom, Nan, and Grampy.

"Clay, you shouldn't have come," I scolded as I passed him.

"Neither should you." He glared at me, annoyed.

"Wait here," I instructed. "Don't engage with him. There are people everywhere, and these are not the kind of people we want to fuck with."

I walked past Clay and towards Blake; his face was pale but he still had a grip on the bag. I couldn't tell if he really wanted it or if he was having a panic attack.

"Give it back!" I demanded.

"What the hell is that thing?" Blake repeated as he moved closer to the road.

"It doesn't matter." I closed my fist. "Give me that bag. Now."

"Anna, I think we have a problem," I heard Clay say from behind me.

I glanced over my shoulder to see all the men from the deck had followed us to the front of the building. Clay was visible, and they were all staring at him.

"What the hell?!" I heard John yell.

The rest of the crew looked shocked to see Clay standing there, in his true form.

"Blake, get away from them!"

"What is that animal?"

"Lock the doors!"

The voices echoed across the parking lot. Clay looked at me—his biggest fear was playing out in front of us. He looked frozen, unsure of what to do. He was trying to catch his breath, just like me, just like…Blake.

"I'm not giving you anything, you freaks!" Blake had made it to the edge off the road.

From the distance, I heard a loud honk and saw headlights flash. I couldn't let anything happen to the journal—no more playing nice. I ran up to Blake, managed to grab hold of one end of the bag, and pulled; he fell forward but kept his strong grip.

"Let go, the strap is going to break!" I yelled.

Maybe I should have just let go. Because what happened next changed everything.

"Anna, let it go!" I suddenly heard Clay scream.

I hadn't heard him yell like that before and it made me pause and look back. He was running towards us. When I turned back to Blake the strap on my bag finally broke. The bag flew into the air, out of all of our reach, and landed in the road.

"Shit!" I yelled.

I looked to the left and saw an eighteen-wheeler barrelling towards us. I pushed Blake to the ground and darted for the bag. It was dark and I knew the truck wouldn't see any of us, but I kept running.

"Anna!" I could hear Blake's voice. "What the hell are you doing?"

Before I reached the bag, Blake grabbed my arm to haul me back. But I twisted his wrist and kicked him in the knee. The lights from the eighteen-wheeler lit me up, and I tried to jump for the bag, but someone tackled me onto the shoulder of the road as the truck's horn blasted.

I looked up to see Clay's face. He was more concerned with saving me than trying to reach the journal.

"I'm sorry, Anna," he whispered, tears running down his cheeks.

"No!" I screamed. "The journal!"

I locked eyes with Clay as his face embodied a pain I've never seen. His whole body tensed, and blood began to drip from his mouth. He staggered, gasping. When he fell, I tried to catch him, but I was too far away. He laid down, his arms and legs moving in jerky, unnatural motions. It was an image that would haunt me for the rest of my life. His body kept twisting and turning, until suddenly he vanished.

"Clay!" I reached for the spot I had last seen him, but he wasn't there.

I scrambled to my feet to see what was left of my bag. It was torn to shreds, decimated by the eighteen-wheeler. I pulled out the journal and saw it had been almost completely torn in half. Pages were falling out and the cover had a deep black tread mark on it.

"Clay, buddy, where are you?" I couldn't catch my breath; tears began rolling down my cheeks. "You can't be gone, you can't be. I can't lose you."

"Are you *stupid*? Who do you think you are? You think you can just jump into oncoming traffic?" Blake grabbed my arm, trying to pull me back to the parking lot. "What the hell is wrong with you, little girl?"

Something inside me snapped. I looked up and planted my fist so hard in Blake's face that blood spurted from his nose. He fell back to the ground, hard.

"My name," I yelled, "is Annaka!" I glared down at him. "My name is Annaka Brooks!"

Everything came out all at once. For so long I had been afraid to embrace who I was meant to be. I had always hated that part of myself, and never really knew why. But I was finally starting to realize the importance of identity, and honouring the people who came before me. The ones who made sacrifices so I could grow. I had been ignorant to it for a long time, but it finally made sense. I was finally growing into my identity, and I wasn't about to let anyone undermine it. As I stood over my father, I knew Clay had been right about Blake. I had been chasing hurt. Even though I was a seeker, I was seeking a past that never wanted me. But now I knew who I was, and I knew all the people I carried with me: Mom, Clay, Grampy, Nan, Tia, the Evanses, all of them. They mattered to me. Not some loser, bleeding on the side of the road. Not that thief.

Clay was nowhere to be seen. Blake was still on the ground, nursing his bloody nose in shock. His deck buddies were yelling incoherently and making their way across the parking lot to him.

"Clay? Clay, where are you?!" I couldn't lose him. Not like this. Not tonight.

I ran for my truck and heard Blake's yelling: "What is wrong with you? What the hell was that thing?" He was still lying on the ground.

I put my keys in the ignition, put the truck in drive, and floored it towards Blake. He scrambled out of the way, and at the last minute I turned onto the road. I never wanted to see that man again. He was toxic. He was poison. He was…the reason why we left Yarmouth in the first place.

I floored it all the back down the main road. I didn't know what to do or where to go. I didn't even know where Clay was; he had just disappeared. The journal was sitting on the passenger side, almost torn apart.

"Come on, Clay!" I yelled while trying to focus on the road. "Give me something. Give me anything. Please."

I couldn't lose my best friend. I could feel my throat begin to clog up.

"No. Not now." I tried to calm myself down but it was only getting worse. An anxiety attack is like quicksand—the more you struggle, the deeper it pulls you down. I could feel myself sinking into it while on the road. It was the worst possible time to have an anxiety attack.

Suddenly I heard a groan from the passenger seat.

"Ohhh God."

I looked over to see Clay holding his stomach. Blood was still pouring from his mouth.

"Clay! Shit, are you okay?" I managed to ask.

"No," he whimpered. "I don't know what's happening."

I knew I had to stay focused. I had to get him back to the house, and repairing the journal would repair him. But when I looked over again I noticed the blue energy rising from him like fog.

"Clay, what's happening?"

"I don't know. But you have to hold on. Keep driving."

I gripped the steering wheel as hard as I could, but that did nothing to keep my mind grounded. The wheel faded into nothing, and so did the seat I was sitting in, along with the rest of the truck. I was floating and Clay was nowhere to be seen.

"Clay? Clay!"

Gravity kicked in like it had been waiting for me, and I fell on my butt.

As I was catching my breath I could feel something, someone, pull my hair.

"Ow!" I closed my eyes, and when I opened them I was back on my grandparents' front steps. "What the fuck!"

"Annaka!" my grandmother scolded. She was braiding my hair. "Who taught you language like that?"

"Nan?"

"Me?! You know I don't use that language."

"No. I mean, why are we here?"

I looked at my hands, and saw I was a little girl again. I didn't know what was going on—why did Clay take me back? Was I still driving the truck in the present? What caused this sudden shift?

"Don't be foolish," Nan said. "We live here."

"No." I stood up, grabbing my hair.

"Wait! We're not done." Nan tried to grab me to sit back down, but I slipped her grip and ran up into the tree house. What was happening? I looked out the tree house window at the lake. There were pleasure boats and warm sun. It was like any other summer day.

"Why are we back here?" I asked aloud. I climbed back down the ladder and saw Nan had followed me and was waiting at the bottom.

"Aren't you gonna let me finish your hair? We can't have you running around looking like that!"

"The journal," I said to myself. I had to find it. It had to be in my room, where it always was. I ran past Nan and made my way inside. When I opened my bedroom door, I spied the journal on the bed. *Yes!*

But when I picked it up, the book began falling apart in front of me.

"No. No. No! Clay? Where are you?"

The bedroom faded into the dark place. The only thing that remained was my closet door. It was open a crack and I could see a blue glow seeping from inside.

"Are you in there?" I asked, approaching the door.

I pushed it open and the light blinded me.

When I opened my eyes again, I was sitting at a table with Laura, Taylor, and Lucy. We were all young. I looked across the table to see Tia at the front.

"Happy birthday, Tia!" Jonathan came in holding a cake.

"Oh no." I put my head in my hands. Was I trapped in the memories?

Jonathan began cutting the cake and placing pieces in front of each of us.

"Aren't you gonna eat, Annaka?" he asked me.

"I'm not hungry," I replied.

I put my head down. How was I going to get out of this? Without the journal, without Clay, there was nothing I could do.

"Oh, come on," Jonathan was saying. "A little cake won't hurt anyone."

When I looked up, Jonathan was gone. So was everyone else. The table stayed, and on it was a slice of birthday cake. I was surrounded by darkness.

"Clay, if you're there," I said, "please bring me back."

"Oh my gosh, Annaka. You're still going on about that imaginary friend?" I could hear Tia laugh, but she wasn't there. I could hear the other girls laugh too, and I felt alone. I didn't respond. I just sat there in front of my cake.

"What were you freaking out about?" I heard my grandfather's concerned voice as the table and cake disappeared.

"Because I'm pregnant." Mom's voice filled my ears. "It's true!" I heard Mom's cries in the darkness. "All I do is let you down. All I do is let everyone down. I am such a fuck-up. I just ruined everything!" Her words echoed.

"Shhh," I heard Grampy reassuring her. "You can never let me down." His humming fill the air, and I couldn't help but cry. I shut my eyes, hoping I could escape this darkness. But all I heard was Grampy humming away. Tears ran down my cheeks.

Eventually my grandfather's humming turned into Aunt Annaka's humming.

When I opened my eyes, I was in the hospice again.

"Oh no, not this one." I shut my eyes. "I hate this one so, so much."

Grampy and Annaka couldn't see or hear me—this wasn't my memory—but I could see Grampy crying as he held on to Annaka's arm, screaming her name.

"Annaka! Come back, Come back, please. Annaka. Please."

I closed my eyes and I felt cool air and smelled fresh grass. I opened my eyes and I was in a park. I looked at my hands and I was a little girl again, just like in the first memory I'd gone back to. I took a few steps and tripped.

"Annaka." Grampy was laughing. "Look at you, tripping all over yourself."

"I wanna go home." I began crying.

"Annaka, what's wrong? You don't want to go to Cape Forchu?"

"No, I just want to see Clay."

"Clay?" Grampy snickered. "Your imagination gets the best of you."

"No." I shook my head. "It's the best part of me." I closed my eyes.

I didn't want to go through these memories anymore. I just wanted to go home. I didn't want to live in the past anymore. I just wanted to be present. Clay was hurt and he needed my help.

"Where are you, buddy?" I whispered.

"What are you doing with the journal? Are you trying to go back again?" I opened my eyes to see Tia facing me on Bobby Noah's back deck. It was the night of the party I had written about in the journal.

"Holy shit," I said out loud.

Tia looked at me closely. "What's up? Are you trying to go back?"

"No, I'm trying to go forward."

"What are you talking about?"

I looked down—I was holding the journal, open to the page I had written about the party. I had an idea.

"I'm sorry if this hurts, buddy. I really am."

"Anna, what are you talking about?" Tia asked.

"It's Annaka," I said as I pulled the page, ripping it clean out of the journal.

I heard Clay scream from somewhere and everything faded away. We were away from drunk teenagers, loud music and from the rest of the world. Everything was dark.

"Clay, I can hear you. Bring me back. Please, try!" I could hear him yelling in pain. I held what was left of the journal and closed my eyes. "Please, please, please, buddy."

When I opened my eyes again I was back in the truck, driving down the road. I heard the loud honk of an oncoming car, and jerked the steering wheel as hard as I could to the right, switching lanes and narrowly missing the car in front of me. I floored it towards town.

"Anna, I can't control it. I can't. Everything is falling out of me." Clay was holding his stomach. His nose was bleeding and his eyes were wide.

I slowed down, pulling over to the side of the road. I looked at his stomach, and there was a stain of blue blood soaking through his dress shirt.

"Oh my God. Oh my God. Oh my God." I was freaking out.

"Take me to the tree house. If I'm gonna go, that's where I wanna go."

"Shut up, Clay. Don't talk like that."

"Just hurry, please."

I hit the gas. I had to get back to the house. We rode past the waterfront, downtown, and through Main Street. I wasn't going to slow down.

I found the dirt road and sped up there faster than I should have. I parked outside the garage.

I picked up the journal. The leather spine was barely holding it together, pages were falling out all over the passenger seat. I tried to pick them all up.

"Clay!" I cried.

"No tears. Not yet." Clay said as he faded. I took the journal and climbed up to the tree house.

"Why here?" I asked frantically. "What do you want me to do?"

"Annaka." He faded into the world and hit the floor. "Annaka, you have to do it."

"Do what?"

"You have to rip it."

"No! No, we can fix it. I'll tape it. I'll—" I tried putting it back together. It was almost completely torn in two.

"No," Clay cut me off. "I can't control what's happening anymore. If you went back again, I don't think I could get you out. It's too dangerous. You have to do this." He looked me in the eye. "Please. Do it for me."

I couldn't. I couldn't do it even if the world depended on it. If the journal was ripped apart, that meant Clay would….

"I can't! I'm sorry."

"Please, Annaka. You don't understand what's going to happen. I can't stop the jumping."

"You shouldn't have come after me!" I shouted through my tears. "Why didn't you just stay here?"

Clay grabbed my hand tight, blood dripping from his mouth. He looked at me, and I knew he was barely holding on. "Because I'm your co-pilot."

Blue fog filled the air. I shut my eyes tight, knowing that everything around me was already gone.

CHAPTER 23

WHEN I OPENED MY EYES, I DIDN'T KNOW WHERE I was. I was lying on grass looking up at the Milky Way. The stars were the only lights illuminating Earth. This wasn't a memory. This was something else.

"Clay?" I called out into the universe. I could hear my voice echo but there was no response. "Clay, where are you?"

I stood up; the sky was full of stars, the grass was dark. I looked down to see a lake.

"What's going on here?"

There was no response.

I turned around to see two silhouettes: the tree house and the house. I walked towards the house, and went straight to the front door. When I opened it, a gust of wind splashed against me and everything was see-through; white lines outlined our home. I caught my breath and could hear a phone ringing somewhere inside. I headed for the living room, where my grandparents' ancient black telephone was ringing off the hook. I hesitated—I didn't know what was happening. I mustered the little courage I had left and lifted it to my ear.

"Hello?"

"Annaka."

I heard the voice I was so afraid of forgetting: my grandfather's. Everything inside of me fell.

"Grampy?" My voice began to whimper. "Grampy, is that you?"

"Yes. Annaka, come here."

I heard his voice echo, and when I turned around he was sitting on the couch, his eyes looking straight into mine. Here was the familiar gentle giant of a man who was always able to put a smile on my face. But in that moment, I couldn't smile. I began to cry.

"This isn't real."

The last time I had spoken to my grandfather was by phone. On my birthday last year, when he told me the story about the first time he heard my voice, as he always did.

"This is just as real as anything," Grampy was saying now.

The terror vanished as soon as I heard him say that. I took a couple slow steps forward, still convinced it couldn't be real. As I got closer, he revealed a smile that made everything okay. I ran and wrapped my arms around him. I let everything pour out. Everything.

"I am so, so sorry, Grampy."

"You have nothing to be sorry about, hon." He patted my back.

"I ruined everything. I shouldn't have gone to meet Blake. I should have tried to come back sooner to see you. I should have—"

"You didn't ruin a thing. You're here now, and that's all that matters."

A shiver crept up my spine. That's when I realized that this was all real. It was all too real, and it was coming to an end.

"Grampy." I forced the words out through my trembling lips, and then my teary eyes got the better of me and I wrapped my arms around him even tighter. Even as a dead man, even as a ghost, he made me feel like a kid again. Safe. I wanted to stay there forever.

"You're so big now," he said. "You're all grown up."

"Yeah," I said through the pain. "I guess I am."

"I guess you know now why I was so emotional the first time I heard your name."

I nodded and stepped back to look at him. "I'm so sorry I went through your stuff."

He chuckled. "No you're not. Besides, it's not like I could take any of it with me."

"I should have just left everything as it was. If I had, none of this would have happened."

"You're a seeker," Grampy replied. "You always were." He smiled. "Just like your aunt."

"The one I never knew of."

"No, one of the secrets I kept close to my chest. Kinda like the friend you have." He winked at me.

He had a point; I guess I couldn't pretend that I didn't keep my own secrets any longer.

"She would have loved you," he continued. "You're just like her, y'know. She was always so eager to find her own way, even if it meant creating a mess. But one thing Annaka always taught me was to keep memories close, even if the ones you shared them with are gone. That's why she gifted me the journal right before she passed, which I eventually passed along to you."

"Woah."

I had no idea my aunt had gifted the journal to my grandfather. She must've known he would need it for the moments he felt alone. But when Grampy found that sense of belonging he had always been searching for, he was able to let go of the past. So he gifted the journal to me. I let that sit with me for a little while. I didn't know what to say, so I didn't say anything. I held on, wanting this moment to last forever.

"Your friend," Grampy spoke. "He needs your help."

"But I don't know what to do!"

"There's only one thing you can do."

I knew my grandfather was right, and that's what hurt. But what hurt even more was knowing there would be a future without him. One I had to navigate on my own. Contrary to what I'd been up to, time doesn't slow for anyone.

"I can't leave him," I said quietly. "I won't leave him."

"Annaka, we can't live in the past. Just like your aunt taught me: all of this, all of us, we're temporary. We don't need a journal to live forever. The people in your life will always be around you, in the memories you share. The good, the bad, all of it." He put his hands on my shoulders and looked me in the eye. "Clay loves you deeply. I know this is the hardest decision you'll ever have to make, but he needs you to do it. He will always be with you, even if his physical presence was temporary."

Everyone is temporary. That thought buried itself deep in my heart. As difficult as it was to hear, I knew it was a truth I had to face.

"He was always there to protect you. Just like my sister was there to protect me. Keep the memories, because those are only gifts that we can keep across time."

I didn't say anything after that. I let silence fill the air.

Grampy eventually whispered in my ear. "It's time."

It was.

I stood up slowly and walked back to the front door. I looked back one more time to see Grampy. He smiled.

"You're a grown-up now. This is the hard part."

"You're right about that." A tear made its way down my face.

"Goodbye, Annaka," he said one last time.

"Goodbye, Grampy. I'll miss you." I opened the door.

"I'm always with you, co-pilot," his voice echoed in the distance.

I walked outside, and headed for the tree house. I knew Clay would be there. Once I made it to the ladder, I glanced back and couldn't see our home anymore. It had faded. It was time to let go. No matter how hard it would hurt.

"Clay!" I called out. "Clay, where are you?" I climbed the ladder and found the damaged journal on the floor. Blue energy flowed all around it.

"Clay," I whispered.

"I'm here."

He appeared in front of me, and he wasn't in good shape. His nose was still bleeding and he was gasping for air.

"I'm so, so sorry," I cried, and took him in my arms.

"You have nothing to be sorry about." He hugged me back.

"You're my best friend." I squeezed harder than I should have. "And I love you so so so much, Clay."

"I love you too." He held on. "But it's time." He rested his forehead on mine.

I looked at the journal and knew it was beyond repair.

"Thank you for coming back, Annaka." He looked at me deeply.

I knew this was it. This was the part where I had to let go.

I held on to Clay with one arm, while reaching for the journal with my other hand. I brought the book around his back, squeezing him as gently as I could.

"I'll never forget you," I whispered, and kissed his soft cheek.

That's when I ripped it.

I did it fast, all in one go. The blue energy blew back and everything around me began to disappear.

"I'm always with you, Annaka. You're always worth the wait," Clay whispered to me as he faded away for the last time.

I looked out the window of the tree house and saw the stars above my head fizzling away. Blue energy was seeping from the ground like fog. I closed my eyes, holding back tears with my fists clenched, resenting the world for being as cruel as it was. For taking away my co-pilot.

When I opened my eyes again, I let my fists go. Everything was back to normal, the stars rested above my head, and I could feel the hard wooden floor of the tree house beneath me.

I was back in reality without my best friend.

"He's gone," I cried aloud. "He's gone."

CHAPTER 24

ONE OF THE LAST STAGES OF GRIEF IS DEPRESSION. AND when I lost Clay, it felt like I skipped over all the other stages. After Clay died, I lost track of time, I lost track of friends, I lost track of family. I felt everything and nothing all at once. It was like feeling numb, but on fire all at the same time. I spent most nights crying myself to sleep. Mom thought I was going through delayed grieving for Grampy. But of course, I couldn't tell anyone the truth except Tia.

Tia tried her hardest to keep me in good spirits, but she understood when I didn't always get back to her. I had dealt with two deaths so closely to each other and was reliving that pain all over again. My entire life felt like one big cycle of grief and it weighed on me. It was so heavy.

So it made sense that one day when I was in bed feeling so far away from the rest of the world, I didn't even notice Tia walk into my room.

"Hey, hey," she said. "It's two o'clock and you're still in bed?"

"Hi." I blew my nose. "What's up in the world of Tia? Coming to visit her depressed best friend?"

"You really think I'd miss your birthday?"

That caught me off guard. I didn't even know what day of the week it was, let alone when my birthday was. "I'm glad one of us remembered." I rolled over.

Tia came close, sat on the edge of my bed, and held me. "How are you feeling?"

"It hurts," I said into her shoulder. "It hurts more every day."

"I know." She kissed my forehead.

I had kept the journal. It was completely torn in half, but I'd kept it anyway. I spent so many nights trying to put it back together in the garage, but nothing worked. I had been hopeful for a bit, but eventually the hope faded away, just like he did.

"I dream about what happened almost every night." I choked up. "But I can't change anything. If I'd just listened to Clay, if I'd just done things a little differently, then he'd still be here. With me."

"Hey, hey," Tia calmed with her voice. "You were doing what your heart told you to."

"My heart was wrong."

"I've heard that before," she replied. "It just means you're human."

I sighed. "Maybe."

"Anna." She paused. "Sorry, Annaka. You've been in your room for a month now. I know it's hard, but we have to try. Is this what he would—"

"No," I interrupted. "He would want me to live my life. He would want me to go to school, become an A+ student, and to strive for greatness no matter what obstacles come my way." I looked away. "But he isn't here, Tia. Clay isn't here to tell me that himself. And it hurts. It hurts so bad."

Tia noticed the ripped-up journal on my nightstand. She went over to it, examining all of the pages that had fallen out.

"There's a lot in here, eh?"

"Yeah," I replied. "He knew all of it, inside and out."

"And you want to keep it?"

"I don't know." I sat up. "I don't know if I can. It just, it hurts looking at it."

"Ahh, I see." Tia set it down. "Have you ever thought of giving it a proper burial?"

I couldn't bury the memories. They were all I had. All those entries, all those times we spent jumping back to them. All the nights we stayed up, hanging out in the dark place like a second home. I couldn't bury them. If I did, that would make all of this real, like when I touched Grampy's urn.

"I can't," I said.

Tia could tell how hard it hurt when I said that. "Oh, Annaka." She gave me a hug. When she pulled back, she tried to change the subject. "Why don't we do something tonight, birthday girl?" She smiled.

I didn't feel like I was in any shape to go out. "Like what?"

"We'll have a girls' night. We don't need a plan. We can just go wherever the road takes us. The skies are going to be clear tonight. Let's take advantage!"

The last few weeks had been mostly rain, and I had spent most of it in my bedroom. It would be nice to maybe get some air, get away from these four walls for a bit.

"Do you want to?" Tia pressed.

"I think so." I nodded. "Text me in a bit, and I'll let you know."

"Whatever you want." She gave me one more big squeeze before getting up. "I gotta head to work, but I'll text you once I'm off. Okay?"

"Okay." I continued to lie in my bed, and looked over to the journal. I knew I had to get rid of it, but I wasn't ready to let go, no matter how hard my fists wanted to be free.

So I stayed in bed. I had absolutely no energy, I couldn't remember the last time I ate or drank, or even showered. My bedroom was a mess, and my hair was even worse. I could hear Mom and Nan moving around downstairs, but they didn't come up. They were good at giving me space, and respecting my boundaries. They knew I was hurting, and that I would come down when I wanted to. Eventually the clock hit five; I slid out of bed and made my way downstairs.

"Shh, she's coming," I heard Mom say.

"She can probably hear you, calm down," Nan answered.

I felt a stupid grin coming, and as I turned the corner Nan blew into a birthday kazoo, and Mom held up a plate of pancakes.

"Happy birthday!" they both said.

As upset as I was, the surprise lifted my spirits. I couldn't believe I had forgotten my own birthday. I was glad I had folks who remembered.

"Thanks, guys." I smiled. "I appreciate it."

Mom placed a plate of pancakes on the table in front of me. I sat down, not exactly hungry, but ate them anyway.

"They might not be as good as your grandfather's," Mom said. "But I'm trying my best."

"I know." I smiled. "Thank you, I haven't been keeping track of time lately. I...honestly forgot my birthday was today."

"You're young, don't let go of your memory just yet," Nan joked.

Through the grief, I was happy Nan was doing better than when we got here. That wouldn't have been possible without Clay.

I smiled and took a big bite of the pancakes.

As nice as it was to see Tia, Mom, and Nan that day, I thought back to what I had been doing a year ago in Halifax. I had gotten home from school and Mom was away. I hadn't had a good day. I was alone, overwhelmed with school, and sad. That evening the phone rang; I picked it up to hear his voice. My grandfather's. It was our yearly routine. One of the hardest parts about losing someone is losing the little things. I got choked up when I realized I wasn't going to receive a phone call for my seventeenth birthday. I wasn't going to hear him tell me the story he told me every year. That wasn't going to happen ever again, and I had to come to terms with that.

I could barely stomach any food; instead, I decided to go outside and sit in the tree house, wishing it could take me away from the rest of the world.

I thought about Clay and I spending so many nights up there, clear sky or rain, soaking in everything. The sky was clear, so I watched the sun begin to set and I could see the universe for what it really was. Healing.

———

A LITTLE WHILE LATER I was surprised by a familiar voice.

"Hey, hon." Mom was climbing up the ladder to the tree house. "Happy birthday."

"Mom, hi?" I sat up. I didn't expect her to come out here.

Mom was trying, I knew. I loved her, and I apologized, and I forgave her. We were a work in progress.

"You've been in your room a lot. Are you okay?"

"I am. Everything is just…everything is just hard."

"I know, hon." She gave me a hug. "I know. Loss isn't always straightforward."

I moved out of the way so she could sit down. She lay back with me and we looked at the sky sprinkled with stars that were so far out of our reach. I never had a chance to sit up there with Mom before. Back in Halifax, we sometimes sat on the rooftop and looked at the streets below because we couldn't always see the starlight. But there was something genuine about this. I think she could feel it too.

"You're still thinking about him lots, aren't ya?"

I knew she meant Grampy. "Yeah. Yeah I am." She didn't know who I was talking about—and maybe I meant both.

"I'm sorry, hon." She held on to me and I rested my head on her shoulder.

I never told Mom about my confrontation with Blake. I thought it might hurt her too much. Mom was more than enough for me—I was realizing that even though I didn't always show my appreciation, I had hit the jackpot when it came to moms.

"You spend so much time alone, I always feel like there's more I should be doing," she said.

"No, Mom. No. You do more than enough. I'm just hurting right now. But you're the best mom anyone could ever ask for." I paused. "I'm sorry about how hard I made coming back for you. I really messed up. I shouldn't have said what I said, and I should have been more empathic."

"Oh, babes. You don't have to apologize for anything. I'm sorry too. I should have been more honest with you." She looked down at her hands and then back at me. "We're different, me and you. I spend most of my time running away from the past, you spend most of your time running straight into it."

I sat with that for a moment. She was totally right: our relationship was like a game of tug-of-war. We spent so much time heading in opposite directions, it caused a rift between us. But there we were, laying in my childhood tree house, finding peace in the middle.

"Is he the reason you want to be called Annaka again?" Mom asked after a while.

"I don't know," I replied honestly. "I spent so much time hating that name. To suddenly understand why I have it, and how much those before me sacrificed…I don't know. I can never be ashamed of our family's past. I can never be ashamed of who I am, or where I come from."

Mom smiled at that. I was done dwelling in the past. I wanted to start anew, focus on the future. But that didn't mean I couldn't keep a small piece of the past with me.

"He would be proud of you, y'know."

They both would be. I knew that. I was also sure I would never be alone—Clay would always be close by, whether I was aware of it or not. Clay might have been able to take me to the past, but I think the most important thing he taught was that I have to stay present. I can't be chasing ghosts. I can't be chasing hurt. I can't be chasing things that can't be changed.

"I'm glad that things are okay between us," Mom let out.

"They'll continue to be okay. I promise, I'm going to finish up school next year, and who knows what the future will bring. All I know is right now, I get to spend time with you, Nan, and Tia." I smiled. "That doesn't sound too bad to me."

Mom smiled too. "I got you something." She sat up, pulled over her purse, and dug into it. "Close your eyes, okay?"

"Okay." I giggled.

"Put your hands out."

I felt her place something in them. It was soft, and felt like leather.

"Open up, Annaka."

When I opened my eyes, I held a new journal in my hands. It was baby blue, emblazoned with "This is for the Seekers." I could tell from the design of the text that Mom totally put that there. The leather was soft. I was a bit shocked at first, but I knew this would make room for the future.

"Thank you, Mom." I hugged her.

"You're welcome." She rested her head on mine.

We just lay there, looking up towards the sky that rested above our heads, knowing that this moment would bleed nostalgia someday. I already knew it would be the first memory I would write about.

Eventually Mom left to put Nan to bed, but I stayed, looking at my new journal. It was different—definitely not the type Grampy would write in—but I was pretty sure this journal was going to start and end with me. Nobody else. It made me think back to what Tia had asked me earlier that day. Was I going to bury Clay?

I went to my room and saw the torn journal resting on my night stand. Beside it was the picture of my namesake, Aunt Annaka, I had found in the attic. That felt like a lifetime ago, but I wanted to keep her close. Maybe I could get to know her.

I picked up the old journal for last time, and carried it outside to a patch of grass beneath the tree house. With a shovel from the garage, I started digging. I knew that's where Clay would want to be. I dug a hole not too deep, but not too shallow. It was in the in-between—just like Clay always was. Between our world and his. I knelt and placed the journal beneath the earth, under the tree house we called home. I didn't cry; I was saying goodbye.

As I smoothed the earth, I heard a voice. "Hey, you ready for that drive?" It was Tia.

"Tia, hey. I thought you were going to text me."

"I did…you didn't reply. But I see you've had your hands full." She pointed to the shovel in my hand. "You did it," she realized. I heard a bark in the distance and could see Taz making his way into our backyard. He jumped on me, barking happily and licking the dirt from my hands.

I chuckled. "Thanks for the birthday love, big guy."

"How about it, captain?" Tia asked again. I knew she wanted to get me away from home, and honestly, that wasn't such a bad idea.

"Let's go." I got to my feet. "We'll take my ride."

We all fit in my truck and I drove towards Cape Forchu. The sky was spitting light, and I followed the setting sun towards the light-house. When we got there Taz ran off, but we knew he wouldn't go too far. Tia and I made our way to the top of the hill, wandered away from the main area, and walked along the rocks. I was a little ahead of her, but she wasn't too far behind. She knew I was quiet for a reason; she had caught me burying my best friend. Now there we were, walking along the rocks above the sea.

"Do you wanna keep conversation light?" she called.

I stopped and let her catch up. "We don't have to," I said, looking onward.

"Do you wanna talk about that night?"

"I thought we already did."

"Yes, I mean, I know you went to meet your dad…I mean, Blake. I know the journal got hit by the truck, I know you were trapped in Clay's world, and you had to rip the journal to get out. But…I don't know." She looked at me and squinted. "What did you see in there?"

I hadn't told her about seeing my grandfather. I was still trying to figure out the how and why of that happening. If everything I had written in the journal was from the past, how did I have an authentic conversation with my grandfather, in the present?

"Clay…before Clay…died, I uh, saw my grandfather."

"Like, a memory?"

"No, this was real. Clay grabbed hold of me, I closed my eyes, and I woke up in my backyard. But not in my reality, it was somewhere in between his and mine. I walked inside the house, and I seen him. I seen my grandfather. We spoke for a while."

"What about?"

"Just everything, I guess. He told me a little about my aunt, he told me I was a seeker, he told me I had to…I had to help Clay."

Tia processed that for a minute. "How did that happen? I thought Clay could only bring things back from the past?"

"I know, me too. But I've been thinking about it non-stop. When the journal was almost ripped in half, I think it created a rift between Clay's reality and ours. Maybe the memories of my grandfather got projected into the present day? Like, how I remembered him, and because of that I got to see him? I don't know. Maybe this is a lot…."

"You're never too much," Tia assured me. "From what I can tell, that doesn't seem too far-fetched."

"I just…I don't know why he did that. I've been thinking about it a lot today, because Grampy would always call me on my birthday. And today, this was the first day I never received that phone call."

"Well, maybe that was Clay's gift to you."

Tia's thought lit up my heart. My jaw dropped. He knew my birthday was approaching, and he knew the tradition Grampy and I kept. He knew I wouldn't receive a call this year, and had one last chance to do that for me.

"I…uh, that's…." I couldn't catch my words. It made sense; Clay had always been selfless. "I think you're right." I finally found the words to say. "It was a gift."

"As far as gifts go, I got you one as well." Tia reached into her backpack and passed me a picture frame. It was a copy of the sketch I'd drawn of her, Clay, and I all those years ago. "It's corny, I know. I just know you're the sentimental type, that's all."

"It's perfect." I gave Tia a huge hug. "Thank you, thank you, thank you!"

She hugged me back with a big squeeze. "And I think, as far as traditions go, we could always start something new."

"Yeah?" I caught my breath as she let go. "What did you have in mind?"

"This isn't so bad, is it?" Tia raised her arms towards the sky. "Just the three of us." She pointed to Taz pissing on the rocks below. I laughed. "How about we come here? Spend all night under these clear skies and create a new kind of nostalgia, a new tradition."

It certainly didn't sound so bad. As I looked around, I saw everything I ever wanted: solid friendship, a place that felt like home, and a place where I finally found what I had been seeking. I found belonging, even if it had taken a long time. I was finally standing in it.

"Besides, it sounds like you have a new canvas for the memories." Tia pointed to the new journal Mom had gifted me, sticking out of my backpack.

"Creating new memories that'll some day be nostalgic." I smiled. "That doesn't sound like a bad journal entry."

"I knew you'd be up for it." Tia grabbed my hand, and we ran into the distance, creating a new memory.

It was the first time in a long while I felt a genuine smile extend across my face. Maybe it was the wind flowing through my hair, or the friends who loved me honestly even on my worst days, knowing that the phase after grief isn't always linear. I was ready to explore these moments I know would grow into nostalgia. I had spent the better part of my life being a seeker, and this was it: I found exactly what I'd been looking for.

I lived my life always so scared of the future, because I left so much of myself in the past. I left friends, family, and mysteries behind. I was scared that the future would somehow bury that part of myself. I was scared to move forward without confronting the things I left behind. I thought the only way to move forward was to dig deep into the mystery, and seek clarity. But one thing I learned is that we all have reasons to avoid the past. We all have events that change us, force us in a different direction. Sometimes it pushes loved ones away; sometimes it brings them closer. It was time to find my own path.

This is me—finally learning to loosen my grip of the past, and creating something new. I knew these moments would become memories, and I would never be alone. Even if we are temporary, I was going to live in this moment, and allow myself to seek something new. I let those thoughts guide me, as we ran beneath the bleeding sky, we knew the stars would heal.

ACKNOWLEDGEMENTS

SO MANY SLEEPLESS, COFFEE-FILLED NIGHTS AND shots of espresso go into a book before readers see it. Add elements of time travel and fantasy, and you'll overthink everything. I guess what I'm trying to say is authors are really, really tired. But this is an experience that I'm so grateful for. I would like to thank Whitney Moran and Terrilee Bulger for believing in this project from the start. It's not every day we see an African Nova Scotian fantasy novel, and this is a very personal project that I have been developing for years. I am grateful that Nimbus Publishing took this project on with open arms.

I would like to thank Emily MacKinnon for being a rad editor throughout this entire process—we made an awesome team. Thank you for everything!

A big thank you to Jenna Giles for driving me to Yarmouth for location scouting, and to Joella Hodder for being supportive all the way through. You two are some of my closest friends, and I am lucky to know you.

To Bria Cherise Miller and Amy Austin: thank you both for being excited about this project, and for letting me ask you so many questions about Yarmouth. A lot of my family is from Yarmouth, but I grew up in Halifax. Those visits I took during childhood summers fuelled the nostalgia for this project. I'm thrilled that both of you wanted to be part of this process, and it wouldn't have been as genuine without your input.

To Sarah Sawler: thank you for being a great friend and helping me through the process when I was new to everything. Making author friends is so important. I'm so grateful we met and bonded so easily.

To Rob Grimes, a former co-worker and close friend: you pushed me to write this book ever since I told you about the premise during a lunch break years ago. I told you I'd put you in the acknowledgments one day! Thank you for motivating me, my friend.

To my mom, Penny Carter: thank you for being my Mom. But more importantly, thank you for being supportive of the work I'm doing. I couldn't do any of this without you in my corner. Infinitely grateful.

And to my grandmother, Dorothy "Dolly" Carter: you were always the inspiration for this project. I miss our phone calls on my birthday so, so much. Thank you for being my Nan, and for being a great co-pilot. One of the last things you told me is that you wanted to see my name in the credits some day. But if I could make a long-distance call to the next plane of existence, the first thing I would say is: this one is for you.

July 21, 1943–June 26, 2015.